MAY, 1996

To Scotty

The
Mayflower
Murder

Good reading!

Best wishes,
Paul Kemprecos

Also by Paul Kemprecos

Feeding Frenzy
Neptune's Eye
Death in Deep Water
Cool Blue Tomb

The
Mayflower
Murder

by
Paul Kemprecos

St. Martin's Press ✦ New York

A THOMAS DUNNE BOOK.
An imprint of St. Martin's Press.

THE MAYFLOWER MURDER. Copyright © 1996 by Paul Kemprecos. All rights reserved. Printed in the United States of America. No part of this book may be used or reproduced in any manner whatsoever without written permission except in the case of brief quotations embodied in critical articles or reviews. For information, address St. Martin's Press, 175 Fifth Avenue, New York, N.Y. 10010.

Design by Scott Levine

Library of Congress Cataloging-in-Publication Data

Kemprecos, Paul.
    The Mayflower murder / by Paul Kemprecos.—1st ed.
      p. cm.
    "A Thomas Dunne book."
    ISBN 0-312-14852-6
    1. Socarides, Aristotle Plato (Fictitious character)—Fiction.
    2. Private investigators—Massachusetts—Cape Cod—Fiction.
    3. Greek Americans—Massachusetts—Cape Cod—Fiction.
    4. Cape Cod (Mass.)—Fiction. I. Title.
    PS3561.E4224M3 1996
    813'.54—dc20   96-34
                                      CIP

First Edition: June 1996

10 9 8 7 6 5 4 3 2 1

For Christi

Thanks to Fred Dunford at the Cape Cod Museum of Natural History for leading me through the intricacies of an archaeological dig.

"The day is for honest men, the night for thieves."
—Euripides

The
Mayflower
Murder

One

MIKE WOODS WAS taking a heavy drag on his Marlboro when the light winked like a firefly's hiccup in the blue darkness around the old fort. He squinted through his new bifocals and cursed the tricks his aging eyes sometimes played on him.

Flicker.

There it was again. The bright amber glow cut through the misty veil of fog drifting inland from Plymouth Harbor. On-off. Real fast.

Mike ran thick fingers through the stiff white stubble of his brush-cut hair and laughed softly. Probably some damned high school kids, drinking Old Mil' and raising hell around the fort. Little bastards needed a good kick in the ass. He took another puff, pinched the glowing end of his cigarette, and put the warm butt in his pocket so the day crew wouldn't find it. Then he started across the cornfield toward the fort.

The thought he might be in danger never crossed his mind. Mike Woods simply didn't scare. He had used up a lifetime of fright forty years ago in a snowy Korean field, bullet hole gaping in his chest, every draft-age kid in China running straight at him, bayonets glistening in the winter sun, so damn close he could see the buttons on those funny padded jackets the Chinks wore, Charlie Fishman, the kid from Brownsville, Texas, standing over him like John Wayne, raking the human wave with staccato rounds from his M-1 as if it would make a dent, then dragging Mike by the collar over the rise to a half-track full of dead men. Old Charlie, who died of a heart attack at the age of thirty-two. Damned good soldier, good buddy.

After Korea, Mike decided his life was charmed. He drove fast, went fishing in howling gales, and climbed ladders like a human fly for his house-painting business. Cars crashed, boats sank, bones broke, but Mike always came back unfazed.

I'm golden, he'd tell his friends, and once again show them the nickel-shaped scar under his grizzled chest hairs. Hell, he'd die in bed, preferably humping Bernice, the waitress with the big, round butt and tits who worked the counter at the coffee shop.

Mike's brags had lost their steam in the last couple of years. The old surefootedness was gone, and he had almost fallen off his rickety scaffolding. Then came the stomach surgery. He sold his paints and brushes to a hardworking Plymouth kid, and took a job as a part-time maintenance man at Plimoth Plantation.

The plantation was on a low hill three miles south of Plymouth on Route 3A, the old coastal road that used to bring the tourists down from Boston to Cape Cod. It was a living museum, a smaller version of Williamsburg, Virginia. Staff people dressed like seventeenth-century English settlers planted crops, hand-churned butter, and raised livestock the way the Pilgrims did three hundred years ago.

The difference was that the staff went home at the end of

2

the day to their VCRs, indoor plumbing, and running water. On the job, though, they took their work seriously. Damned good actors, Mike thought. You couldn't get them to admit it was any later than the year 1627 if you stuck a blunderbuss up their ass.

Mike was a townie, born and bred in Plymouth. He took grudging pride living where the Pilgrims settled, but he considered the local lore about John and Priscilla Alden, the Rock, and Squanto as hoopla to separate the out-of-towners from their money. As somebody whose ancestors did *not* come over on the *Mayflower*, Mike always thought of the Pilgrims as tight-lipped religious nuts who invented Thanksgiving and went around preaching from the Bible at the poor damned Indians.

With the clarity that sometimes appears with old age, Mike had come to appreciate and identify with the raw tenacity and stubbornness of the First Comers, especially since he started his job at the Plantation. If he were younger, and a little quicker with his wits, he'd love to dress up in costume and play at being a Pilgrim for the tourists. Not a Goody Two-shoes like Elder William Brewster, he teased his wife; he'd play John Billington, the first person hanged for murder in the New World.

Mike often worked after hours, which is what he was doing on that warm summer night. He pounded a loose nail into a sign using the hammer end of a hatchet he'd wheedled from a young Indian down at the Hobbamocks' homesite on the Eel River, just below the plantation, then glanced at his watch. It was ten o'clock.

Mike stuck the hatchet in his belt, stepped outside, and lit up a cigarette from a pack he kept at the workshop. His wife enforced a strict no-smoking zone at home. Mike strolled past the big gambrel-roofed visitors' center that housed the ticket offices and gift shop, and followed an ascending dirt path. At the cornfields, he stopped and drew in a deep breath. The smell of newly turned earth and manure mixed with the kelpy low tide vapors from the harbor. Stars glittered like rhinestones in the velvety sky. Below the fort, on the gradually sloping hill, was the quiet thatched-roof village of Plimoth.

Mike often wondered what it was *really* like living in one of those dirt-floored shacks, sleeping on crowded straw mattresses, your house stinking of wood smoke, livestock, and unwashed bodies, wondering if the rustling outside your door was just the cow or some half-naked heathen savage waiting for you to take a leak so he could tear your scalp off and nail it to the doorflap of his tepee.

Goddamn, they were some tough bastards. He savored his cigarette and chuckled in wonderment, letting his glance drift a couple of hundred yards distant to the two-story fort, whose cannon protected the village below. That's when he saw the light and went to investigate.

The dirt path through the cornfields led to the gate in the stockade fence around the fort. He stood at the opening and listened, drawing on his old deer-hunting instincts. For all his bearish bulk, Mike Woods could sneak close enough to a tenpointer to yank its tail. But, like his eyesight, Mike's hearing had gone to hell in a teakettle. He tensed his ear muscles, as if that would help. All he heard were the insects buzzing and birds down at the Eel River calling out in their sleep.

Mike crept stealthily into the fort compound. The blockhouse loomed above him. Cannons poked out through openings in the palisades on the roof. He leaned against a corner of the building. Again he listened.

The soft rustling sounded like cellophane being crushed.

4

The noise came from the other side of the fort. He edged along a wall. The crackling grew louder. Ghostly shadows danced on the fence. There was the acrid smell of wood smoke. He trotted around a corner, his heart pounding. Yellow flames licked at the base of the log foundation.

Jeezus!

The fort was on on fire.

No time to run for a fire extinguisher or call for help. The fort would be a pile of ashes by then. Mike stripped off his sweatshirt and beat at the blaze. Sparks exploded in his face and stung his eyes and bare skin. He ignored the pain and slammed the shirt against the sheets of flame again and again.

Whack . . . whack. . . .

Mike lacked the stamina of his youth, but he was still a powerful man. After a few minutes, the fire retreated under the smothering blows. But the second he slowed his efforts, a hot orange tongue shot out laterally along the logs. He attacked the hissing streamer, cutting the blaze into two pockets of fire. He went after the larger fireball and beat it down. Then he attacked the smaller one.

Mike tossed the sweatshirt aside, scooped dirt from the ground with his hands and threw it on the dying flames. Then he stamped the last sizzling embers under his heavy-soled work boots. Only after he was sure the fire was *in extremis* did he stop. He wiped his stinging eyes with the back of his hand. He took great hoarse gulps of air and coughed the smoke out of his lungs. Sweat poured off his soot-blackened face. He was so damned mad that he ignored the sharp pains racking his rib cage.

Christ, he couldn't believe it. Some sonofabitch tried to burn down the fort!

The sweatshirt was a blackened rag. He was going to catch

5

hell from his wife for ruining perfectly good clothing. He'd worry about that later. Mike was exhausted, but he set his anvil jaw at a determined angle and walked around the fort. He peered in windows and made sure the doors were locked. Then he went to the front gate and looked down on the roofs lining both sides of the short dirt road that served as the plantation's main street.

He swept the compound with his watery eyes, letting his gaze move past the elevated watchtowers to the far end of the stockade fence and back again. The darkened village was as still as a crypt. Even the cows and chickens had turned in for the night. He heard only the hum of traffic on the Route 3A, less than a quarter-mile distant, and his own hoarse breathing.

The fire was a personal assault. Mike had taken a proprietary interest in the plantation. The tourists had it all day, but at night it was his. That's why he was so angry. He knew the village layout by heart, better than the costumed staff. He could identify every one of the more than two dozen houses enclosed within the stockade fence. He thought of them as still being occupied by their long-dead owners.

Old Miles Standish had his place close to the fort so he could rally the troops in case of an attack. John Alden's and Governor Bradford's houses were just down the hill. Mike had memorized the names. Cooke and Allerton, Brewster and Browne. All the others. And, of course, old John Billington, who crammed a family of four into a shack no bigger than a bathroom.

He tensed. The puddled yellow circle from a flashlight zig-zagged across the main street.

Mike's shoulders hurt, and his arms felt like deadweights hanging by his sides. But the adrenaline high from beating out the fire gave his old muscles new energy. He moved noiselessly down the hill, sniffing the wind as if he were stalking a big buck.

The light ducked in behind the Miles Standish house. Mike was only yards away now. His hackles rose at the odor of gasoline. Rounding the corner of the fence, he saw a squatting figure hunched over a flaming cigarette lighter. Mike whipped the hatchet from his belt and lifted it high.

"All right, you fucker, one move and I'll bash your head in."

Mike heard the voice roar out of his throat, enjoyed the power of it, moved in, unafraid.

The figure jumped to its feet. Mike flicked on his flash-light, caught the surprise in the man's face a second before the intruder launched his body at him. Mike tried to step aside, knowing his reflexes were gone, his reactions slowed by fatigue. The man's shoulder slammed into his midsection. Mike toppled back and hit the ground hard. The impact knocked the wind out of him. The flashlight flew from his hand.

Fingers grabbed at his throat. Mike flailed with his left arm. He felt the warm wooden shaft of the hatchet in his right hand. He had only brandished the hatchet as a threat, but the guy was trying to tear out his Adam's apple! He raised the hatchet and blindly aimed the blade at the man's head. The swing was short and lacked strength. His assailant deflected it with his elbow and wrenched the hatchet out of his hand. The man shifted his weight. Mike rolled out from under him and struggled to his feet.

"You sonofabitch!" he yelled. "I'm going to rip you a new asshole!"

It was Mike Woods to the last, defiant and unafraid.

He moved in with his head lowered like an enraged bull. The hatchet came up, then arced down. With a sickening sound, the blade caught Mike behind the left temple. His legs turned to rubber. The momentum in his heavy body carried him forward. He plowed a furrow in the dirt with his jaw. His lungs coughed once.

After four decades, the IOU Mike Woods signed in blood on a snow-covered Korean field had finally come due.

Two

THE *MILLIE D.* was midway between the mainland and the low, silky dunes of the outer beach when Sam stepped away from the helm and eyeballed the pale sun from under the dark green visor of his duck-billed cap. He took a bead with his long nose and fixed our position with the mental sextant he carries around in his head.

"Hey, Soc," he called over the guttural rumble of the 360-horsepower Detroit diesel engine. "This bearing okay?"

I stood in the *Millie D.*'s stern, peering through binoculars at the sandy bluff a half mile distant. The lenses framed the picture window of a rambling two-story house due west of the boat. Sam was on target.

I raised my arm and yelled, "This'll do it."

Sam cut back on the throttle. Keeping our speed at a crab-scuttle, he steered the forty-eight-foot tub trawler in a big lazy circle. The cloud of herring gulls darting in our foamy wake squalled like children playing in a schoolyard, then wheeled in a great shimmering cloud to keep pace. When he had it just right, Sam reduced engine power to an idle. The trawler rocked gently in the easy green swells.

On long winter nights, when the sawtooth winds from the Atlantic try to pry the shingles off the roof of my house, I dream about mornings like this. The puffy white clouds pasted onto the hard blue bowl of the sky had been lofted from swansdown. I drew in a deep intoxicating lungful of sea-sweetened air like a coal miner coming off his shift. Then I went below to fetch Maggie Eaton.

The cardboard box stashed on a bunk looked much too feeble to hold Maggie's remains. I pictured her just a few days ago, a blowsy big-boned woman shocking her private-duty nurses with ribald jokes. Using a screwdriver, I pried the top open and carried the box on deck. My foot caught on a step and I imagined Maggie's lusty barrelhouse laugh roaring through the thin cardboard walls: *Hey, be careful with me, Soc, I break easy.*

Balancing the box on the port rail, I pivoted it slowly to give Maggie a last view of the harbor. *Her* harbor. Maggie wanted her ashes scattered on the waters where she'd dared the winds in the sleek, twenty-eight-foot Morgan she loved almost better than anything.

Sam came over and slipped the tan canvas cap off his close-cropped snowy hair. He rested a gnarled brown hand on the box and held the cap over his heart. I followed his lead, with my Boston Red Sox cap. Sam's blue eyes squinted at the jadeite water through wire-rimmed glasses, his untamed brows furrowed in thought. Something was troubling him.

"Dickie Hopkins, the undertaker, got me to do this a couple of times before, Soc. But that's always been with strangers, off-Cape people." He shook his head like an old plow horse.

"This is different. Don't quite know quite what to do. Seems like it ought to be something more than just 'Good-bye, Maggie, nice knowin' you.' "

"Did the senator ask you to say anything special?"

"Nope. Said everyone got a chance to sound off at the memorial service. He just wanted Maggie's ashes out here where she loved to sail her boat. I respect his wishes, but it seems we ought to give the old girl a proper send-off."

"Let's start with a moment of silence, and I'll think about it."

"Finest kind," Sam said. We bowed our heads and I dug into the corners of my memory. After about thirty seconds, Sam looked up hopefully.

I nodded. "No problem, Sam. This is by a poet named Homer. He wrote it two thousand years ago. It's about the birth of Aphrodite, the goddess of love, which was what Maggie was all about." I cleared my throat and raised my voice over the grumble of the engine and the wet cough from the exhaust. Gulls piped and swirled overhead as I began: *"The breath of the west wind bore her/Over the sounding sea,/Up from the delicate foam . . ."*

When I was finished, Sam said, "Knew you could come up with something, Soc. It says a lot. The senator would've liked it. Maggie, too."

Maggie would have *more* than liked it. The thought of being poured off the stern of a fishing boat to the words of Homer's poem would have sent her overboard with laughter.

Sam gazed pensively at the crystal sun sparkle on the puckering waves.

"Makes you think, doesn't it?" he said.

"Think about what?"

"Dunno, just makes you think," he said enigmatically. Sam was a Yankee. His emotions rarely surfaced, but they were there.

He put his cap back on and tugged the long visor down until it almost touched his nose.

"Time to put Maggie to rest. Stand upwind when you tilt her over. Pokie Eldridge got drunk when he was planting his wife Helen in the harbor near the lighthouse and dumped her ashes into a six-knot wind. Got the whole mess in his kisser. Old Pokie swore up and down Helen'd done it on purpose." A grin slashed Sam's weathered face. "Knowing the way Pokie treated Helen, I think maybe he was right."

I checked the wind direction again. Then I tipped the box over the side. A light gray ribbon flowed out, fanned as it was caught on the light breeze, then dusted the lacy billows.

"Sleep well, Maggie," I said. "Go on the breath of the west wind."

" 'Bye, Maggie," Sam said. "We're gonna miss you."

When the box was empty I tapped the bottom. "That's all."

"That was real nice. Promise you'll do the same for me."

"Hell, Sam, you'll be scattering *my* ashes to the sea. Remember one thing, though."

"What's that, Soc?"

"Don't stand downwind."

Sam gave me a sour look and shuffled back to the wheelhouse. A minute later, the engine flexed its muscles, and the steel hull swung around so its bow pointed toward the channel. Around eleven o'clock, Sam eased the *Millie D.* into the little jog just south of the fish pier, and brought the boat alongside the bulkhead with that sure and delicate touch I admired but could never duplicate. We tied up, secured the boat, and walked across the parking lot.

A black Lincoln town car was parked next to our pickup trucks. There was a quick toot on the horn, and the door on the driver's side opened. A pair of legs with metal braces on them swung onto the tarmac, followed by the wide shoulders of Senator Alan Eaton. The senator pulled himself out and erect, then reached in for two aluminum crutches. He pushed his forearms through the grips and moved toward us in swinging arm-driven strides, as if gravity to a man with useless legs was an inconvenience, but no big deal.

Sam said, "Morning, Senator."

"Good morning, Sam. You too, Soc." We shook hands all around.

"Well, we put Maggie to rest," Sam said.

The senator smiled sadly. "I was watching from our house. That was exactly where she wanted her ashes to go. Thanks to both of you."

Sam nodded his approval. "We said a few words. Soc came up with them. Tell Alan what you said, Soc."

A eulogy loses something in the parking lot of a working fish pier, but the senator looked interested. I pretended the pickup trucks and eighteen-wheelers weren't there and repeated the quote from Homer I had delivered before we gave Maggie to the sea.

Senator Eaton took my hand and crushed a few bones. "Thank you, Soc. I really appreciate that. I know Maggie would, too."

"Glad to do it," Sam said. "Millie and I had some good times over to your house many a night. We're going to miss Maggie."

13

"Me too," Eaton said. "Me too."

The friendship between the brawling, powerful Democratic U.S. senator from New York and the quiet-spoken, rock-ribbed Republican from Cape Cod went back to the days when Sam ran a small charter fishing boat. Alan Eaton, then a young congressman from Manhattan, was one of his first customers. Margaret Eaton and Sam's spouse, Mildred, found mutual consolation in their fishing widowhood, love of bridge, and the sense of humor that came with living with strong-willed spouses.

Senator Eaton has red hair that has gone mostly to gray and a craggy face that would have looked good on Mount Rushmore, which is where it might have ended up if fate hadn't called time out. Eaton got hit by a degenerative disease, but it was only a temporary diversion from his ascent to the upper reaches of the Senate. He would have stayed there until they carried him out feet first. Only after Maggie was diagnosed with breast cancer last year did he slow down. They began to spend more time at their summer home on Cape Cod. It was there that Maggie died.

"Soc and I were talking on the way in," Sam said. "We want you to come out fishing on the *Millie D.* We can rig it up so you can get around, and we'll catch some stripers and blues like we did in the old days."

I didn't hear Eaton's answer. Joe Lombard, a Princeton summer kid who packed fish at the pier, was yelling my name. I excused myself and went over to the fish-company office.

"You got a call," Joe said. "Guy named Flagg." He picked up a sheet of letterhead from the cluttered desk under the *Sports Illustrated* swimsuit calendar and stuck it under my nose. "Meet me 1 P.M. today at the Powwow," the message said. I looked up at Joe.

14

"When did he call?"

"About half an hour ago. You were out with Sam. I said you'd be back soon, and he asked if I could give you a message. No, that's wrong—he *told* me to give you the message and to make sure I got it right. Made me read it back to him three times before he was satisfied. You owe this dude money, Soc?"

Joe was clearly annoyed as only an Ivy Leaguer could be miffed at being treated like Mickey the Dunce. I could have explained that John Flagg was a very careful man in a business where being careless could make him dead. Instead, I thanked Joe, stuck the message in my pocket, and walked back to my truck.

Sam and Eaton were still talking. They were going to Sam's house for lunch and a game of cribbage. They asked me to join them. I excused myself and said I'd call Sam later to talk about fishing the next day. I gave final condolences to the senator and got into my 1977 GMC pickup. The engine started with only five or six pumps of the gas pedal. I drove north on Route 28 along the shores of Pleasant Bay and turned off at a cranberry bog. The dirt road ended in front of a boathouse that looked as if it would tumble into the bay if someone leaned against it.

People who live on the water on Cape Cod sometimes give their houses clever names like *At Last* or *Dun Roamin'*. I can't see carving *Toobroketofix* onto a quarterboard. I simply call it The Boathouse. The place wouldn't get past the building inspector today, which is plain crazy, because it's withstood every kind of dirty weather thrown at it since going up as part of an estate back in the twenties.

I went around to the deck and looked out over the bay, a body of shallow water separated from the Atlantic Ocean's moody waters by the fragile embrace of a slender barrier beach

15

that runs north and south. A round black furry blob that looked like a giant foozeball with legs came over to rub against my ankles.

Kojak is a Maine coon cat, a breed supposedly descended from a love affair between a feline and an amorous or near-sighted raccoon. His tail alone is as big as most cats, and he spends a lot of time lying around watching butterflies, so he is on the chunky side. Kojak was having internal-plumbing problems, and the vet had him on a low-ash diet. I went in the kitchen and spooned some glop into his dish. He stared at his food like a kid over a helping of spinach. I poured myself a glass of cranberry-raspberry juice and took Flagg's message back onto the deck.

The bay was busy with pleasure-boat traffic, which wasn't unusual in near-perfect weather. Power boats cruised back and forth, burning up gallons of gas as they looked for sailboats to terrorize. I read the message again. If I had any brains, I would rip the paper to shreds and tell Flagg it was that snotty kid Joe Lombard's fault for not giving it to me. I was fooling myself. There was about as much chance of blowing off Flagg's summons as the motorboat cowboys out on the bay had of learning good manners.

Flagg's note was short on detail, but there was only one powwow I knew of. Every year the Wampanoag Indians in the town of Mashpee at the other end of the Cape get together for dancing and drumbeating. Year-rounders like me try to dodge the summer crowds, and I had never been to one. Flagg is a Wampanoag Indian from Martha's Vineyard who has redis-covered his cultural past with the gusto of a born-again Pente-costal, and at times he can be a royal pain when he goes on about his Native American roots. But I couldn't see him at any-thing that was even faintly touristy.

16

You never know about Flagg, though. Let me take that back. One thing you *do* know about Flagg: trouble sticks to him like burrs on a hound dog.

Maybe I was being overanxious. Hell, I chuckled, nothing can go wrong at a quiet little old powwow with some friendly Indians.

Looking back on it later, I figured General Custer must have said the same thing just before he rode off to the Little Big Horn.

Three

A WOMAN WITH russet potato cheeks relieved me of an entry fee, stamped my hand, and let me through the chain-link fence around the combination baseball and soccer field where a sign out front announced the annual Wampanoag Powwow.

A booth just inside the gate offered buttons and bumper stickers that said: "Columbus Wasn't First." Nobody from the Sons of Italy was buying. More booths were selling turquoise and silver jewelry, pottery, furs, beads, and tapes of Native American music.

Behind the stalls was an encampment of trailers and RVs. The license plates were from every state in the Northeast, and there was a good sprinkling of cars from southwestern states like New Mexico and Arizona.

I followed the low drumbeat to powwow central, a roped-off area in the middle of the field. Dancers dressed in feathers, loincloths, and buckskin moved counterclockwise in a big slow-moving circle. A wrinkled grandmother in leather led a little girl in a Pocahontas dress through the paces. A dozen young guys were seated on the ground around two tom-toms, each drum as big as a bathtub. They pounded the skins and chanted, "*Hi-yeh, Hi-yah.*"

The drumbeat and the chanting stopped suddenly. A young woman with café-au-lait skin stepped up to a microphone. Dark brown hair plaited tight in a braid and decorated with feathers hung down the back of her heavily beaded dress to her slender waist.

The woman sang a couple of Earth Mother numbers. Her voice was strong and mellow. She gave her tongue a workout with an ululation. Then she explained the Indian chants and closed with a wolf call that would have given Little Red Riding Hood the goose bumps. As the echoes faded, she pointed into the eastern sky. A winged shadow glided silently above the treetops like a dark angel.

"Look over your heads and see what has come to watch us," the wolf lady shouted. "The Great Spirit has given us His blessing for this gathering."

A chorus of oohs and aahs rose from the crowd. The bird had a white head and its big wings ended in fingerlike feathers. A bald eagle. It circled several times and disappeared toward the east.

The wolf lady handed the microphone to the leader of the Wampanoag Nation. He offered his official greetings and introduced a sweet-faced teenaged kid as the Powwow Princess. A pair of cute little girls did a jingle dance that was more jingle than dance. Then everyone joined in, including some tourists who did the funky chicken.

Someone tapped me on the shoulder. "May I have this dance?"

I turned and saw a distorted double image of myself in the silver lenses of a pair of reflecting wire-rimmed aviator sunglasses. A Washington Redskins cap a size too small for Flagg's head rode at anchor on a sea of wavy black hair worn longish over the ears.

"This number's a little fast for me," I said. "Maybe they'll play a fox-trot if I ask them nicely."

Flagg's thin lips widened in a tight smile. "Don't bet on it."

We shook hands. "I was beginning to think I was at the wrong powwow."

"I knew you'd figure it out." He gazed up at the sky. "How did you like the eagle?"

"The timing was a little too good to be true," I said skeptically. "Sure it wasn't a kite or somebody with a remote control?"

"I wouldn't have believed it either, but he comes back here every year at this time. Maybe it *is* the Great One giving us His blessing."

"It's lunchtime. How about blessing me with some genuine Native American cuisine," I said.

We walked past a line of food booths and canteen trucks. "Take your pick. We've got buffalo burgers on Indian bread, venison steak, Seminole pan potatoes, Indian fries. We got quahog chowder, clam cakes, and Wampanoag wing dings."

"I never knew spiced chicken wings were an old Wampanoag recipe."

"They're not. Navajos invented them."

"I hope your feelings won't be hurt if I have a hot dog."

"Naw, that's a Choctaw invention." He ordered two dogs and a couple of Cokes. We piled on the mustard, relish, and chopped onions and took our lunch to a picnic table whose top wasn't any more sticky than a sheet of flypaper.

Flagg usually wears a navy suit and wing-tipped shoes polished to a spit shine. Today he was in a tangerine-colored pocket T-shirt with the name of a gym on it, old jeans, and beat-up moccasins. Flagg is built like a steel wood-splitting wedge, with a barrel chest, narrow hips and short powerful legs. He looks as if he could jump out of a plane without a parachute and land safely on his feet.

He chewed the hot dog thoughtfully, taking his time. When he was finished eating, he removed his sunglasses to reveal the hard black eyes behind the silvered lenses.

"I got a friend who's in trouble," he said. "Cops say he killed somebody."

"That *is* trouble. Is your friend anybody I know?"

"Not likely. His name is Joe Quint. Hails from the Narragansett tribe down in Rhode Island. We were in the Airborne together back in 'Nam."

"That must have been before we met at Quang Tri."

He nodded. "Joe and I met on a mission near the Cambodian border. We used to wonder why a couple of Noble Redmen like us were fighting on the side of the cavalry. Got to be good buddies. Then he got wounded in an ambush and they shipped him home. I mustered out of Airborne a couple of months later, and you know the rest."

The 'rest' was Operation Phoenix, a shadowy counterinsurgency group Flagg worked for when I met him in a bar in the Quang Tri City citadel.

"How did Mr. Quint get himself charged with murder?"

"Lemme back up first. After 'Nam, Joe went to college to get his law degree, and I went to work for the feds. We'd hear from each other once in a while. Mostly I'd read about him in the papers. Joe got involved in Native American causes. A week ago, he called me. He said he might need my help. That he was onto something big."

"What was it?"

21

"You've got to know Joe. He's a one-man show. That's probably what got him wounded in 'Nam. He said he'd get back to me. Next thing I know, Joe's in deep shit. You hear about that killing up at Plimoth Plantation?"

"I've been pretty busy fishing. Haven't read the papers. You'll have to fill me in."

"Worker at the plantation was murdered. Killed with an Indian hatchet." Flagg's window-shade lids dropped so I could barely see his dark eyes. His mouth curled into a mirthless grin. "Cops figured it must have been the work of a hostile native."

"Your pal, Mr. Quint?"

He nodded.

"Why him? There must have been more to it than a hatchet."

"Joe's got a big mouth. He's been making waves, being a royal pain in the ass up in Plymouth town. Got his face on TV in front of Plymouth Rock and the *Mayflower* replica. Said the Indians were getting shafted all over again."

"I'm still waiting for the punch line."

"Here it is. The cops say they can connect Joe with the murder weapon."

"You could stop right there."

"There's more. They can place Joe at the scene."

"Double whammy like that is hard to beat, Flagg. I'd advise him to hire the best lawyer he can get, plead guilty to manslaughter and throw himself on the mercy of the court."

"I'd give him the same advice, except for one thing."

"You think Joe is innocent?"

"He's not the kind of guy who'd do something like this."

"Doesn't make any difference what you or I think. It's what the law thinks."

22

"No argument there. That's why I called you. I want you to look into this thing. If I go in and start asking questions, pretty soon people will want to know who I am and what I do. My bosses wouldn't like that."

Flagg had pulled me out of trouble a few times, and I had done the same for him. I didn't know whose marker was due. It didn't matter. If Flagg needed a favor, I'd oblige him.

"No problem," I said. "I'm getting sick of looking at dead codfish all day."

"Glad to hear you say that. This would mean a lot to me."

"I understand. You and Quint are brothers of the blood, bonded by war."

"Something like that, Soc. Joe saved my ass more than once back in 'Nam. I owe him."

I chewed on a chunk of ice. "Something might come out of digging around that you won't like, Flagg."

"I know. You might find Joe's guilty as sin. I've been in this business too long to get surprised at anything. But like I said, I don't think so. Thanks for trying to prepare me for a hard landing."

"Okay, pal, you know your friend better than I do. I should talk to him. Is he in the slammer, or out on bail?"

"Neither. He did a dumb thing. When the cops started looking for him, he ran."

I let out a low whistle. "You're right. That *is* dumb."

"He knows it looks bad, so he's going to turn himself in."

"Any idea where he is?"

"Yeah, he should be sitting in my car." Flagg put his glasses back on. I found myself staring at my reflected face again. "C'mon, I'll introduce you."

We dropped the paper plates and napkins in a barrel and walked across the field. The kids were still thumping on the tom-toms, and dancers stomped around the ring freestyle.

"There's one thing," Flagg said as we headed toward the parking lot. "Joe can be a little tough to get to know. He's uptight about Native American stuff, but a lot of it's just noise. He's not stupid. Be patient with him. He talks a lot, tries to be hard-ass, and you've got to cut through the crapola."

"I'll be the epitome of patience, Flagg."

"Huh," Flagg said noncommittally. "My car's over here." We cut behind a booth that was basically a couple of folding tables set up under an oversized open-front tent.

I passed a big, square-shouldered man going the other way. He moved slowly and deliberately, like somebody walking on mashed potatoes. His mouth was fixed in a grim line, and he was intent on something I couldn't see. He wore southern-sheriff sunglasses like Flagg, but it was his jacket that rang the warning bell in the back of my mind. The baggy black windbreaker wasn't something you wear when the temperature was in the eighties.

I spun on my heel and followed him around the corner of the booth. He stopped and, with his right hand, he reached under the back of his jacket and pulled out a pistol. He held the gun in both hands, bent his knees in a wide-legged target stance and squinted along the barrel.

The muzzle pointed at a man who was running for the woods that edged the field. He was about a hundred yards away and seemed to be moving in slow motion.

I took three long steps and threw a cross-body block. My technique wasn't anything you'd see in the NFL. The guy was hard as a frozen side of beef, and he took his time going down. I landed on top of him and groped for the gun without much success. The guy waved his gun arm like someone signaling a

New York cab. He had become a rolling mass of knees, elbows, shoulders, and curses.

The gun swung toward my head. The muzzle looked big enough to handle a cannonball. Time for unconventional warfare. I sank my teeth into his wrist. There was a loud yell of pain. The fingers unclenched. The gun dropped to the ground. I kicked it six feet away. People were shouting. Maybe one of them was me.

Getting rid of the gun wasn't such a hot idea. Now the guy had two hands free. He scrabbled forward on his belly, reaching for the gun. I dove onto his back. An elbow crashed into my midsection. Trying not to vomit, I got my legs under me and my hands below his chin, then pulled up, using the leverage of my body. His hands clawed in search of my face. I got one knee into his back. Another second, and he'd say uncle.

I've been known to count my chickens before they're out of the egg. It's a fault that goes back to my old Marine days. Marines always think they have the situation under control. I should have remembered that the corps invented the term SNAFU. Situation Normal, All (expletive deleted) Up.

Then I wouldn't have been so surprised when a house landed on my head.

Four

My EYEBALLS STOPPED spinning like slot-machine cherries and the blurred features of the wolf lady's face arranged themselves more or less where they should be.

"Are you all right?" she said. There was worry in her bottomless dark eyes.

My head was cradled against the softness of her thighs, and the buckskin fringe of her dress tickled my nose. I sat up slowly. Tweetie birds twittered above my head. Little men were trying to punch their way out of my stomach.

Judging from the wall of legs gathered around us, I had edged out the jingle-dance girls as the powwow's main attraction. I picked Flagg out of the crowd and didn't like what I saw. He was talking to the guy I'd tackled. They looked chummier than delegates at an Elks convention.

A sound like an asthmatic bullfrog singing *La Traviata* tried to escape from my throat and barely made it past my front teeth. Flagg heard my defiant croak. He came over and kneeled on the ground beside me. The wolf lady got up, checked to make sure I didn't fall backward, and went over to talk to some people in the booth.

Flagg came over. "You gonna be okay, Soc?"

I felt like a baseball at a Little League practice, but the aches and pains took second place to the anger burning in my gut. "Why isn't that dirtbag in jail?" I glared at the guy. He stared fiercely back at me. Then he said something to another man in a windbreaker. I don't read lips, but I guessed he wasn't composing an Elizabethan sonnet in my honor.

Flagg said, "Got to do some talking, friend. Can you stand?"

This is the part where the punch-drunk pug says, "Lemme at him." I didn't feel like a rematch at the moment, though. "Yeah. Just point me in the right direction."

Using Flagg as a ladder, I pulled myself vertical. The guy saw me get up and came over. I clenched my fists and raised them a few inches. His green eyes flickered to my sides, and he stopped out of range.

Flagg stepped in between us like a referee at the Saturday-night fights. He gave me a level gaze that told me to slap a lid on my mouth. "Soc, I want you to meet Stanley Rourke. Mr. Rourke is an agent with the FBI."

At the moment, Mr. Stanley Rourke didn't look like an agent for *any*thing. His clothes were covered with grass and mud. His ginger hair was mussed, and his mustache was higher on one side than the other. He was rubbing his right hand where I'd bit him.

"FBI." I can be lightning quick with a riposte.

"That's right," Rourke snarled. "FBI."

"What's an FBI agent doing waving a gun around at a family gathering?"

"I was pursuing a suspect in a felony," Rourke snapped. "I

would have had him if your friend here hadn't interfered."

"Look, Agent Rourke, this was an honest mistake," Flagg said.

I unholstered my lip and let fly. "Shit, Flagg, it was no mistake. This guy had his gun out. No badge. No uniform. No warning to halt."

Rourke took a step forward, cold fury in his eyes. "Look, you sonofabitch, you're lucky I don't take you in for assaulting a federal officer and obstructing an arrest."

I looked at the bite marks on his hand. "You're lucky I don't have rabies."

Flagg grabbed my shoulder, muscled me over to the booth, and told me to stay put and keep quiet. He went back and they talked some more. Rourke grimaced, waved his fists in the air and pointed at me. Flagg listened impassively.

With the wrestling match over, the crowd had drifted off. The wolf lady was standing a few yards away. She handed me my Red Sox baseball cap.

"I found this," she said. "I think it's yours."

I brushed the pieces of grass and dirt off the navy blue crown, paying particular attention to the red "B," and replaced the cap carefully on my aching head. With her full lips and brown-sugar skin, the wolf lady had the kind of peaceful exotic look Gauguin used to capture in his South Seas women.

"Thanks," I said. "How'd *you* get in the middle of things?"

"I was coming over to the booth. I saw you and that . . . gentleman struggling. Then his friend hit you with something. You were lying there. I've never taken first aid, but it seemed the least I could do was to keep your head off the ground."

Flagg returned, his mouth curled in a wistful smile.

"Should I pack my bags for Leavenworth?" I said.

"You're off the hook this time. I kept showing him my IDs until I found one that impressed him."

"Wonderful! I'm glad you had the opportunity for some G-men bonding. Tell me what happened? I was taking a nap and I missed most of the action."

"I can put it together. Joe was waiting in the parking lot. He saw these guys, figured them for cops, and beat feet. Rourke and the other agent saw Joe heading for the woods. Rourke says he was about to fire a warning shot when you invited yourself to the party. While you were chewing on his hand, the other agent came up and crowned you."

"How come they're still hanging around here? I'd think they would have the hounds crashing through the woods looking for your pal."

"Hell, Soc, you were just the opening act. Joe really pissed these guys off. While you and Rourke were getting to know each other, Joe walked over to one of the town cops directing traffic and turned himself in."

"It would have saved me a couple of jars of Tylenol if he'd done that in the first place."

"You can still pull out, Soc. This FBI thing might complicate matters for you."

I looked around for the wolf lady, but she was gone. I had forgotten to ask her name. Flagg was waiting for an answer. There was really only one I could give him.

Five

KOJAK JUMPED ONTO the driftwood coffee table on my deck and went boneless. Puddling his body into a seventeen-pound, furry black jellyfish, he completely obliterated the file I was reading. I stared at the back of his head a couple of seconds, briefly entertained thoughts of trading him for a pair of Vietnamese potbellied pigs, then went inside and mixed some Nine Lives tuna and egg with his low-ash glop. He heard the can opener and followed me into the kitchen. While he sniffed his dish suspiciously, I grabbed a cold green bottle of Rolling Rock from the fridge, went back onto the deck, and dug once more into the life and times of Joe Quint.

Flagg had given me the file before he left for parts unknown. He said he'd be out of town a few days on business, jotted down a number where I could reach him, and warned me not to bite any FBI agents until I got my rabies shots.

The file read like *The Leatherstocking Tales.* Quint covered more ground than the Last of the Mohicans. He was born in

Charlestown, Rhode Island, got drafted in the army and volunteered for the Airborne. He graduated from URI in Bristol, picked up his sheepskin at Suffolk University in Boston and immediately started representing Indian reservations in the West and Southwest. He went head-to-head with the Bureau of Indian Affairs, flirted with the radical American Indian Movement in its waning days, and eventually crossed the line from purely legal to political.

Quint developed a knack for getting his name in the papers. One *Boston Globe* clip was typical. The city of Boston wanted to build a sewage treatment plant on an old Indian burial site. Quint quashed that. He led a "death march" along the route the Mahheconneuk tribe took when the colonists drove them off their land onto "plantations" in 1675.

The *Globe* quoted Quint as saying: "These plantations were the first concentration camps. This was the start of the Indian holocaust." Not bad.

I picked up another clip. Quint helped organize a Columbus Day party at the Esplanade, the little Charles River park around the bandstand shell where the Boston Pops plays. This is sacred white man territory hallowed by countless Fourth of July concerts and the ghost of Arthur Fiedler. The state had put some Columbus Day billboards around that said: "Celebrate Discovery." Quint blasted the white historians who said Chris discovered America.

"If the Micmac tribe from Maine had canoes that would have taken them across the Atlantic Ocean to Europe, could they say they *discovered* England or Spain? Columbus was a cruel and greedy man," Quint said, "and violence against Native Americans continues to this day." Not bad at all.

There was a picture of Quint standing with a group of peo-

31

ple on the stage of the Hatch Shell. He wore a wide-brimmed Western hat and dark shades, so it was hard to tell what he looked like.

Quint had popped up in the middle of Indian controversies around the country. He was a mediator in upstate New York when the state cops tried to close down tax-free cigarette sales by the Senecas. He was in the background after a couple of people were killed in a Mohawk shoot-out over gambling casinos. In Arizona, Quint was at the barricades with the Apaches who blocked roads after the feds grabbed gambling machines and tried to take them off the reservation.

In the Apache case, he said: "How would you like it if someone busted into your house and took off with your TV and VCR because he said they were illegal?"

There was much more. Quint was in federal court as part of the legal team representing an Abenaki claim to one-third of New England. He fought an attempt to put a nuclear-waste site near a reservation in Minnesota. He was embroiled in a battle over Sioux fishing rights. Whenever you found Indians on one side of the fence, and the white man on the other, Quint was in the thick of it. I wondered how Quint could fit a murder into his tight schedule. Hell, he hardly had time to grab a sandwich.

I watched a blue heron glide gracefully over the marsh grass until it flew out over the bay and I couldn't see it any more. Then I picked up the cordless phone and called information for the Plymouth state-police barracks.

Major-crime investigations in smaller jurisdictions of the Commonwealth are handled by CPAC, the Crime Prevention and Control unit. The staties told me to talk to Lieutenant Bacudas at the Plymouth County DA's office in Brockton, an old shoe factory city near Boston that serves as the county seat.

A few minutes later I was giving the lieutenant my name. I said I was a private cop looking into the Joe Quint case and asked if I could make an appointment to see him.

He consulted his calendar. "You free at lunch tomorrow?"

I told him I was.

"I'll be in Plymouth. There's a little takeout clam joint on the waterfront that's got great seafood. Place next to the whale-watch boats. Can you make it around noon?"

"I'll see you there."

Tires were crunching loudly into my clamshell driveway. I put the phone down and walked around to the front of the house. Senator Alan Eaton was getting out his town car. The week before, I'd dumped a truckload of new quahog shells into the driveway, and they hadn't been pulverized into small pieces yet. Eaton's crutches slipped on the uneven surface. I waited as he made his way slowly across the drive to my front door. He'd be insulted if I tried to help.

"Damn it man, good thing this isn't a public building!" he barked. "You'd have to have a handicap-access ramp."

I started to mumble an apology, but stopped when I saw the wide grin cross his tanned face. I held the front door open and said I'd meet him out on the deck with a cold beer. He said that was fine. I popped a couple of fresh bottles. He was sitting in my chair.

"I didn't interrupt your work now, did I?"

"No problem, Senator, I was just finishing up."

"Well, that's good. It doesn't do to work too much. Taking a little break from your fishing?"

"Some of the private-cop stuff I do. God, that reminds me. I've got to call Sam and tell him I can't go fishing for a day or two."

Eaton laughed heartily. "Young Mr. Sam may be able to

retire on his cribbage winnings. He cleaned my clock today."

"I stopped playing cribbage with Sam a long time ago. He'd peg twenty holes to my one. My get-rich dream is to form a syndicate and back Sam as a cribbage ringer. Are you interested, Senator?"

"You bet I am, Soc. "Now," he said. "The reason I dropped over. I wanted to say good-bye and let you know I'll be back in two weeks. Sam expects there will be some good striper fishing then, so we're going to give them a run for their money."

For the next hour, we traded fish stories. We talked about bait and moon tides, fishing tackle and boats, monster fishes that have gone down in history. The sun had disappeared over the trees to the west when Eaton looked at his watch. "Got to be going. I'm catching a late plane back to the capital tonight."

I walked him to his car. "See you in two weeks, Senator."

He stuck his hand out the driver's window and gave me a warm handshake. "Two weeks, Soc. One more thing. I just wanted to thank you again for the nice words you said over Maggie's ashes this morning. It meant a lot to me."

"She meant a lot to me, Senator."

"I know she did. Now, if there's ever anything I can do for you, let me know. I mean that quite sincerely, Soc; you give me a call."

"I will, Senator," wondering what the chairman of the Senate Judiciary Committee could do for a raggedy fisherman. You never know. Maybe he could get me a job with the FBI.

After Senator Eaton left, I went in and called Sam. I told him I had a case and had to take a couple of days off from fishing. Sam and I have an understanding. He said he'd get the Nickerson kid to fill in.

Sometimes people ask me why a commercial fisherman has

a private-eye business on the side. Usually I pass it off with a flip answer. I say an ex-cop has a hard time fitting his flat feet into rubber boots. But the real reason is a lot more complicated than that.

My mother clucks her tongue and says it was preordained by my Cretan blood; I take after her grandfather Nikos, a gentle farmer who helped a neighbor and ended up as a fierce mountain fighter who gave the occupying Turkish army nightmares. Ma is a lot more sophisticated than she looks. But when she named me Aristotle Plato Socarides, she still believed people lived up to the names given them. It's an old Greek failing. Greece is full of wiry little guys named Herakles and homely women named Aphrodite. My mother is a quick study. When my younger brother was born, she played it safe. His name is George.

Ma has been the prime force in my life. She pushed me into college to study the classics. It was her apron strings that I was trying to cut when I quit school, joined the Marines, and went off to Vietnam to save the world. I wish I could say Vietnam matured me, but mostly what it did was screw up my unformed brain. When I mustered out of the Marines, I became a cop in Boston. I met a woman named Jennifer who persuaded me lovingly that I didn't have to go into a defensive crouch every time a car backfired. I seemed destined for marriage and kids, what Zorba called, "the whole catastrophe."

As Sophocles says, fate is stranger than anything. Some city kids high on pills ran a red light in a stolen car. In one fiery second, my fiancée was dead and my life changed forever. I would have withered to dust if I hadn't found the boathouse on a weekend fishing trip with some guys from Vice and Homicide. I used the money I'd been saving to get married for a down payment. I quit the department and moved in year-round after a politically connected young jerk I'd arrested got off on a drunk-driving charge.

Sam and I met in a coffee shop named Elsie's. He was looking for a deckhand. I had no experience and lots of enthusiasm. We've been together ever since. He and his wife Mildred had one kid, a son, killed in the Mekong Delta, who will always be twenty years old. They've sort of adopted me, which shows that they have more kindness than brains.

Every year I say I'm not going to renew my private investigator's license, and every year I do. I tell myself I do it to pick up some extra cash, but the money I get in fees often doesn't cover the cost of the license. Sometimes I think the real reason I play at being a cop has to do with the car crash that changed my life. I'm still trying to make sense out of a senseless thing. If being a private cop means I can help somebody in trouble, maybe Jennifer didn't die in vain. Or maybe this is all merely rationalization and my mother is right; it's in the blood.

When I'm not fishing or sleuthing, I do some commercial diving. I started diving for recreation in Vietnam and have kept my certification through the years. People hire me to retrieve a lost outboard motor or to check the bottom of their boats.

I have a lady friend named Sally Corlin whose continued association with yours truly is a source of continuing amazement.

Sally is a dolphin trainer who works at a marine theme park called Oceanus. She has lovely chestnut hair and eyes that are somewhere on the spectrum between ocean blue and marsh lavender. The only flaw I can see in her otherwise high intelligence is a tendency to waste her time with unpromising men, although she is learning.

Sally and I have occasionally been what is called an item, although if our relationship were drawn on a chart it would resemble the peaks and valleys a side scan sonar might draw of the undersea canyons at the edge of the Continental Shelf. Sally tolerates a lot from me, more than I would expect any human being to tolerate. She never says anything about the way I dress. She only complains about my cooking when it gives her a stomach ache. She worries that my work as a private cop might expose me to bodily harm, but balances this off with the knowledge that sometimes I help people in trouble. Only one thing bothers her.

Two weeks ago, it bothered her a great deal. I didn't show up for a date. I had a perfectly good reason. I was too drunk to drive. She did not buy my argument that she should be glad I didn't get into my truck where I would have been a hazard to myself and others. Not long after that she told me she was going to a marine mammal conference for a weekend with Mike, a muscle guy who helps train dolphins at the aquarium. We haven't talked since then.

Otherwise, my existence is pretty routine. Occasionally something shatters this peace. Like a hurricane, a northeaster, or a boat wreck. Or a call from John Flagg.

Six

A BURLY STRAW-HAIRED guy sat alone at a picnic table next to the Plymouth town pier. He was reading a newspaper. I went over and asked him if he was Lieutenant Bacudas. He squinted up at me with sky-blue eyes that were too old for the fat-cheeked baby face and buttery complexion.

"How'd you guess?"

"I used the amazing deductive skills I picked up as a Boston cop. One, you're reading a paper published in Brockton, where the Plymouth County DA has his office. Two, you're wearing a tie." I gestured at the other tables under the canopy. "And three, you're the only person here who doesn't have at least one kid with him."

Bacudas showed a full set of crooked teeth, shook hands, and told me to have a seat. "Good thing I'm not on stakeout duty." He handed me a menu. "I recommend the fillet of fish sandwich. My treat. Coke okay?" I nodded. He didn't have to ask me twice. Delicious smells were wafting from the kitchen. He went up to the takeout counter. I glanced at the Red Sox box scores in the paper. Sox fans are stoical by nature, but it's never easy to have your hopes dashed every year. The Olde Towne Team was continuing the slide it got into each summer since the Sox sold Babe Ruth to the Yankees. I pushed the paper aside glumly and glanced toward the nearby town pier.

The news was better there. For all its tourist trade, Plymouth still has a working waterfront. The gill-net boats tied up at the pier were sea-beaten. The tractor trailers waiting in line to haul their catch away to market were grungy and grimy. A smell of diesel fuel, barnacles, and old fish hung in the air. The ticket booths were busy signing up people for deep-sea fishing and whale-watching trips. There were no boutiques selling overpriced designer resort clothes. No restaurants making sandwiches named after people. No whimsical descriptions on the menu that say: "The Captain Neptune is a delightful blend of white tuna meat, Gouda and Brie, with dressing *a la française* and alfalfa bean sprouts, all on a crusty focaccia . . . "

Before long, Bacudas came back carrying a plastic tray with two golden slabs of cod on hamburger rolls. New Englanders have a low tolerance for fish that's not fresh. What's passable in other places doesn't cut it in these parts; a fish has to be practically wiggling when you sink your teeth into it. Bacudas sampled his sandwich, grunted approval, and wiped tartar sauce off a blond mustache that was too nearly invisible to be useful as face decoration. "Jesus!" he said. "Why does the good stuff always have to be so frigging fattening?"

I took a bite that burned the roof of my mouth and cooled it down with a slug of Coke. The lieutenant watched me as if his mother's reputation depended on my approval. "Fresh enough for you?" he said.

"Any fresher and I'd have to stab it to death with a fork."

He nodded his approval and devoured half his sandwich.

39

"So, tell me," he said between chews, "how'd you get into Indian Joe's case?"

"A guy I knew from Vietnam asked me to check it out and see if I could dig something up that might help Mr. Quint."

"No disrespect intended, but tell your friend if he wants to help Joe, he'd do better baking a file into a cake."

"I think you're telling me Joe Quint shouldn't make any travel plans."

"Not unless he sprouts wings. Joe's tracks are all over this one, and he's going to have to do a hell of a rain dance to wash them out."

Not a bad metaphor for a cop, especially a state cop. "That's why I wanted to see you. All I know is that somebody was killed at Plimoth Plantation, and Quint's the only suspect."

He nodded and polished off the rest of his sandwich. "You been to the plantation?"

"Once, years ago. I didn't stay long. Every second-grade kid in Massachusetts was on a field trip the day I was there."

"Fucking crazy," Bacudas said with a shake of his head. "People come from all over the world and pay major bucks to see how the Pilgrims lived in shit. They should talk to my grandmother. That's all I heard about when I was a kid, how bad it was back in Lithuania before she came over on the boat." He belched. "You remember the layout at the plantation?"

"It's been a while, but I recall there was a fort with cannons at the top of the hill, the old village built on the slope, and a lot of chickens and ducks running in and out of the houses."

"You got it. About a week ago, a town guy named Mike Woods kissed his wife good-bye and went over to the plantation to do some maintenance work he couldn't get to during the day. He tells his wife he'll be home by eleven. Eleven-

40

thirty, and Mike's not there, so she figures he's stopped off for a beer. She wakes up at two A.M. He's still not home. She gets worried and calls the cops. They send a car to the plantation. It's bad news for Mrs. Woods."

"Mr. Woods is dead."

"Very."

"Cause of death?"

"Medical examiner says his skull was split."

"I heard someone used a hatchet on him."

"Yeah, that's right. Belonged to the victim. They got a little Indian settlement outside the village compound. Gives people an idea of how the other half lived. Got a couple of huts. Some of the Wampanoag Indians from around here hang out. They make canoes and cook up food for the tourists. Mike Woods was over there once and saw one of the guys using a tommyhawk. Said it would be real handy in the shop."

"You've talked to the Indian?"

"Yup. He says Woods admired it so much, he gave it to him."

"Any prints on the hatchet?"

"Naw, it was wiped clean."

I finished my sandwich and took a sip of Coke. "I'm missing something here, Lieutenant. What's the connection to Joe Quint?"

Bacudas glanced longingly at the food going by on trays. He asked if I wanted another fish sandwich. When I said no, thanks, he went in the fish market and ordered one for himself. He was nice enough to bring me a refill on my Coke. While he waited for his sandwich to cool, he answered my question.

"Okay, you want to know the connection. It's a pisser. But first you've gotta go back a couple of weeks to when Quint shows up here in town and starts making noise about how the

41

white men have been screwing the Indians."

"Quint is pretty well-known around the country as an Indian activist. He's good at getting people's attention."

"No argument there. He knows what buttons to push. He stands in front of Plymouth Rock and tells the tourists how they should be ashamed over what he calls a symbol of the white man's oppression. Does the same thing over by the *Mayflower*. He complains that the Pilgrims were corn thieves, land rustlers, and plague carriers. Naturally, he's invited a TV camera crew to record his comments for the six-o'clock news."

"Naturally."

"Joe tells the whole world he wants to get rid of Plymouth Rock and sell the *Mayflower* to a toothpick factory."

"Plymouth Rock is one big boulder. Good luck to him if he wants to move it."

"He's got other plans for the Rock. He wants someone to tickle it with a jackhammer and break it into bite-sized pieces. Then he'd sell the itty-bitty rocks as souvenirs and use the money for Native American causes."

"Not a bad marketing idea, really, but I can't see the locals letting their big tourist draw hammered into gravel."

"You wouldn't *believe* the reaction. Every so often some jerk spray-paints the old rock, but at least you can clean the stuff off. But *destroy* it? Hell, some people around here would sooner sell their kids than destroy *the* Rock. By the time of the murder, they're really cranked. They think the Indians are gearing up to rape and pillage. Probably got loaded muskets under their beds."

"So Joe Quint got some attention and bad eyes from the folks at the Mayflower Society. The last time I looked, this was a free country. A big mouth doesn't automatically mean a murder rap."

42

"There's more. One day Joe sets up a one-man picket line outside the plantation gates. Tells everybody going in that it's a—lemme see, what was the phrase he used? Oh, yeah—it's a monument to oppression. Like building a replica of Auschwitz and leaving out the ovens and gas chambers. He says if they want to be accurate, they should have an Indian's skull stuck on a pole outside the plantation. Some of the plantation people wouldn't mind it if Quint volunteered *his* head for the job."

"Quint's used the concentration-camp analogy before. It's strong stuff, but as I said a minute ago, it's a big leap from working the TV cameras to killing someone. What makes Joe the prime murder suspect?"

"Coupla things. First, Joe was in the vicinity of Plimoth Plantation the night of the murder."

"Someone actually *saw* him?"

Bacudas backtracked. "Actually, no. They *think* they saw him."

"Jury won't buy that."

"Yeah, I agree, but somebody definitely made his car."

"Reliable witness?"

"The best. A cop."

I thought about it for a second. "Let me see if I've got this right. Nobody is actually sure they saw him at the actual scene of the crime, and there weren't any fingerprints on the murder weapon. You might be able to get an indictment, and I've been around long enough to know that most evidence is circumstantial, but this is a pretty thin case. Do you really think this would hold up under a smart lawyer?"

"Naw. I can think of half a dozen guys who could tear it apart. That's why you've got to hear the rest of the story. After the cops found the body, they looked around. They figure somebody tried to burn the fort down. The wood near the foundation was charred. The arson boys picked up traces of accelerant. Gasoline. Mike Woods's sweatshirt was lying on the ground near the fort, all burnt to shit. Arson thinks he beat the fire out, then went down into the village. The body was found near the Standish house. More gasoline, a Bic lighter with no prints, but no fire. We think Woods surprised the fire-bug and got killed."

"You said there was a connection to Quint."

"Yeah, and it's a real pisser. You know that hatchet I mentioned?"

"The one Woods got from the plantation Indian."

"Yeah, well, they found it in Joe's car. The blood on the blade came from Woods. More bad news for your pal. There was a can of gasoline in his car."

"You're right—it's a pisser."

"Sews the whole thing up as far as I'm concerned."

"I dunno."

Bacudas raised his eyebrows in surprise. "You've got doubts?"

While Bacudas talked, I had been making a little paper tower out of the empty tartar-sauce holders. I looked up from my creative work. "Do you know anything about Joe Quint?"

"Just what I get from the other PDs."

"Then you might already know that Quint was in one of the toughest military units in one of the toughest areas of operation in all of Vietnam. He came out with a Purple Heart and put himself through law school, graduating with honors. He has been a highly visible Indian activist who's walked in to mediate situations where the bullets were flying and the bodies were dropping. And he's won a number of court suits against platoons of federal lawyers."

"So he's a hot shit. What's your point, detective?"

44

"My point is, that a guy that brave, dedicated, and smart is not going to blow into town, court the TV cameras by threatening the town's pride and joy, then go out and try to fry the chickens at Plimoth Plantation, kill someone with a stolen tomahawk, get spotted by a cop, and be so flustered he leaves highly incriminating evidence in his car."

Bacudas looked at his empty plate as if he thought of getting another sandwich and changed his mind. "Maybe he's a good soldier and lawyer and a lousy crook."

"What do you think, Lieutenant?"

"My job is to just lay out the facts. Jeezus, I sound like Sergeant Joe Friday."

"What about Quint? What does *he* say?"

"He's said he's not guilty, for one thing. And that he was at his girlfriend's house on the Cape."

"Did you talk to her?"

"Of course. She backs him up."

"What about the car being seen in Plymouth?"

"He has no explanation."

The whale-watch boat was leaving the pier. I followed it into the harbor with my eyes and brought my thoughts back to Joe Quint, putting myself in the defense counsel's place. "His lawyer might be able to create doubt in a jury's mind about the hatchet and the gas, but the car places him near the scene. He'll have a tough time with that one."

"I thought you knew. Joe's not using a lawyer; he's representing himself."

I raised an eyebrow. "Maybe Joe's not as smart as I think. That's not generally a good idea. Did the judge allow bail?"

"She set a bail of $500,000. Word around the courthouse is that Joe could have raised it through his Indian-group connections, but he's still in the slammer, so I don't know what's going on. Guess he likes jail food." He looked at his watch and got up. "Got to get back to the DA's office. "Anything else you need, give me a call."

I thanked him for his time and lunch. He said it was no problem. After he left, I strolled past a fish restaurant that had a cutout of an old salt sitting on the roof in an open boat, then along Water Street, which borders the harbor, to the *Mayflower II.*

The replica of the old ship that brought the Pilgrims to Plymouth has a shiny mahogany hull and pretty red, white, and blue trim topside. It looks like an overgrown three-masted bathtub, too small and too top-heavy to go anywhere, much less across the Atlantic Ocean. The ticket to Plimoth Plantation gets you aboard the *Mayflower* as well. The decks were loaded with people.

I picked up a brochure that said the ship was built in Devon in 1955, and sailed to Plymouth harbor two years later. It was 106.5 feet long, with a beam of 25.5 feet. Alongside was a 33-foot shallop, a replica of the workboat the Pilgrims used for fishing and trading and exploring. A diagram of the *Mayflower* told me what I already knew, that there wasn't much space for the Pilgrims who made the sixty-six day journey. I didn't know it then, but I would wish later that I had looked at the diagram a lot more closely.

Plymouth's pet rock is a couple of hundred yards from the *Mayflower* under a gray stone Doric canopy that looks like a Victorian mausoleum and is almost as exciting. I bought a scoop of heavenly hash in a sugar cone at a little ice-cream stand across the street, then went back to the canopy. Plymouth Rock sits in a sandy pit whose harbor side opens to the sea. It's protected by metal bars that let the water in and keep people out.

46

The rock is about six feet long and five feet wide. It looks like any boulder you'd find in a harbor breakwater, except for the date 1620 carved in letters about ten inches high on its flat sloping surface, and a crack right across the middle that has been filled with concrete. Lying in the sand around the rock were hundreds of pennies, some bottle caps, and an empty Busch beer can. I'd guess the people who threw the stuff in figured that there had to be more to it than just staring at a dumb boulder.

Plymouth Rock is where kids learn about truth in packaging. I couldn't have been older than ten when my parents drove the family down from Lowell to see the Rock. I don't know what I expected, but the boulder simply lying in the sand certainly wasn't it.

Some tourists whose caps said they were veterans attending a navy destroyer crew reunion were taking photos of the Rock as if it were something they felt they had to do, having come all this way. When I finished my ice cream, I walked across the street and climbed a low hill past the Pilgrim wax museum.

Near the museum is a tall statue of an Indian. A plaque says the statue was put up to honor Massasoit, the great sachem of the Wampanoag, who helped the Pilgrims, and was erected by the Improved Order of Red Men. I wondered what the *unimproved* order was like. Massasoit was looking out into Plymouth Harbor, his back to the Mayflower Society headquarters, probably wishing the immigration laws in his day had been stronger. The hill offers a good view of the waterfront. I lingered a few minutes, taking in the sweep of the harbor and Cape Cod Bay beyond. I checked my watch, walked back to where my pickup was parked at the town pier, and drove to the Plymouth County House of Correction on the edge of town to talk to a real, live Indian.

Seven

"Indian Joe says he doesn't want to see you and wouldn't, even if he knew who you are, which he doesn't."

The House of Correction guard sounded like an underpaid country-club majordomo snottily putting an upstart nouveau riche in his place. I scribbled in a notebook, tore out the page, and stuck it under the guard's nose.

"If Quint doesn't want to see me after he reads this, I'll go quietly."

The guard scanned the note, decided it wasn't the blueprint to the jail's underground sewer tunnels, and went back through the steel door.

A few minutes later he returned, trailed by a guy of medium height who was wearing denims, a black Harley-Davidson T-shirt and Chinese slippers. The guard pointed to a plastic-topped table and read the rules for visitors and prisoners. The guy took a seat on one side of the table, I sat opposite and we sized each other up like a couple of stray mutts fighting over a fire hydrant.

His long black hair was parted in the middle and pulled back into a ponytail tied unfashionably by a rubber band. His face was the color of new buckskin, and his fleshy nose was slightly off-center, as if he'd run into a wall. He drilled his gaze into mine and fingered the tip of the thin mustache that crowned his wide mouth. After a stare contest that ended in a draw, he pushed the lined notebook page across the table.

Glaring narrowly at me with street-smart eyes, he said, "What's *this* crap supposed to mean?"

The message was pretty straightforward. It said: *Flagg sent me.*

"It means that I'm the guy you were supposed to meet yesterday at the powwow."

"I told Flagg I'd talk to him. He never mentioned anyone else." His voice was edged with suspicion.

"John likes to surprise people." I pulled my business card out of my wallet and put it on the table like a riverboat gambler laying down his fourth ace. "He asked me to help you."

The line under my name says Private Investigations. It impresses some people; Quint wasn't one of them. "I don't need your help," he said flatly.

Flagg said to be patient with Quint. Okay, I'd been patient. Looking around at the white-washed cinderblock walls, I said, "Maybe you don't need *any*body's help. But in thirty seconds, when I walk out of this place and they slam that big steel door behind me, I can go straight to the nearest bar and get a beer. I can stop off at Mickey D's for a Big Mac if I want to punish my stomach. I can call up a woman and try to make a date. Or I can just go home and take a nap. What are you going to do when you go back to your cell, cross another day off your calendar and watch *Wheel of Fortune* on the telly?"

He shook his head and smiled thinly in spite of himself.

"Where the hell did Flagg find you, at The Comedy Connection?"

"No, he found me the same place he found you. Vietnam. You'd been sent home with a hole in your leg and he needed a pal to gripe to about the war. We met in a bar up north. He was glad to talk to me. We were both young and foolish and wished we were anywhere in the world but 'Nam. I was in the Marines, he was with Operation Phoenix and wasn't sure he liked the way they did things. Flagg and I became friends, and when he got out, we worked on a few cases together."

He picked up the card, read it, and clucked. "You don't look smart enough to be an Aristotle or a Plato."

"I'm not. That's why I'm wasting my time here with you. What's your Indian name?"

He paused. "Running Deer. That was before my leg got shot up in seventy-one."

"Bad call. I saw you humping it for the woods yesterday, and it wasn't your leg that was giving you trouble. You're too flabby around the waist to run any farther than the refrigerator. Do you want to play another round of sticks and stones or get down to why I'm here?"

"They've got a rec room here, and I can play games anytime. Okay, tell me why Flagg brought you in."

"He can't touch your case because of his government job. He wants me to find out what happened. He thinks you're innocent."

His heavy eyelids blinked, then drooped. He gave me a hard look through the slits.

"I was nowhere near the plantation that night. It's as simple as that."

"I talked to a state cop a while ago. He said a witness saw your car in Plymouth."

"The witness is wrong. I was with a friend all night in Mashpee. My alibi's solid. No one actually saw me at or near the scene of the crime."

I leaned forward with my elbows on the table. "I know you're pretty good at torts, counselor, but have you practiced much criminal law?"

"My area of expertise is federal Indian law. That's no secret."

I nodded. "Then believe me on this one. The jury will hear that your car was in the neighborhood, and to them, a car and person are the same thing. They'll also be told that the hatchet and gas can were found in your car. Any idea how that happened?"

He leaned forward and hissed the answer. "Do you really think I'd risk my ass to burn down that fucking thatched-roof Disney World, split some poor bastard's skull in, then leave bloody evidence in the vehicle that was supposedly used in the commission of the crime?"

"If you had a lawyer, he'd tell you stupidity is a lousy defense."

"Look, Mr. Socarides—"

"Call me Soc. It saves time."

"Okay . . . Soc. It's perfectly obvious this was a setup. That stuff was put in my car to frame me."

"Who would do that?"

He snorted. "I've made a lot of enemies doing what I do."

"Anyone in particular?"

He clamped his mouth shut. If Quint knew, he wasn't saying.

"What brought you to Plymouth?"

"I was on Cape Cod."

"Doing what?"

"Vacation."

"Why did you break off your vacation to terrorize the Mayflower Society?"

"Something set me off."

"What was it?"

"None of your business."

"Here's another thing that's not my business. I heard you could have made bail. How come you're still here in the clink?"

Quint sat back in his chair and crossed his arms. "This stuff is out of your league, Mr. Private Eye."

"Try pitching a ball slow and easy, and maybe I'll hit it."

I waited.

Quint snorted softly and shook his head. "You familiar with the Leonard Peltier case?"

"I've read about him. He's in jail for murdering a couple of FBI guys. Some people say he's innocent."

"There's no doubt in my mind that he's innocent. But as long as he stays in jail, he'll be a martyr and a symbol of injustice and the white man's oppression."

"That's a little tough on Peltier, isn't it?"

"He understands."

"Let me see if I get this straight. You're doing the same thing, proving that the justice system is a sham when it comes to Native Americans, hoping that maybe Robert Redford will make a movie about you."

"We're dealing with four hundred years of injustice. We use what we've got."

My slim layer of patience was wearing thin. I jerked my thumb at the guard who had ushered me in. "Do you know what the guards call you here?"

"Yeah, they call me Indian Joe."

"Do you think being made a joke of is going to further your cause?"

Exposed nerve. Quint stood up. "Interview's over," he growled, signaling the guard that he wanted to go back to his cell. "Excuse me, pal, I've got some calendar days to cross out."

I said, "What do you want me to do?"

As he was being led off, he turned to give me my instructions. "Go fuck yourself."

"Quint," I called after him. "Did you really mean that, about busting Plymouth Rock into gravel?"

Just before the door slammed behind him, he smiled and said, "Of course."

And you know, I don't think he was kidding.

Outside, I sucked in huge breaths of fresh air. I get depressed by prisons, hospitals, nursing homes, zoos, anyplace you can't leave very easily. I didn't stay depressed for long. A man in a gray suit strode toward me from the parking lot. It was Rourke, the FBI agent I did the tango with at the powwow. He came over and stuck his face in mine. Rourke would never make an FBI recruiting poster. He was neither handsome nor clean-cut. He had a wide homely face, ears like pitcher handles, a mouth like Willy the Whale, and the kind of thuggishness you see in cops who have been dealing with hard cases so long they imitate them.

"What the hell are *you* doing here?"

"Are you asking that in a physical or a metaphysical sense?"

He glowered. "I'm asking it as a federal law officer."

"In that case, I heard this is a good place to meet single women who come to visit their boyfriends."

"You know," he said quietly, "all I have to do is go inside, flash my badge, and I'll know everything you did in there."

I don't know why I was baiting him. Maybe it was just the spillover from dealing with Joe Quint.

"I wouldn't want to put you through all the trouble." I reached in my wallet and gave Rourke my card. He wasn't any more impressed than Joe Quint was. He handed it back. "Your buddy Flagg said you were a private eye. Tell me something I don't know, like what you were doing inside."

"I was here to see a client."

A light bulb seemed to go off in his head.

"Joe Quint," he said. "Right, it's Joe Quint, isn't it?"

"I don't mind helping you out, Agent Rourke, but I'm not going to do all your work for you."

His face turned the color of boiled beets. He jabbed a stubby forefinger into my chest. "Look, you little puke, stay out of this case."

That was only the warm-up. He went into a detailed account of what would happen if I didn't heed his advice. It included every kind of painful infliction visited by one human being on another, and then some. Dismemberment was the only one he left out, and he would have gotten around to that if there was more time. Nobody has ever called me a puke before. I didn't know whether to get mad or laugh. I laughed. That made him angrier. He jabbed some more with his finger. I was getting sick of being taken for a doorbell.

"If you stick that thing in my chest again, Agent Rourke, you'll be pulling the trigger with your nose at target practice."

His eyes bulged. He couldn't believe someone would threaten one of Hoover's boys. I wouldn't have believed it myself. But I wouldn't have believed I'd tackle an armed FBI agent, either.

"I'll just warn you once. Stay out of the Joe Quint thing.

It's just another case with you. This is personal with me. If you get in my way, I'll run right over you like a bulldozer."

It wasn't smart to take on the federal government, but the best way to keep me interested was to warn me off. I'm not a complete fool, though. I resisted my impulse to answer him with one of my usual witty comebacks.

"Thanks for the warning," I said respectfully. "I'll think it over."

"You do that." He spun on his heel and marched toward the jail.

I watched him go inside, thinking that maybe I had pushed him too far, not really caring if I had.

Eight

Route 3 is a four-lane highway that runs north-south between Cape Cod and Boston, slicing through the sprawling wooded hills of Miles Standish State Forest a few miles west of Plymouth. Although its official name is Pilgrim Highway, the road wasn't there when the Pilgrims came ashore and neither was the Mexican restaurant off Route 3, where I sat at the bar drinking Dos Equis beer.

The place was empty, except for me and a man wearing a rumpled business suit and a face to match. He sat a few stools away enjoying a solo happy hour. He kept glancing in my direction as if he wanted somebody to talk to. *Cheers* was on the wide-screen TV; an old episode, because Coach was still tending bar. I munched nachos and cooled down the high-octane salsa with sips of cold beer, reflecting on my jailhouse interview with Joe Quint.

Quint said he had stayed the night with his girlfriend. I dug out my notebook. The name Lieutenant Bacudas gave me was Patricia Hoagland. The guy at the bar slid one stool closer.

Time to go. I paid for my beer and got on Route 3 south, crossing the Cape Cod Canal at the Bourne Bridge. The Cape is shaped like an arm curled up in a gesture that could get you killed if you made it in some countries. I live just above where the elbow would be. Plymouth is the shoulder. The town of Mashpee is the triceps.

Mashpee is laced with skinny back roads. I drove down every one of them at least once. I found the town forest and the town dump. I asked three different people for directions, but they were lost, too. I looked in my road atlas and got lost again. I would have missed the mailbox if it weren't a fire-engine red. The name Hoagland was painted on it in drippy black letters.

The dirt driveway ended after a couple of hundred feet at a boxy one-and-a-half-story house sheathed in asphalt shingles of insipid green. What the real estate people call a fixer-upper and carpenters call an opportunity. Parked in front was a dusty white Subaru station wagon decorated with bumper stickers. The kind that say: "Arms Are For Hugging." I went up the walk and rang the bell. A dog started barking in the house. Seconds later, the door opened. It isn't polite to gawk, but I couldn't help staring stupidly at Patricia Hoagland. She and the woman I had flippantly dubbed the wolf lady were one and the same.

"Miss Hoagland?"

"Yes," she said. My reaction must have shown in my face. "Is there a problem?"

"No," I said, tightening up the slackness in my jaw, "I'm just surprised to see you here."

"I don't know why that should surprise you. This *is* my house."

"We met yesterday at the powwow." I touched the visor. "You returned my cap."

"Yes, of course. I remember."

"Maybe I should explain why I'm here."

"Maybe you should."

I gave her my business card. Her brow creased. "You're a private investigator?"

Her question had an incredulous tone, as if I'd told her I was a nuclear physicist. I tend to dress down, but for the meeting with Bacudas I'd exchanged my shorts, T-shirt, and sandals for a clean shirt, slacks, and Nikes. The public is conditioned by TV and she may have been expecting something more traditional.

"Slouch fedoras and Aquascutum trench coats went out with Humphrey Bogart, Miss Hoagland."

"I'm sorry, I didn't mean to be rude. It's just that I've never met a private detective before. What can I do for you?"

"I've been asked to look into Joe Quint's case. I wondered if I could ask you some questions."

"I'm not sure. I think I'd like to know who hired you first."

"A mutual friend."

"May I ask what this friend's name is?"

"John Flagg."

An overweight chocolate Laborador retriever who'd been barking spastically in the background poked his head from behind her legs and sized me up. The white fur around his muzzle made him look like a friendly old sailor, long home from the sea. He squeezed past her and sniffed my hand.

Patricia Hoagland smiled at the dog. "Please come in," she said.

She led the way into a living room done in earth colors: russet, ocher, and brown. The thick rug had a geometric Aztec design. The white walls were hung with Indian weavings and sand paintings. A mask with a face like a drunken buffalo leered at me from over the flagstone fireplace.

I settled into a comfortable fabric and wood frame sofa. The dog came over and drooled on my thigh.

"If Cochise bothers you, tell him to sit," Patricia said.

She removed a limp marmalade cat from a wing chair and sat down with the animal on her lap.

"Nice kitty," I said.

"Far from it. Her name is Sitting Bull, and she'll tear your heart out if you irritate her."

I glanced warily at the cat, but she closed her eyes and slipped into a peaceful snooze.

"I enjoyed your chanting demonstration at the powwow, Miss Hoagland."

It was a self-serving lob that was partly genuine but mostly intended to show Patricia Hoagland what a sweet, caring guy I am. She took it for what it was worth—practically nothing—and batted it back to me with an even sweeter smile.

"From where I was watching, you were more interested in mud wrestling."

"I've given up wrestling. I can't afford the cleaning bills."

"That's probably a good idea. Would you like some iced coffee?"

I nodded. Patricia set the sleeping cat down and went into the kitchen. She had put aside her buckskin dress and beads for denim cutoffs and T-shirt. She was maybe five-two, well-proportioned in just the right places. What they were thinking about when they said good things come in small packages. She came back a few minutes later.

"How do you know John Flagg?" Patricia asked, handing me a tinkling glass.

"Flagg and I were in Vietnam together. We've worked on a few cases since then. Do you know him?"

"I've heard Joe talk about him. I hoped to meet him at the powwow."

"You'll get another chance, I'm sure."

She stroked the cat's head gently. "What is it you want to know?"

"I dropped by the jail and talked to Joe a little while ago. He said he was with you the night the man was murdered at the plantation."

"That's right. He was here in this house."

"His car was seen in Plymouth. Any idea how that might have happened?"

"It was a mistake on someone's part."

"The identification was pretty solid."

"It was a *mistake*," she said emphatically. "There was no way Joe could have left without my knowing it."

"Could somebody have taken his car?"

She thought about it. "Possibly, I suppose, but highly unlikely. It was parked out in the drive. The keys were in the house."

"Did anybody else see him here that night?"

"No. Let me take that back. My kid brother came by."

"What's his name?"

"Peter Hoagland. He's a real-estate man in town. He was here for a short while that evening."

"When did Joe leave?"

"Early the next morning. He went off with a friend. The police showed up with a warrant around nine o'clock and searched his car." She patted her knees impatiently. "Mr. Socarides, this is the same story I told the police. Forgive me for seeming annoyed, but I don't see why it's so difficult to understand. Joe was here. He could not have killed that man."

"How long have you known Joe, Miss Hoagland?"

"Three years."

"Are you good friends?"

"*Very* good friends."

"Do you love him?"

Her cheeks turned the color of ripe golden plums. "I don't see—"

"You're right, it's none of my business. But it *is* the DA's. He'll ask you the same question. He'll want to attack your credibility. He'll paint a picture for the jury of a woman so deeply in love she is willing to perjure herself to protect her man. The jurors might admit to themselves that they would lie, too, if they were in your place. They might even think it's noble and admire you for it. Just because they empathize doesn't mean they will think it's right. Your testimony could be worse than useless; it could show you've got something to hide."

I expected an argument. Instead, she said, "Why do you care about Joe, Mr. Socarides?"

"I don't. I just met him today and he impresses me as a guy who's going to pop like a balloon if he gets more full of himself. But John Flagg is a friend of mine, and he asked me to do him a favor."

Patricia Hoagland's almond eyes got bigger and more beautiful. "What about justice?"

"What about it?"

"Would you let someone go punished for something he didn't do?"

"It happens all the time, Miss Hoagland."

"You still haven't answered my question," she probed.

"I'll try again. I wouldn't let someone be punished for

61

nothing, but it's not always within my power to stop it, and I'll be damned if I'll spend the rest of my life looking for windmills to tilt at. Now let me ask you something."

She hesitated; she still wanted to play third degree. "All right," she said.

"I went through the clips on Joe. Every time he went public, it looked to me like a well-planned attempt to get some ink. Whether he was trying to make the feds back down or making claim to all land west of the Mississippi, it was done deliberately and carefully. Then comes this Plymouth thing. He's rolling around like a loose cannon. Getting the local folks so stirred up, they're priming their muskets. It seemed out of character. What set Joe off? What got him going around threatening to pound Plymouth Rock into sand?"

"Joe doesn't tell me everything. All I know is that he went to Plymouth one night, and when he came home, he was very upset and angry. I asked him what the problem was. He said he'd explain later."

"Do you know where he went in Plymouth?"

"Only that it was an auction someplace."

"So the next day, after the auction, he started making headlines."

"Actually, it was a few days later. He made some telephone calls and went to Boston."

"Any idea who he talked to or saw?"

"In Boston, it was somebody in the state government. I overheard some of his calls. He was talking to museums and archaeologists, I believe. I was trying not to eavesdrop."

"Do you remember hearing any names?"

"Yes, one, because it was unusual. Zane."

"Just Zane?"

"Yes."

Brakes squealed softly in the front drive. My back was to the window. Patricia glanced over my shoulder, but didn't get up. The front screen door creaked open, and quiet footsteps sounded in the hall. Cochise lifted his head off my knee and went over, tail wagging, to greet two men who came into the living room. The taller one was a lank, big-handed guy dressed in jeans, work shirt, and cowboy boots. He moved with the easy sureness of a high-wire walker. He had a round tanbark face and a profile like an ancient Roman. The other guy could have been his twin, put under a pile driver and squashed down half a foot; his deep chest barreled out over stumpy powerful legs. The tall man looked at Patricia Hoagland, then skewered me with flinty eyes.

"Everything okay, Patty?"

"It's fine. Tommy and Ed, this is Mr. Socarides," she said.

"We dropped by to talk to you, Patty. We'll come back later."

"No, stay. Mr. Socarides, are there any more questions I can help you with?"

"You've already helped a great deal. Thanks for your time."

Patricia offered to walk me to my truck. A blue Ford Ranger pickup with New York plates was in the drive. "Your friends, Tommy and Ed, they're not local Wampanoag?"

"No, they're from out-of-state. They're friends of Joe's."

I nodded, thanked Patricia, asked her to call me if she remembered anything more, and went to get into my pickup.

She put her hand on my arm. "I want to thank you for yesterday at the powwow. You may have saved Joe's life. I think that man was going to shoot him."

"Why would an FBI agent be chasing Joe with a gun?"

"I don't know. As I told you, Joe doesn't always confide his business in me."

"Does that bother you?"

"I can understand why he might want to keep his client cases confidential, but sometimes I don't know what he's been doing until I read about it in the papers. That hurts."

"Is he telling you all there is now?"

"No. I think he's involved in something very serious that he's keeping to himself."

"What makes you say that?"

"Something else was weighing on his mind, even before that man was murdered. But I don't know what it was."

I got into the pickup and started the engine. "Let me know if you find out, Miss Hoagland."

"Call me Patty."

"Only if you call me Soc."

"All right, Soc. I'm glad you still want to help. Especially after what you said about tilting at windmills."

I smirked and put the pickup into gear. Why do nice ladies like Patty end up with men who are jerks? I started to think about the women in my life, didn't like where it was taking me, and switched to another topic. How had Patty described it? *Something Else.*

Nine

THE SECRETARY AT Peter Hoagland's real-estate office said I could find Patty's brother at a Route 28 building site next to a convenience store and liquor market. I parked in front of the store and wandered over to a construction trailer. Two guys stood outside the trailer talking. One was a heavyset man in work clothes and a hard hat. The other, wearing a suit, was a head shorter, twenty years younger, and a hundred pounds lighter. It was pretty clear who the boss was.

The younger man was drawing imaginary pictures in the air with his hands. Squares. Circles. Trapezoids. Figure eights. He danced lightly around the heavy guy as he talked.

"Tom, we've got three weeks to finish phase one of this project," he said, raising his voice over the racket made by the backhoe chewing a hole in the earth behind them. "The banks are on my ass, the lessors are on my ass, and *I'm* on my ass. I don't want to be cutting ribbons for the new liquor mart after every tourist has gone home and taken his checkbook with him."

Tom nodded like a spring-necked car doll in a rear window. "Our problem is gonna be the subcontractors, Pete."

The younger guy drew an imaginary Z in the air. "Correction, Tom. Our problem is *not* going to be the subcontractors. If they can't guarantee they'll be here when I want them, get somebody else."

A big cricket chirped. Pete reached into his pocket, pulled out a flip phone, and stuck it in his ear. He listened a second, then barked, "Tell Mr. Peterson it's the best offer he'll get for his house in this market. If I were him, I'd sell, pronto."

He snapped the phone shut, and picked up his conversation without missing a beat.

"Here's what I want you to do, Tom. Fire the framers. Fire the drywall boys. Hire Jackie Crowell. Hire Frankie Souza. Tell them we'll pay two percent over their regular criminal rates if they drop their other work and get this job done on schedule."

Tom heaved his bulky body. "Done deal, Peter," he said and lumbered off.

Hoagland turned his quick dark eyes to me. His mouth snapped wide in a hair-trigger smile, and he shot his hand out. "Peter Hoagland. What can I do for you?"

"I stopped by your real-estate office. Your secretary said you'd be here."

"I just talked to her. She called to say somebody was looking for me."

I told him who I was and that I was a private cop. "I'm looking into the Joe Quint case. I just talked to your sister. I wondered if we could chat a few minutes."

Peter gave me a wary look. "A private investigator? Are you working for Joe?"

"In a way."

"Joe's in a hell of a mess."

"Maybe you know something that will help him out of it."

"I hope so. Joe is like my big brother. Only thing I got against him is he's not married to my sister. Excuse me a second." He pulled out his phone and punched a number. "Denise, hold all calls till I get back to you. Yeah, no exceptions. I know, I'm supposed to talk to McGrath about the Snow property. The bastard charges me two hundred bucks every time he says hello, so of course he likes to talk. Tell him I'll see him at four o'clock sharp. I'm looking for more money or it's a no go."

He snapped the phone shut and stuffed it into his pocket. "Denise is worse than a mother, but my office would come to a screaming halt without her." He grinned engagingly. "How do you like working with Joe?"

"It's a challenge."

"I'll bet." He shook his head. "He can be a real pain."

"Actually, I'm doing it as a favor."

"An altruistic private eye. I like that. Do I have to call you Aristotle?"

"You'd be the only one who does, outside of my mother and father. Most people call me Soc."

He reached in the open window of the black BMW parked next to the construction trailer, pulled out a small aluminum case, and extracted two stogies each about a foot long. "Havanas. A friend brings them in from Montreal. Try one, Soc."

I told him to light up without me. He blew a smoke ring toward the sky. "These cost ten bucks apiece. That's about a dollar a puff, but what the hell."

Peter had the same dark shiny hair and dusky complexion as his sister. Where Patricia was serious and studied, though, he had a quicksilver smile and an easy charm.

"Your sister says you were at the house the night of the murder."

"Yeah, I stopped by, had a chat with Joe, and a beer."

"How long were you there?"

"Only about an hour. I got into an argument with Patty and left."

"Do you mind if I ask what the argument was about?"

"The usual thing." He gestured at the growling backhoe. "She doesn't like what I do. She says I'm raping the town and being disrespectful of my Wampanoag heritage. I tell her she's going overboard on the Indian cultural thing. You've seen her house. It looks like a gift shop at a Hopi reservation."

"If you don't get along, how did you happen to drop by?"

"I've been really making an effort to get closer to Patty. Our parents are both dead, so there's just the two of us."

"That's why you were there, to do some family bonding?"

"To be honest, I went to see Joe. We don't see eye to eye, but he doesn't make it a personal thing, like Patty. He's cool. He says I'm an Indian gone wrong, but it's a joke between us. I'd do anything to help him. With Patty, maybe it's just the kid-brother thing."

The kid-brother thing. I knew about that from the stormy relationship with my younger brother George. "Sibling rivalry?"

"That's part of it, but it's more complicated." He looked at his watch. "I could show you better than tell. You got a few minutes?"

"I've got all day."

He opened the passenger door of the BMW. I got in and he slid behind the wheel. "You know much about the history of Mashpee?"

"Only that it used to be an Indian reservation, and that it's been growing faster than mushrooms."

"Fastest-growing town in the state, in fact." He started the engine and pulled out onto Route 28. "My sister thinks I don't understand the situation. I was a history major at Cornell. I know damned *well* what's going on. You familiar with the big land suit we had here in town back in the 1970s?"

"The Wampanoag claimed most of the town as tribal land. They went to court and lost."

"Right as far as it goes. You have to go back three hundred years for the big picture. Miles Standish came down from Plymouth and offered to buy the Indians' land. The locals didn't have a clue what private ownership meant; it was all open land to them. But it seemed like a good deal, so they let it go for a couple of copper kettles. When they found out they couldn't fish and hunt, they went back to Miles. He showed them the contract. Said that's what they signed."

"Too bad the Indians didn't have your lawyer."

"Hah. That shyster would have charged them *two hundred* copper kettles an hour. Anyhow, a white guy named Richard Bourne felt guilty and got twenty-five square miles put aside for the Indians and their kids forever. He set up the Mashpee plantation for good Christian 'praying Indians.' After Bourne died, the land pirates came in again, trying to nickel-and-dime the Indians out of their plantation."

Peter inserted the BMW deftly into the flow of cars circling a busy traffic rotary, and we cruised south toward Nantucket Sound.

"One day the Indians woke up and found the whites owned more land than they did. Most of the whites lived off-Cape, though, so the Indians could still run things. There was Indian consciousness-raising going on at the time. The Indians took a closer look at their old customs. They started the summer powwows. But while they were banging on their drums, the whites took over control of the town hall and real estate. The Indians fought back. They organized the tribal council. That's their headquarters over there." He pointed to a small building set back in the woods. "Same thing was happening as with Miles Standish. Look around and you'll see what I mean."

We went by developments named Sea Mist and Sandalwood. Soon, the woods on either side of the road were thick with buildings. Peter stopped at a couple of signs: Residents Only or No Trespassing.

"What's that tell you?"

"The rabbit hunters and the fishermen are out of luck again?"

"Right." He hooked a U-turn and headed back toward Route 28. "These used to be all woods," he said. "Now look at it. There are hundreds of condos and houses. Couple of terrific golf courses. I play them both. Jacuzzis. Swimming pools. The tribal council said enough was enough. They'd been bilked out of the land illegally, and they wanted it back. All the real-estate people were scared shitless. Not a land transaction went on for three years. Then the feds say, nope, you're not a tribe. You lose. The dam breaks. Wham. Mashpee becomes a boomtown. Subdivisions. Malls. Even got a strip joint."

"Tough break for the Indians."

"Yes and no. They should have seen it coming, but being told they were a nontribe sucked the wind right out of their sails. Hit 'em right in their pride. They pulled back. Gave up what was left of their political power."

Peter took us around the traffic circle again. We headed toward the village center. The houses were older and had a tired look. We went past the small white First Pentecostal Church of Jesus Christ, Inc., hooked a left at the trading post, and drove past a brick building.

"Town hall," Peter said. "Anglo country now."

"Tell me about your sister," I said. "How come you two are so different?"

"Sis is no dummy. She's got her master's degree in psychology and teaches at the community college. What my sister is into—the born-again Indian stuff—that's nothing but a reaction to losing power in town, if you ask me."

"How come you didn't react the same way?"

"Mr. and Mrs. Hoagland were poor, but they didn't raise any stupid children. It's a matter of pragmatism, Soc. Like I said before, you've gotta look at history. Back in 1620, when the Pilgrims showed up at Plymouth, the Wampanoag said, 'Uh-oh, there goes the neighborhood,' but they looked at the guns the white guys were carrying and started smiling and shuffling their feet. Our people gave the Pilgrims a hand surviving, and what they got in return was musket balls, TB, and smallpox that wiped out thousands of Wampanoag."

"Don't forget Thanksgiving. They gave them that, too."

"Now *there's* a scam. Sure, the Pilgrims invited the Indians to their party for a few days, but Massasoit's guys brought in five deer, so it wasn't a free lunch. And you know what Massasoit got for his trouble?"

"A condo on the beach in Mashpee?"

"You wish. I'll tell you what he got. Few years later, the Pilgrims tell Matacomet, Massasoit's youngest son, the one they named King Philip, that his people couldn't sell their land without an okay from Plymouth, and that they had to turn in their guns. Then the white men pushed us into a war they couldn't lose, killed Philip, drew and quartered him, and stuck

71

his head on a pole up at Plymouth. They sold his son and wife into slavery, and executed or enslaved hundreds of Indians, including the Mashpee Wampanoag, who had signed a non-aggression treaty with the Pilgrims. You tell *me* who the savages were."

"Sounds as if the Pilgrims and the Indians never really liked each other."

"That was only part of the problem, Soc. The Indians played into the white men's hands. The tribes were always fighting among themselves, so the white men pitted one group against the other, then took it all."

"So the whites exploited the Indians. Your big sister is saying the same thing."

"Oh, sure, we both agree that the Indians are still being victimized. Just a couple of years ago, a town cop stopped a local guy, Wampanoag, after a car chase, and filled him full of lead. The cop was cleared by the inquest and stayed on the force until the tribe started raising so much hell they got rid of the guy. They gave him a hefty severance package—almost like a reward for killing the Wampanoag."

"That was tough, but I still don't understand where you and Patty differ."

"Patty thinks you use moral persuasion and education to get your way in the white man's world. That once you have enough powwows and bake sales, the whites are going to come around and give you what was yours in the first place."

"So what's your point?"

"My point is it's stupid to use reason on the white guys, because it's never worked, and that it's even dumber to fight them, because you're going to lose. Do you think it makes any difference how many Wampanoag we have in the selectmen's office or on the planning board?"

"I don't know, you tell me."

"It doesn't mean crap. If the Anglos want to do something in this town, they'll bring in their corporate lawyers and engineers, they'll pull strings at the state house or in Washington, and they'll get what they want. We are still outnumbered and still outgunned, just the way we were back when they were chopping King Philips's head off."

"I think you're about to make another point."

"You got it. My point is that the best way to get back at the whites is to use their own greed to suck the money out of their pockets. My sister thinks it all comes down to a question of identity."

"You can't discount identity entirely."

"I don't, not by a long shot. If it will get me what I want, I'll dance around in a feathered headdress. I'll wring every last shred of guilt I can get out of White America. But let's be realistic, Soc. Look at me and my sister. We're like the mestizos in South America. People intermarried through the years. They made it with the Cape Verdeans that came in to work the cranberry bogs, and with the Anglos. I can look in the mirror and see pure Wampanoag around the cheekbones and eyes." He pressed his nose. "But my skin's got more of Africa and Yankee in it than Indian. I know damn well I'm not going to find my profile on a nickel."

"There's more to a tribe than skin color."

"Shit, Soc, I know that. But you can't drag the feathers and drums out after all these years and say, 'Hey, we can beat a tom-tom, so we're Indian.' Hell, what are you, Greek? I don't see you running around in a toga."

"Greeks didn't wear togas. That was the Romans."

"Whatever. You know what I mean."

Peter gestured toward some timeworn houses. "People

who own these places go back generations in this town and mansions like this are what they've got. Patty's content living in the old family house. I've got a place on the water that would knock your socks off. If this is what they want, they can have it. The only difference is, this time Miles Standish and the white men are going to pay through the nose. Hah. Listen to me, white men. Hell, maybe Patty and I are more alike than I think."

He pulled up to his real estate office, an ocean blue one-story clapboard building. Out front a sign shaped like an arrowhead said Maushop Realty.

"Is that sign supposed to be a statement of your Indian identity?"

He laughed. "I'll use my heritage where it counts. We've got great beaches and pretty scenery in this town, but you can get the same stuff dozens of places on the Cape. So we sell image. You name a condo complex Paukawananee. People like that. You can even make up an Indian name, like I just did."

Inside, three brokers were crowded into a small space working the phones.

"I'm back, Denise," Peter said to his attractive blond receptionist. "I'll take those calls in a few minutes."

We went into his office and Peter picked up the pile of pink message slips on his desk. "I'm going to have to do some business, I guess. Anything else I can tell you?"

"Getting back to Joe. Is there any way you can verify he was at the house all night?"

He spread his hands. "Damn, I wish I could. I'd lie for the guy, but who'd believe a real-estate broker?"

I plucked his business card from a holder and wrote my name and telephone number on the back of it. "If you think of anything, give me a call. I don't have an answering machine, so just keep trying."

He shook my hand. "Thanks for trying to help Joe."

"Thanks for the tour. And the history lesson."

Denise stuck her head in the door. "Peter, it's Mr. McGrath. He says he can't be there at four, and he wants to talk to you."

Peter flashed his bright smile and shook hands. "Duty calls, Soc. I've got to go back to raping the town."

I drove home and called Flagg. It took a minute for his answering service to patch me through. I was on my deck, feet propped up on the driftwood coffee table, sipping lemonade from a tall tumbler. Yellow light from the late-afternoon sun painted the bay and the outer beach. When Flagg came on, I told him I had seen Joe Quint.

"How did you two get along?"

"We were civil to each other. More or less."

"I'll tell him to calm down."

"It would be in his own interest. He's in more trouble than he knows. On the bright side, I met his girlfriend, Patty."

"What did you think of her?"

"Attractive. Smart. Attractive."

"That's nice. Was she any help?"

"Not much. She's Joe's alibi. She'll make a good presentation on the witness stand, but a jury will figure she's protecting Joe. She doesn't know why Joe raised a ruckus around Plymouth, but she may have given me a lead. I talked to Peter, her little brother. He was at Patty's house and saw Joe there the night the guard was killed. Problem is, he went home early and can't corroborate his sister's statement."

I told him about my conversation with Carl Bacudas, the state cop.

"Huh," he said. "Bottom line, Soc."

"You might be able to convince a jury that the hatchet and the gas can were plants, but they're still going to wonder what Joe's car was doing in Plymouth that night. If they think Joe is lying about the car, they'll figure he is lying about everything else. I'll see if I can punch holes in the car story, but I'm not hopeful."

"Well, do your best. Call if you need any information."

"I will. I want to talk to the cop who saw Joe's car. And I want to visit the crime scene. If I think of anything else, I'll go back and see Joe and we can have another smile contest."

"Sounds good. Keep in touch." He hung up.

I had some more lemonade and called the Plymouth Police Department. I said I was a private investigator working on the Joe Quint case and asked if I could speak to the officer who saw Joe's car. Defense attorneys sometimes hire private eyes, so they weren't surprised by my call. They relayed my request to Officer Petrillo. He said he'd meet me the next morning at a coffee shop in town.

Kojak hadn't touched his food from breakfast. I gave him a fresh batch, got down on my hands and knees, and made loud munching sounds, as if I were going to eat his supper. The con job didn't work. I decorated the special food with a smily face made out of Tender Vittles. I made myself some Where's Waldo SpaghettiOs and hot dogs then went over to Sam's place, where I got my tail whipped at cribbage.

When I got home, the Tender Vittles were gone, but Kojak hadn't touched the low-ash.

Ten

OFFICER JACK PETRILLO was a clean-cut kid in his early twenties who looked as if he'd be more at home in a Boy Scout uniform than cop's blues. He was jawing with some regulars when I arrived at the coffee shop. We moved over to a quiet table where we could talk. Petrillo recommended the egg breakfast sandwich with sausage and cheese. Every cop I met lately thought he was James Beard.

"How'd you get into the Quint case?" he asked. "Court appoint you?"

"A friend of Joe's asked me to poke around."

He chuckled softly. "Some friend. No offense, but I don't envy you on this one."

"You're not the first one who's said that. That's why I wanted to talk to you. A major part of the state's case will be riding on your testimony. You saw Joe's car near the plantation the night of the murder."

He nodded. "I was going off-duty. It had been a hell of a long day. Hot and muggy. The *turistas* were everywhere. I did traffic control, then spent the rest of my shift patrolling in the cruiser to around eleven o'clock. I live south of town and was on my way home, going by the plantation. I stopped at an intersection. There was a black Jeep Cherokee in front of me. Rhode Island plates. He turned off, and went down the road that takes you toward the state forest and Route 3." Petrillo grinned ruefully. "Guess I shoulda made a pinch, but there wasn't any reason to."

"Quint drives a black Jeep?"

Petrillo nodded.

"There must be more than one black Jeep around, even some with Rhode Island tags."

"Yeah, but how many have a WAR PAINT license plate and a bumper sticker that says 'Indians One, Custer Zero?' "

No help there. "When did you find out about the murder?"

"Next morning. I was having breakfast, listening to the seven-o'clock news. I knew ol' Mike from around town. Nice guy, he'd give you the shirt off his back. Just for the hell of it, I called the PD and got someone to run the plate of the black Jeep. Figured maybe the driver saw something. Turned up Joe Quint's registration. I knew who he was because his name had been in the papers. I called the sergeant up with the info. We went down to the Cape with a search warrant and ID'd the car. It was the same one I'd seen in Plymouth."

"That's when you found the hatchet and the gas?"

"Uh-huh. They were in the Jeep."

"Where was the hatchet?"

"It was just lying on the back seat under some newspapers."

"What about the gas can?"

"That was in the luggage space."

"Any prints?"

"Nah, must have been wiped clean, or they used gloves."

I leaned back in my chair and cocked an ear to the talk at the next table. The Red Sox were on a one-game winning streak. Satisfied that all was right in the world, I brought my thoughts back to the case. The comedy of errors Petrillo described didn't click with what I knew about Quint.

"May I ask your opinion as a cop?" I said. "If you killed someone and tried to torch a place, would you wipe your prints off the murder weapon and the arson stuff?"

"Sure," he said laughing "Anyone who watches cop stuff on TV would know enough to do that."

"I agree. Now, assuming you had the brains to clean your prints off the evidence, what would your next step be?"

"I'd get rid of the evidence. Throw it into the Cape Cod Canal."

"Would you leave it in your car for the cops to practically stumble over?"

"Hell, *I* wouldn't, but people do stupid things. I see it all the time."

"Joe Quint is not a stupid man."

"That's what I hear." He shrugged. "Maybe he panicked."

"Panicky people tend to do crazy things. They may do the *wrong* things, but they act. They might throw the stuff out at the first rest stop they see, or toss it by the side of the road, but they aren't passive. They wouldn't just leave it in a car."

"Got a point there. So what's your opinion?"

"I don't know." I took a sip of coffee and stared off into space. "Could you show me where you saw the Jeep?"

Officer Petrillo was obliging. His cruiser, with the words "America's Hometown," painted on the rear fender, was parked around the corner. I followed him south out of town on

Route 3A. The windy old coastal road that runs along the bay shore used to be the main north-south highway to Cape Cod before the state built Route 3. We pulled over at an intersection. He pointed out where he was coming from and showed me where he saw the black Jeep. I thanked him for his time and followed the signs to Plimoth Plantation.

At the visitor center, a big gambrel-roofed building with an observation turret, I bought a ticket, picked up a brochure, and followed the crowds along a path that ran between agricultural fields to the fort. I walked around the fort until I came to a place where the lower outside wall was blackened by fire. Then I went into the first floor of the blockhouse, past the rows of pews, and climbed some stairs to a flat roof that was open to the sky. Cannons poked their ugly muzzles through slots in the wooden balustrades.

From the top of the fort, I looked down on the village. More than a dozen small houses with thatched and wooden roofs flanked the dirt lane that ran down the gradual slope of the hill from the blockhouse. Behind the houses were gardens, and corrals for cows and sheep. A stockade fence, with raised platforms built into it to give the Pilgrims a clear shot at any pesky redskins, surrounded the whole village. About a half mile beyond the village, Plymouth Harbor and Cape Cod Bay shimmered in the morning sun. I left the fort and walked down the main drag.

The village was thick with tourists who flowed in and out of the houses, or stopped to chat with the staff people dressed up in seventeenth-century costumes. The men wore puffy pantaloons and broad-brimmed hats, the women close-fitting linen caps and full skirts to the ankle. A guy pitchforking hay to some cows was telling a camera-toting Japanese group, "Aye, 'tis seven years since we come over on the *Mayflower*, arriving here safely by the grace of God. . . . " Chickens roamed freely the way they used to before Frank Perdue got hold of them.

The Miles Standish house, where Mike Woods was murdered, was a two-story place just down the hill from the fort. I walked around the house a couple of times, but nothing popped into my head. I continued on through the village, then followed a nature walk along the Eel River to the Hobbamock homesite. Some reed houses were set up here. A couple of young guys in Indian costume were burning the core out of a log to make a canoe. Another was chopping firewood. I watched him for several minutes, paying particular attention to the iron-headed hatchet he was using.

It was getting hot and buggy. I climbed the trail that took me back to the visitors' center. Maybe I should get a dartboard and put names on it. I was walking by the gift shop, on my way to the exit, when a voice called my name. A slim woman with dark red hair and a dazzling smile was walking toward me. She came over, wrapped her arms around me, and kissed my cheek.

"I can't believe this, Soc. I never thought I'd see you again. How *are* you?"

The last time I had seen Eileen Barrett was on a Provincetown pier. She was mourning the death of her brother Michael, who had murdered a few people over an old treasure ship. Michael had been my client, and his story did not have a happy ending.

"A little stunned, Eileen. Last I knew, you were headed for Kansas."

"I got as far as Pennsylvania and came back."

She gazed at me with appraising cobalt blue eyes that simultaneously invited you in and kept you at a distance. "You're looking good," she said.

"You *always* look good, Eileen."

I wasn't indulging in empty flattery. Eileen wore plain black frame glasses. Her hair was longer than I remembered, and it was tied back in a tight bun like a country schoolmarm. If the intent was to make her less desirable, it was a waste of time. Her long legs and slender arms were bronzed from the sun and the color went well with the baggy oyster-shell shorts and the oversized coral shirt. She had gained maybe five pounds, but it had settled in the right places.

I could say, "Nice to see you again," and go on about my business. Or I could suggest we sit down. Eileen took the decision out of my hands. She pointed to a table in the courtyard restaurant and suggested we get out of the foot traffic.

Over tall glasses of iced tea, we caught up with our lives. After her brother's death, she finished her graduate studies in anthropology at Harvard and taught at the University of Pennsylvania. Her New England roots tugged her back to Boston. Now she was working in archaeology. The summary of my life took about thirty seconds.

She pinched her chin between her thumb and forefinger. "You still dive commercially?"

"Occasionally, when someone asks me."

"*I'm* asking, Soc. I need a diver—quite desperately, in fact."

I thought about Joe Quint and my pledge to Flagg. "It would be tough to fit in, Eileen. I'm up to my eyeballs with work."

"This wouldn't take long. It's nearby." She saw me wavering. "You might be doing some good."

The Eileen I used to know had an overbearing self-assuredness she wore like a suit of armor. Now she seemed more vulnerable. Not in a weak sense, just more human. And more attractive. The sad softness of our last encounter still lingered in her eyes.

"I'd have to know more about it before I made a decision," I said. She smiled and was polite enough not to gloat over hooking me so easily.

"Fair enough." She extended her hand, and we shook on it.

We finished our tea and went out to the parking lot. Minutes later, we were in Eileen's Dodge minivan heading south on Route 3A. Several miles past Plimoth Plantation, Eileen turned east and we bounced along a glorified cowpath through a dense stand of tall pines. After a quarter of a mile, the trees thinned out into scrub growth. The road ended in a rolling grassy field dotted with red cedars. We parked at the edge of the field behind a Toyota Land Cruiser, an Isuzu four-wheel drive, and a red Mustang convertible.

Eileen led the way down a gradually descending path for about two hundred yards. A guy in his early twenties was shoveling soil into a strainer made out of wood and wire mesh. A woman about the same age shook the dirt through the framework and picked through what was left on the screen. A short man in a safari shirt and English military shorts, like the ones Abercrombie & Fitch used to sell, stood nearby, making notes in a clipboard.

Eileen approached the short man. "How is it going, Doctor?"

He removed a grimy white cotton sun hat and wiped the sweat off his bald head with the back of his hand.

"As you can see," he answered in a voice as dry as dust, "it is going very well. Except for some bloodthirsty female greenhead flies who would like to incorporate my blood protein into their reproductive cycle, and this blistering sun, which is rendering all unexposed parts of my body the color of London broil." He paused to swat a greenhead on his leg. "Our young assistants here are doing all the hard work."

The woman at the soil screen brushed some pebbles aside and plucked something from the wire mesh. Excitement danced in her eyes.

"It's been worth it, Eileen. We've found several pieces like this." She handed Eileen a ragged black object.

Eileen examined the chunk in her palm. "Part of a ceramic pot. Probably conoidal." She traced some lines on the piece with her fingernail. "Fairly elemental incised marks. This looks very promising." She turned to the man with the clipboard. "Doctor, I'd like you to meet Aristotle Socarides, an old friend of mine. Soc, this is Dr. Emery Zane, project director here."

Zane. Patty Hoagland overheard Joe Quint mention someone named Zane on the telephone.

Dr. Zane swung his beak of a nose in my direction. His darting green eyes made short quick assessments through the thick wire-rimmed lenses, like a sparrow examining an acorn. He had let the gray monk's fringe of dandelion fuzz around his tanned head grow unchecked, and now it framed his pate like a halo. I guessed he was in his late fifties or early sixties, but the pale green orbs that blinked from behind Ben Franklin glasses had the intensity and wonder you see in a child.

"My congratulations, Eileen. I offer you respite from this backbreaking labor with an assignment to find some Gatorade, and you return with this gentleman with the philosophic name." He was smiling, but there was mild reproach in his voice.

"The Gatorade is in the truck, Dr. Zane. I stopped by Plimoth Plantation to see somebody in their research department and ran into Soc, who was a friend of my brother's. Soc is a *diver*, Dr. Zane."

His eyes widened behind the thick lenses. "Ah! Sorry for my bad manners." He tucked the clipboard under one arm and came over to shake my hand. "Well, a *diver*. I should have known Eileen would come back with more than I ordered. She's proven herself very resourceful throughout this entire project."

I glanced around the field. An area about three hundred feet square was sectioned off into checkerboard squares by parallel strands of white twine stretched a few inches above the ground. Rectangular pits about a yard across had been dug here and there between the twine markers.

"What exactly is this project?"

"Condominiums. A major complex," Eileen said. "The contractor was digging a trench for the percolation tests and hit a prehistoric shell midden. There were artifacts in it. Pottery, arrowheads. State law says the site has to be examined for archaeological significance. Dr. Zane was hired as a consultant. The tests showed that the site is significant."

"I put in the winning bid for the inventory phase as well," Dr. Zane added. "It was unrealistically low, but I thought this site might prove to be interesting, and I wanted to work it. We've dug one-by-one-meter holes to determine site integrity. That is, whether it has been disturbed. Our initial survey indicates the area is generally pristine."

"From the looks of it, I'd say you need a ditchdigger, not a diver."

"Oh, this isn't the really fascinating part, Soc." Eileen looked at Dr. Zane for his approval.

"By all means, Eileen. Once you have a fish on the hook, reel him in." He headed toward the Jeep. "Please excuse me while I have a gallon or two of Gatorade."

Eileen smiled. "Dr. Zane is the president of Northeast Archaeological Services. I'm the project manager here." She introduced me to the young couple. "Dillingham Hoxie and Norma Lang are Brown University grad students helping out on the project." We walked over to a tall man in a waist-high pit. He had the kind of body you see in health-club weight rooms on guys who pop steroids like candy. He was unenthusiastically scraping out a layer of dirt with a trowel that looked like a toy in his hand.

"How are you doing, Rick?" she said.

He picked up a Ziploc bag and handed it to her. "This is all I've got for a morning sweating in the trenches."

Eileen examined the black object in the bag. "It's a nice shard, Rick. I'd say, go down another layer and if there's nothing here, try another hole." She turned to me. "Soc, this is Rick Mason. He's our all-purpose factotum: surveyor, photographer, keeper of journals, and digger. Rick, this is my friend Soc. He's a diver."

Rick looked at me as if I reminded him of somebody he once argued with in a ginmill. He had a ruddy booze-burned face, black hair curling down his neck, a drooping mustache, a wide choirboy's forehead and a sly, narrow chin.

His round watchful eyes sized me up. "You going to help out on the project?"

"I told Eileen I'd lend a hand."

"Good. Maybe we'll be out of here before Christmas."

Eileen cut in. "Thanks, Rick. I'll show Soc where we need his help."

As we walked away, I said, "Rick doesn't seem like a happy camper."

Eileen shook her head impatiently. "That's just Rick. He

doesn't like being here. Frankly, I don't know why Dr. Zane puts up with him." She smiled. "There's something else. He's asked me out a couple of times. I refused. Then I show up with you. I think he's jealous."

We walked toward the edge of the field. Eileen continued, "We're not sure yet whether this was a permanent occupation site. We haven't found the big numbers of cooking utensils which would indicate that it was a true village. It is near fresh water and a herring run where people might have come in the spring to catch the fish. There's a major Indian 'highway' running through the woods nearby. We think the site was occupied at least three thousand years ago during the Early Woodland Period, but it may be much older. It could be a seasonal rendezvous where people from various villages came to trade, gossip, and celebrate religious festivals."

The field ended in a bluff a few yards beyond the perimeter of the dig. From there, a muddy slope dropped about fifteen feet to a circular pond that was about a quarter of a mile in diameter. Driven into the ground a foot from the edge of the cliff was a stake with orange Day-Glo tape tied onto it.

Eileen tapped the stake with the side of her sneaker.

"This may be the most important part of the dig." She waved her arm at the pond. "We're really standing high on a hill that must have overlooked low-lying pasture at one time. Over there, near those trees, is a river. Cranberry growers dammed it up, creating this pond. We think there's a big clay deposit underneath because the water has held."

She got down on her knees and leaned over the edge. "Look at this." I followed suit. The banking below the grass was covered with thousands of bleached and broken white shells.

"This must be where your Indians had their clambakes."

"Right. This shell midden is huge. You find your best artifacts in a midden heap. It's where they threw broken pottery or chips from making weapons and tools. We wondered whether any artifacts had washed into the water. Rick had done some diving and volunteered to go down and take a look. That's when he found the fairy hole."

"I was told not to believe in fairies, but go ahead anyway."

"It's a silly name for a rock shelter. The Indians would stay there on hunting or fishing expeditions. The opening is in the cliff below here. A cave, perhaps. Rick found some tools and potsherds near the entrance. We think it's a small indication of what's inside. Rick wanted to make more dives, but Dr. Zane said no, not alone."

"That was smart. Cave diving on your own is asking for trouble."

"We've been looking for a diver, but they've all been tied up. So when I met you—"

I gave an exaggerated sigh. "And I thought you were simply glad to see me."

The sunlight caught the burnished copper highlights in Eileen's hair. She wore a perfume that smelled like flowers in the spring. We were still kneeling like supplicants. Eileen shifted her weight from knee to knee. Her gaze brushed my face.

"I *am* glad to see you, Soc."

Without my telling it to, my arm slipped around her shoulders. "I'm kidding, Eileen. You know me, always with the jokes."

Her eyes probed mine. "You never called me."

"I didn't have your number," I said. But I knew it was more than that. I have a tendency to see things in black and white. Probably my Cretan blood. I'd been attracted to Eileen, not just by her good looks and sweet body. But challenged, as well, by the cool exterior I was sure covered a fiery core. Then she lied to me. I took it personally. Now she was asking me a favor.

"How deep is the pond?"

"Around sixty feet, according to the topographical maps. Rick says the cave is forty feet down."

"What would you want me to do?"

"We'd like you and Rick to check the area immediately around the cave to see whether any material has washed down. Then we'd like you to go inside. Based on shelters in other places, we suspect it's fairly shallow, maybe a dozen feet or so. If there are artifacts, we can deal with the question of removal later."

"Why not remove them right away?"

"People think everyone in the field is like Indiana Jones, digging up golden artifacts when we're not dodging spears and arrows. We're conservation archaeologists. Archaeological sites are a limited resource. You may want to dig up a site if there's going to be an impact, like the condominiums that are going here. But if you can't get all you want out of a site, it's best to take the artifacts you need to evaluate it, and leave it alone for now. This shouldn't take more than a day or two."

"Are there any other archaeological digs around besides this and the one at the plantation?"

She shook her head. "Not that I know of. The archaeological community is a pretty small one. Everybody knows everybody else. We'd be aware of it if there was."

I helped Eileen to her feet, scanning the pond and the excavation site quickly.

"Okay," I said. "You've got a diver. I'll squeeze a couple of hours in here and there."

She put her arms around me and kissed my neck. A tingle traveled down to the tips of my Nikes.

"I *knew* you wouldn't let us down. The pay is good. And we've rented a house in Plymouth. You could stay with us, and wouldn't have to commute." She paused. "It would be nice to talk. We parted on rather abrupt terms last time."

I like to think I'm a fairly simple guy. Give me a beer and a burger at the end of day, and a winning season for the Red Sox, and I'm in pig heaven. But at times like this, I know I'm a phony.

Maybe I was obliging Eileen to make up for being too harsh in judging her. But my brain cells had put in a long-distance call to the Joe Quint case. If Eileen hadn't asked me to help out, I probably would have volunteered and grabbed a trowel. Joe started beating the war drums after he tripped over something having to do with an archaeological dig and a person named Zane.

"It would be very nice to talk," I said. I'd always felt there was something unfinished between Eileen and me. Instead of making calf eyes, I should have been listening to the little voice in the back of my head. It was doing its best to remind that all Joe Quint managed to dig up from his inquiries into a man named Zane was a bucketful of trouble.

Eleven

SAM WAS AT Elsie's restaurant talking to a couple of gill netters. They were complaining about the low wholesale price of cod. I plunked onto the stool beside him and ordered iced coffee. The conversation switched from fishing to the Ms. Eelgrass contest, an annual spring rite where young town women dress up in seaweed and shells to raise money for local charity. Some of the guys still argued that this year's winner should have been the sexy lobster in the red body suit and not the quahog lady who kept inviting the boys to bring their hoes to her clam bed. I said I favored Madonna the Mermaid, but got shouted down by those who said green-skinned mermaids with yellow kelp hair were a dime a dozen.

Switching to a safer topic, I said, "How'd the fishing go today without me, Sam?"

"Guess the fish like you better'n they do the Nickerson kid. They didn't jump out of the sea into the boat the way they usually do. Had to work for a change."

"Sorry I missed it." The iced coffee came. It was lukewarm, and oily globules floated around in the slightly sour cream. I wrinkled my nose. "How does Elsie manage to screw up something as simple as iced coffee?"

"Just naturally good at it," Sam replied.

I ladled sugar into the glass until it almost showed at the top. "This case may go longer than I thought, Sam. I'm going to need the rest of the week."

"More complicated than you expected?"

"Yeah." I took another sip of iced coffee, decided nothing could help it, and pushed the glass away. "You know anything about Indians, Sam?"

"Just what I've seen in the John Wayne movies on TV."

"I mean Cape Cod Indians."

He stuck his lower lip out. "Let me see. Sure, there was a fella years ago. Called him Cherokee Charlie. Crazier than a loon. The police had his name on a list so he couldn't buy liquor in town, but he'd pay someone to get it for him, and go off on a whiskey toot for one or two weeks. All gussied up in buckskin and feathers, went around waving a wooden tomahawk, talking about how General Custer and the cavalry was coming over the canal bridges. Never hurt anybody. People stopped paying him much mind after a while. Remember him coming in here, in fact. Place used to be called Lonzo's back then. Different ownership."

"Was the food any better?"

"Lonzo was Elsie's father. Taught her everything she knows about cooking. What do *you* think?"

"I think you just answered my question. What was a Cherokee Indian doing on Cape Cod, Sam?"

"Shucks, he wasn't *really* a Cherokee. Syrian, or Lebanese fella I think. But if he wanted to be an Indian, we didn't want to spoil his fun. In a small town you make do with what you got. Try the iced tea, Soc."

The tea tasted burnt. More fishermen came in and the discussion turned to town-hall politics. I bid Sam good-bye, told him I'd keep in touch, and went back to the boathouse.

A FedEx envelope was tucked behind the screen door. I tossed it on the kitchen table, fed Kojak some low-ash food, and made myself a pot of Celestial Seasonings peppermint iced tea. I sat at the table and ripped open the FedEx package. Inside was a one-sentence note from Flagg: "Thought you could use this stuff." Kojak sniffed his dish and came over to rub against my ankle, hoping I'd decorate his food with Tender Vittles again. I scratched his bony head between the ears.

"This is one crazy case, Kojak. My client wants me to take a walk. The FBI would prefer it if I moved to Madagascar. The state cops say it's open-and-shut. The town cop says he definitely saw Joe's car. Joe's girlfriend says he was with her. And I've just volunteered to dive for a bunch of archaeologists, including Eileen Barrett. You remember Eileen, don't you?"

Kojak crumpled into a dusty heap. The packet Flagg sent me included an autopsy report on Mike Woods. The medical examiner said the victim had been killed by a blow to the head from a sharp-edged instrument. The trauma was consistent with the hatchet found in Joe's car. Traces of blood and hair on the weapon matched the victim's. No fingerprints. The report pretty much tallied with what I knew.

I sat back and assembled events as the cops saw them. Joe goes to his girlfriend's house for dinner, has a beer with her brother, then hits the sack around eleven. He gets up in the middle of the night, drives to Plymouth, torches the plantation fort, murders the guard, and his car is seen by a cop. He returns home, leaves the gas can and the weapon connecting him to both crimes in his car, and goes back to bed. It's hard to believe he could have left Patty without her knowing. Women have a radar that rings an alarm. If you leave the bed even for a *minute*, the arm starts groping for the missing warmth of a body. If Patty *did* know Joe was gone, she was lying to the police, and to me.

I went through the reports again looking for inconsistencies. It didn't take long to find one. Patty said the cops were at her house around nine A.M. looking for Joe. Waitaminute. Petrillo, the cop who saw Joe's car, heard about the murder on the radio while he was eating breakfast. That was on the seven o'clock news. He ran the plate on Joe's car, which must have taken a few minutes, because it was a Rhode Island tag. Then told his sergeant. The cops had a search warrant when they arrived in Mashpee, which was about a half-hour drive from Plymouth. Plus the time to call the local cops, as a courtesy, to let them know you were coming in on their turf. How'd they get everything together so fast?

If Petrillo's story didn't sic the cops on Joe, what did? I wrote the question on a corner of the FedEx envelope. Another funny thing. In the police report, Patty Hoagland said Joe came by her house around three in the afternoon. But she didn't mention that her brother Peter stopped by that evening.

I called the Plymouth Police Department, and asked for Officer Petrillo. They said he'd be back in a little while. I left a message to call me. Next I dialed Patty's number. She was home.

"I've been going over some police reports and I had a question," I said.

"I'll be glad to help if I can."

"Well, the cops quote you as saying Joe came by about three, you ate around seven, watched television until the news at eleven, then went to bed."

"That's right. What's the problem?"

"There's one thing missing, Peter. Your brother's visit isn't mentioned in the report, so I must assume you never said anything about it. Did you forget?"

"No. I just didn't want Peter involved. I didn't think it was important. Besides, Peter left long before he would have been able to substantiate or refute Joe's alibi. Do you think I was wrong not telling the police?"

"A good prosecutor will look for any omissions in your story, Patty. It's just one more thing the DA can use to convince a jury that your testimony is not to be trusted."

There was an audible sigh on the other end of the line. "You're right, of course. Do you think I should tell the police now?"

"Give it a day or two. They may be back to see you again. Kind of slide it in so it gets on the record. Do an 'oh, by the way . . .' Tell them you were upset and forgot. Be as helpful as possible. It's damage control at this point, but it'll probably be okay."

"Thank you, Soc." There was a pause. "I just want you to know I appreciate your interest in Joe's case. He can be difficult, but please bear with him."

"I intend to. While I've got you on the phone, Patty, can we back up a bit? Joe came to stay with you a couple of weeks ago. How did he happen to be in this area? He lives out of state, doesn't he?"

"Joe keeps an address in Rhode Island, but he's rarely there. He had legal business to take care of in Boston. This was going to be a vacation, a chance to see each other, go boating, have picnics, and take it easy. The weather's been wonderful. We were having a nice time."

"Then Joe was pretty relaxed and happy?"

"As relaxed as he ever is. But yes, I'd say he was happy."

"Okay, let's go over some old ground. One minute Joe was content as a quahog at high tide. The next, he's going around Plymouth like Geronimo on the warpath. I know we discussed this, but was there one single point where things changed."

"Yes, I know what you're saying. It began with a phone call. Somebody called Joe here."

"Do you know who it was?"

"No. Joe seemed more bemused than anything at the time. It was a different story after he came home that night."

"Exactly what did he say?"

"That he'd been at an auction. He was furious. The next day he made those telephone calls I mentioned, then started his rampage, as you call it."

"He never told you what angered him?"

"No. As I said, he told me he'd give me the whole story when he had it."

"You say he mentioned someone called Zane. Are you sure that's what he said?"

"Yes, quite sure. It's an unusual name. Is any of this of help?"

"It will be. I'd like to know more about the auction. Could you talk to Joe again? Maybe you can pry it out of him. Also, see what you can find out about Zane."

"I'll do my best. What do you intend to do next?"

"I'm going to follow up whatever leads I have. I'll keep in touch."

She said she'd appreciate that and thanked me again for

trying to help Joe. I crossed off the note about Patty's brother, penciled in the word "auction," and stared into space. Then I remembered my promise to Eileen. I went to the closet and dug out my dive duffel bag. My air tanks were empty. I called up the dive shop. They said they'd have full tanks waiting for me in the morning. I spread my dive suit, regulator, fins, weight belt, and buoyancy compensator out on my bed. The phone rang. It was Officer Petrillo.

"I had a question," I told him. "You were coming off the night shift when you saw Joe's car, correct?"

"Correct."

"I think you said you didn't come on duty again until the next afternoon. You ran Joe's plate and talked to your sergeant after hearing about the murder while you were eating breakfast."

"Still correct."

"I can't figure out how you managed to be in Mashpee with a warrant by nine o'clock, given the normal time it takes to pull things together."

"Can you hold on?" I heard him fumble with the phone. A minute later, he came on again. "Hi." His voice was hushed. "Sorry, I had to switch to another phone. Run that by me again, okay?"

I repeated the question.

"Here's the story," he said. "They got a call."

"A call?"

"Yeah, an anonymous phone call. Came in around six that morning. Guy said if we wanted to know who was behind the fire and the murder at the plantation, see Joe Quint in Mashpee. Gave us the address. Sarge was checking it out, started the wheels moving; he'd asked the Mashpee cops to keep an eye on Quint, just in case. When I called with the info on the plate—"

"Placing Joe's Jeep in Plymouth?"

"That's right. Sarge figured that was the clincher. We got the judge out of bed to sign the warrant and zapped on down to Mashpee. They downplayed the tip here at the station. Wanted to give the impression that the case was solved by fast police work. The evidence we found was pretty solid that he was the perp. Hell, you don't blame us, do you?"

"Naw. You would have caught him anyhow."

"I think so. Look, I could get in trouble if this gets around that I told you."

"Mum's the word."

"Thanks. Anytime I can be of help, let me know. Got to go now."

I thanked him and hung up. *They got a call*, Petrillo said. If one assumed that Joe Quint was innocent, only one other person would know Mike Woods was dead. The murderer. And there was only one reason for chancing a tip to the cops. To frame Quint. Sam was right about Cherokee Charlie. Things aren't always what they seem.

Twelve

A OLD WARNING kept running through my mind on the drive from Cape Cod to Plymouth. *Ignore the past at your peril.* Every time I poked into Joe Quint's present, I tripped over the past.

Mike Woods died at a reproduction of a three-hundred-year-old village. The murder weapon was modeled after an old Indian hatchet. Quint was cranked up over Plymouth Rock, circa 1620. Patty Hoagland dresses up like her ancestors, singing their chants and seeing auguries in the flight of a big bird. Patty's brother Peter was retaliating for the predatory practices of generations of white men by beating them at their own game. Now Eileen and her crew were sweating under a hot sun in search of garbage left behind by people who had been dead so long that their bones were dust.

America's Hometown was just awakening. I drove up a hill overlooking the commercial section into a quiet residential neighborhood of narrow streets and old houses. I parked at the foot of Burial Hill near a big flagstone church that looked as if it belonged in an English vicarage. The plaque out front said a church had occupied that spot since 1620. It was about where the original of the blockhouse reproduced at Plimoth Plantation would have been. I pondered the quote on the sermon board: "We are each of us responsible for the evil we might have prevented."

Pilgrim Path was a tree-shaded walkway that led to the top of Burial Hill. The summit offered a view of the sweep of the town, the county and courthouse buildings, and the harbor. Centuries of gravestones crowded the burying ground. They were carved with biblical names like Jabez, Mercy, and Bathsheba, and "That virtuous woman, Mrs. Ruth Turner." I wondered if virtuousness would still be considered a virtue today.

The old stones told me nothing. I descended the hill and walked back to the pickup. I passed a memorial to Elder William Brewster, Patriarch of the Pilgrims, who died in 1644; a marker for Edward Doty, a passenger on the *Mayflower;* and another showing where John Alden lived. The past again. Despite all the hokey tourist stuff, the wax museum, the postcards and the overpriced trinkets in the gift shops, this town took its history seriously.

The house rented by Northeast Archaeological Services was on Sever Street, near the probate court. It was a two-and-a-half story Victorian with gingerbread trim and a cylindrical turret at one end that looked like a missile silo. Eileen was waiting on the veranda. She saw my truck pull in front, came down the steps, kissed me lightly on the lips, and grabbed one of my bags.

"Dr. Zane and the others are already at the dig," she said, leading the way through the front door. "Have you had breakfast? There's blueberry pancake batter left. Freshly picked blueberries."

"Thanks," I said. "I stopped at a five-star Dunkin' Donuts for a coconut-covered and coffee."

The front door opened onto a generous hallway with floors waxed to a high gloss. Eileen bounded like a gazelle up a wide staircase that led to the second floor. My room was wallpapered in a morning-glory print, complete with hummingbirds. It was furnished with a couple of old-fashioned dark wood dressers and a desk. Light streamed in through two large-paned windows.

"How do you like it?" Eileen said.

I pushed the white cotton Cape Cod curtains aside. I could see the pier where I had a fishwich with Lieutenant Bacudas, the dark-hulled *Mayflower* moored at its dock, and the granite canopy over Plymouth Rock.

"I may never move out." I hoisted my duffel bag onto the brass bed. "Give me a couple of minutes to get organized."

"That's fine. When you're through, follow the hallway to the end. I'll be working in the lab." She paused at the door like Lauren Bacall talking to Bogie in *To Have and Have Not.* "We'll be neighbors. That's my bedroom across the way."

Unpacking took no time. I travel light. T-shirts, underwear, and toothbrush. I peeked through the open door to Eileen's room. The room was similar to mine, except that it had more pink and it smelled deliciously like Eileen: spring flowers, shampoo, and body lotion.

A portal opened into the turret at the end of the hallway. Eileen sat in the center of the perfectly circular room, pecking away at a computer keyboard on a desk made of a door resting on two filing cabinets.

Thick textbooks and manila folders were piled everywhere on the desk. More books spilled off shelves built from two-by-eight boards and cinder blocks. Taped to the curving walls were topographic maps of Massachusetts and Plymouth and sheets of paper with wavy lines on them, like a kid might make. On a dresser was a microscope, tons of slides, and assorted Ziploc plastic bags with little black or brown hunks in them.

Eileen looked up from her glowing computer monitor and swept the air with a slim arm. "How do you like our lab?"

I swiveled on one foot. "You need an assistant named Igor, some big noisy spark coils, and a few glass jars with brains in them."

"I'll call Dr. Frankenstein and ask if he has any hunchbacks he can spare." She clicked off the computer. "Speaking of mad scientists, we'd better go before Dr. Zane's blood pressure reaches critical mass."

We stowed my dive gear in Eileen's minivan. Twenty minutes later, we were at the excavation site. Dr. Zane and his crew were under a tent, clustered around a folding field table like army generals in an old Civil War photo. Zane strode briskly over to greet us.

"Good to see you, Soc. Has Eileen got you comfortably ensconced in your quarters?"

"I couldn't have done better at the Hilton," I said, hoisting my tanks and gear bag out of the van.

"Good." He rubbed his hands together. "We were just going over Rick's report."

Zane guided us to the table and handed me a sheet of paper smudged with dirty fingerprints. "This is the standard excavation-permit. We've adapted it for underwater use." He flattened the form on the tabletop. "Rick, would you explain your scribblings to the gentleman?"

Rick said, "Doc Zane has me fill out this excavation form, but it's a waste of time—"

"Not so," Zane interjected. "Proper procedures have to be followed."

Rick ignored him. "You can disregard this stuff about levels and excavation categories because there aren't any. I drew this rough diagram. This arrow is the stake near the edge of the cliff." He ran his finger along a wavy diagonal line. "This is an underwater profile of the cliff. There's mostly clay on the outside, but it looks to me like solid granite underneath."

I pointed to an X about halfway down the jagged line that defined the cliff profile. "Is this the rock shelter?"

"That's right." He tapped the form. "That's the entrance. It's around four feet feet high, about the same wide."

"How did you happen to find it?"

"I was swimming along the base of the cliff looking for Indian stuff. I saw some shells and swam up to check them out. On the way, I found the cave."

"Did you go inside?"

"No frigging way! Not alone."

Dr. Zane had been smoldering quietly while Rick stole the show. "Based on experience in other locations," he cut in, "it's probably a shallow opening, rather than a cave. Our thinking is that it was a temporary abode, thus won't offer a great deal in the way of permanent settlement artifacts. But archaeology is a crazy business. One tiny significant piece of ancient junk can set the whole establishment back onto its posterior. Well, shall we begin?"

Rick nodded and started to put on his wet suit. I stripped down to my bathing suit and got into my neoprene bottoms. Then I walked to the edge of the cliff and looked out over the pond. Morning sunlight sparkled on its quiet surface. I reminded myself that complacency is the biggest danger when you dive in freshwater. There aren't the currents and tides that keep you alert in the ocean. But freshwater can drown you just as dead as the salty stuff.

"What's the visibility like down there?" I asked Rick.

"Not bad near the top. Fifteen to twenty feet, maybe. The water is pretty clear even near the bottom, except for some plant junk floating about. There are piles of weeds on the bottom. I had a hell of a problem seeing when my fins stirred up the silt. Couldn't move until the stuff settled down."

"We'll just move real slow. Does the slope to the cliff face go down gradually or drop off sharply?"

"It goes out gradually for a few feet, then drops off."

I nodded. "I'll run a line for us." I dug a small Danforth anchor out of my duffel, carried the anchor over to the cliff, swung it like a bola, and let it splash into the water about ten feet out. After it sunk to the bottom, I yanked on the line to make sure the anchor had caught. Then I tied the slack end of the line around the stake.

"The line will be our guide. This is your party, so I'll let you lay out the dive plan."

He squinted against the water's glitter. "We'll follow your line down to the bottom. Then we head off to the right facing the cliff. When we get to where I think the rock shelter is, I'll come up. If I'm wrong, we drop down again and do it over."

"Sounds fine to me." I zipped into my wet-suit top. Dil and Norma, the Brown University grad students, came over. Norma was a thick-bodied woman with a blunt nose over a wide, friendly mouth, her straw-colored hair drawn back into two pigtails like an Amish maiden. Dil was a darkly bearded man with big horsy teeth. He looked more like a Greek monk than a grad student. They helped us on with our air tanks. Eileen had faded into the background while Rick and Dr. Zane filled me in. Now she stood silently off to the side.

104

"Is there anything wrong?" I asked.

"This has been a little difficult, watching you and Rick suit up. It reminds me of you and Michael getting ready to dive on the *Gabriella*."

I squeezed her hand gently. "That's behind you, Eileen. This is not the *Gabriella*. This is Rick Mason and me."

Dr. Zane came over to see if we were ready. He glanced at Eileen's hand in mine, but said nothing, and bent over the stake. I explained the reason for the anchor line.

"Ingenious. You've done some underwater archaeology?"

"Some. This is just common sense."

"We could *use* some common sense in this discipline." He handed me a specimen bag and a trowel. "This might come in handy."

I hooked the bag onto my suit and attached a white plastic slate and black crayon to my wrist. Rick and I went through the routine predive inspection, checking out our buoyancy compensators, weight belts, and regulators.

The black wet suit held my body heat in under the hot sun. I felt like a baked stuffed lobster. "I'm set if you are," I said to Rick.

Rick nodded. We sat on the edge of the cliff, swung our legs out, then slid down the bank into the pond, holding onto the anchor line. The water felt like ice when it first hit my overheated skin, but it warmed to a comfortable temperature quickly.

We spit in our masks and rinsed the lenses to prevent fogging, tested our regulators again, and bit down on the mouthpieces. Rick gave me the thumbs-up sign. I curled my thumb and forefinger in an okay. He pushed off and sank feet first in an explosion of bubbles. I waved to Eileen and the others, who were leaning over the top of the bank, hit the release valve to let air escape from my buoyancy compensator vest and sank, one hand sliding along the anchor line.

The cliff was faced with clay, broken here and there by outcroppings of dark rock probably deposited by Ice Age glaciers. Rick accidentally brushed the cliff face, and I lost him in a muddy cloud and pieces of vegetation. He waited for me on the bottom, squatting off to one side of the anchor.

I made sure the anchor was firmly set. On the message board attached to my wrist, I wrote: "I'M READY.

Rick pointed to the right.

We swam above the spinachy weeds, with the cliff on the left and me slightly behind and off to Rick's right. He moved his head back and forth like a hunting alligator. After a few seconds, he stopped and pointed vigorously at the cliff. He picked up a small bleached fragment of clamshell. He gestured above his head, then kicked upward, with me following. He hadn't gone fifteen feet when he stopped, flicked on his flashlight, and played it along the face of the cliff.

A toothless black mouth yawned in the gloom.

We moved closer and stuck our head in the cave's entrance. I unclipped my flash and its narrow yellow beam joined his.

I wrote: AFTER YOU on the wristboard, and did an Alphonse-and-Gaston wave of my hand.

Rick headed in. Silt covered the floor of the cave. The slightest eddies created by his fins stirred up miniature volcanic eruptions.

We rounded a curve and stopped to reconnoiter. We were in a space around a dozen feet across and six feet high. Brown vegetation hung from the rocky ceilings and walls. Rick was checking out the far nooks and crannies with his light when he spotted something on the floor.

Using a three-inch paintbrush from his pack, he fanned the muddy bottom. Black silt enveloped his hand. This was going to be tricky stuff. Luckily, the silt was heavy and settled quickly. The brushstrokes revealed more white clamshells. Rick plucked a dark object from the mud, rubbed it with his gloved fingers, and held it close to his face mask.

Lying in his glove was a hollow cone-shaped blackish piece of what looked like pottery. He mimicked someone smoking. On the wristboard he wrote the word: PIPE.

Rick tucked the specimen in his waist bag and glided forward, stopping half a dozen times to brush the floor. He kept some specimens. Others he examined and discarded. Our flashlights cast grotesque shadows on the dark stone walls. We came to a small domed room and a blank wall. At first glance, it appeared to be the end of the cave. As Dr. Zane expected: maybe this was only a shallow opening in the rocks.

I noticed something unusual at the lower left of the wall, where the seven is on a clock face. A pocket of darkness didn't disappear when the light hit it. I swam over and probed it with my flashlight beam. It was a hole.

Rick followed my lead. He scribbled on my wristboard: TUNNEL?

I nodded. He started to swim down. I touched his shoulder and pointed to my watch. The rule is that you plan the dive and dive the plan. We hadn't planned to do any *spelunking*. He pointed to his watch and pressure gauge to emphasize that we had time to explore. Okay, I nodded. Just being cautious. I reached into my bag and pulled out a roll of white twine. I had never done any cave dives, but I knew it was easier to get into trouble than out of it.

I tied one end of the twine to a knobby protrusion about a foot high, unrolled a couple of yards of string, then pointed into the tunnel. Rick tried to go in head first, then backed out and took off his specimen bag. I did the same. This was going to be a tight squeeze.

He slithered into the passageway. With misgivings hanging around me like pilot fish on a shark, I followed him in.

Thirteen

BOINNG. . . . KABONK. . . . BONK. . . .

Our air tanks banged and scraped against the tunnel walls. My latent claustrophobia kicked in. My heartbeat tripled. Hundreds of tons of dirt and rock pressed in from all sides. What if there was a cave-in? What if I got stuck? What if Rick got stuck?!

Kaboinng. . . . Skreeep. . . . Bink.

Deeper into the earth. This was crazy. There was no place wide enough to turn around. If we hit a blank wall, we'd have to back out! Rick plugged ahead. I vowed to count to thirty, and if he didn't stop, I'd grab his fin and drag him out. I was up to twenty-five when Rick disappeared.

It was like a blip going off the radar screen. One second Rick was going around a turn. The reflection of his light bounced off the brown walls of the tunnel. The bubbles from his regulator streamed back. His fins moved up and down. Then he was gone. Ahead was only darkness.

Not total. There was a yellow glow against the gloom. I

headed toward it. The tunnel ended. Just like that. I popped out into an open space like a watermelon seed being squeezed between somebody's fingers. The glow came from Rick's flashlight, which hovered in the blackness a few yards away. We moved closer together. The sensation was like being in free fall in a spaceship. Not knowing up or down. We seemed to have broken out into a chamber. We played our flashlight beams around. They bounced off a wall. Then froze, as they found a leering face. The face was painted in white against the dark rock of the wall. It was a drawing a child might make. The eyes and mouth were horizontal lines, like a minimalist jack-o'-lantern. Next to it was a handprint and a stick figure of an antlered deer pursued by stick figures of men with spears. There were pictures of birds and moons, half and full, more spears or arrows, bird and animal tracks, diamonds and triangles. There were zigzag lines and squares.

We spun, slowly, getting our bearings. The underwater chamber was about twenty feet across. It was like a prehistoric version of a wraparound movie screen like those in science museums.

Suddenly it dawned on me that we were not in the comfort and safety of a museum. We were deep under the earth and running low on air. I grabbed Rick's elbow and pointed to my pressure gauge. The needle was near the red section that corresponds to the reserve on a car's gas tank. He nodded. It took us another minute to find the opening where we'd come in. We bounced through the tunnel to the main cave. Then into the pond again. We kicked our way to the surface. On top, I inflated my BC and floated, blinking my eyes in the sunlight and taking wonderful breaths of fresh, uncompressed air. Rick was a few feet away.

We had come up around twenty-five feet from the staked

guideline, a couple of yards off the face of the cliff. Eileen, Zane and the others had been watching for our bubbles and were waiting for us. We handed up our buoyancy compensators and masks. The crew helped us climb the muddy side of the cliff. I got out of my wet-suit top and sat on the grass, basking in the welcome heat of the day.

"Well," Dr. Zane said eagerly, "did you find any artifacts?"

"A few." Rick handed Zane the bag and walked away.

Zane pawed excitedly through the pottery scraps like a child opening presents on Christmas morning.

"Aren't you going to tell them about the drawings?" I asked Rick.

"You tell them," he said over his shoulder. "I need something to drink."

"What kind of drawings?" Eileen said.

"Miró. Picasso. Birds. Moons. Stars. People. Hex signs. Lightning."

Dr. Zane dropped the net bag and put his sweaty face close to mine. "Young man, if you don't tell me immediately in detail what you found down there, I shall relieve you of your trowel and insect repellant on the spot."

"There's an inner chamber connected to the rock shelter by a tunnel. The walls are covered with pictures."

I gave him a summary of our dive, starting with our first foray into the cave. His sharp sparrow eyes went into a high-speed blink when I got to the details of the wall pictures.

"Were these drawings scratched in or painted?" he said.

"Beautifully painted. It reminded me of the cave art they found in France years ago."

He removed his glasses. "Do you know what this means? Rock art is *extremely* rare in the Eastern Woodlands Indians.

Especially specimens as sophisticated as you say these are."

"Dr. Zane," Eileen said excitedly, "this site could be ten thousand years old. Maybe twenty."

"I share your enthusiasm, Eileen, but whatever happened to careful scientific analysis?"

"It went out the door when Soc started describing those wonderful things."

Zane laughed. *Wonderful* things. How appropriate. That's what Howard Carter said to Lord Carnarvon when asked what he saw in King Tut's tomb. Very well, Eileen, enjoy your imaginative frolicking for now. This discovery will come under the hard glare of scientific scrutiny soon enough." He slapped me on the back. "Congratulations, Soc. Your first day, and you make a monumental discovery."

"All I did was hold the flashlight."

"No matter. You and Rick showed a great deal of resourcefulness and courage."

"Thanks. What happens next?"

"You'll have to go down again with a camera," Dr. Zane said. "Damn! I never imagined we'd be doing any underwater photography. All we have here are a few point-and-shoot cameras to record the site. I have a colleague in Boston who has the proper equipment. I'll go back to the house and call him."

'You won't need me for a while," I said hopefully.

"Take a few hours' rest, and we'll put you to work when I get back. Not a word of this to anyone. Every time rock art is discovered in New England, we have people saying it was done by the Norsemen or denizens from the lost continent of Atlantis, as if the Indians didn't have the brains to draw. Lord knows what they'd make of this."

Eileen and the grad students elected to stay at the site. Rick said he'd hang out too, but he didn't look enthusiastic about it.

I hitched a ride back to Plymouth with Dr. Zane. He gave me an extra house key, warned again not to blab about the pictographs, and got on the phone.

While Zane tried to track down an underwater camera, I planned to follow up on another Patty Hoagland lead. She said Quint came back to Mashpee upset over an auction in Plymouth. I changed into a fresh T-shirt and shorts and drove to the library, a one-story brick building on the outskirts of town. The reference room had copies of *The Old Colony Memorial*, the local weekly newspaper. I went through the papers for the last three months. In less than half an hour, I found a display ad with a big boldfaced headline that said: *Important Estates Auction*. A smaller headline said: *Americana, clocks, guns, silver, Oriental rugs, paintings*. The ad was for a place called Heritage Auction Galleries. The name of the auctioneer was Claude Renault.

I ran my eye down the small dense type that described the Salem Chippendale, Oxford chests and blue Fitzhugh soup tureens until I came to a line that said: *American Indian collection*. The ad said the documented auction items came from a private estate.

The librarian gave me directions to the auction house in Kingston, an old town a few miles from Plymouth. Heritage Auction Galleries was in a two-story antique red house that had a large corrugated steel building grafted onto its backside.

A pink-faced receptionist impaled me with hard green eyes and asked accusingly if I was there to inspect the items for the Saturday auction. From the snapping-turtle set to her mouth, I guessed she was dying to tell me to beat it. She looked disappointed when I said I was interested in some antiques auctioned a few weeks earlier. She said I would have to talk to Mr.

Renault and gestured toward a door. I could find him in the gallery.

I walked down a hallway until I came to a sign that said Gallery and went through a door into a space as big as a blimp hangar. The gallery smelled of wood finishes and moldy cloth. Hundreds of pieces of old junk were stacked on broad shelves that ran along the gallery walls. Two men dressed in work clothes were sticking numbered labels on auction items. A third man checked the labels against a scrolled computer printout. He wore slacks the color of ketchup and a plummy purple silk shirt. He was around six foot three inches tall and almost as wide. A cloud of musk cologne floated around him.

He regarded me with sad, watery eyes. "You're a day early for the inspection."

"Yes, I know. This isn't about Saturday. I wanted to ask you about some items you sold off earlier this summer."

He made a fluttering can't-you-see-I'm-busy gesture of impatience. "I'm afraid I can't talk to you now. We've got to finish this inventory and coding."

"That's too bad. I'm passing through, and don't know when I'm coming back."

Renault looked up from his printout, studied me for a moment, then passed the paperwork to his assistant. His moist dark eyes seemed to be on the verge of tears. He extended a pudgy hand that had more glittering rings than fingers and gave me a pulpy handshake.

"Please forgive my abruptness. We've got staff out sick, and we have to have these items ready by tomorrow."

"I understand." I gave him my name. "I appreciate your taking the time. This is a pretty impressive collection."

"Not what you'd expect to find in the middle of the woods, is it?" he said proudly. "We specialize in early American furniture. Being close to Plymouth is a plus, of course. You can claim every piece you sell *may* have belonged to John Alden and Priscilla Mullins."

"Early American is okay, but I've been fascinated in Indian stuff since I was a kid."

"Indian, you say?" He tapped a dimpled chin with his forefinger.

"Yes. I've got some great pieces at my house in Weston," I said, using the name of a pricey suburb near Boston. "I sold my software business a couple of years ago, so I'm semi-retired. The new owners asked me to stay on as a consultant. I bop back and forth to my place on the Cape, do as much sailing as I can on my forty-one-foot Morgan, and kind of keep an eye on things via the fax and cellular phone. I was out of town when your Indian goods went on the block, but a friend told me about it."

The quick and completely fictitious financial picture I created started Renault's greed meter running.

"It's unfortunate you didn't know about the auction," he purred. "Quite a nice collection, really. A rich gentleman in Michigan had acquired the pieces through the years. When he died his nephew inherited the estate. He simply wanted to liquidate it as quickly as possible. He has a summer home nearby and asked us to handle the sale."

"I'm going to hate hearing about what I missed out on, but do you remember any of the items that were in the collection?"

"Oh, yes, of course. They had great historical value. They were from Wounded Knee."

"The *original* Wounded Knee?"

"That's right. Tools, Indian clothing, jewelry, just about everything that you would have found in an Indian village back then. Very good condition, too."

115

"Damn! I could kick myself for missing that one."

"Don't despair. There's always the chance we might acquire more in the future. It's not what I specialize in, but frankly, I'm more interested in cultivating repeat customers than selling to people who want a Colonial table for their living room because their friends have one. I'll give you a ring if anything comes up. Leave your number with Betty, our receptionist."

"Definitely. If you let me know before you auction the goods off, perhaps we can work out a deal."

He fingered his chin dimple again. "Perhaps we can. Now, if you'll excuse me . . . "

On the way back to Plymouth I tried to remember what I knew about Wounded Knee. Not a hell of a lot. Cavalry massacred some Indians there. Later, there was a big battle between the FBI and Indian activists. It was an emotional name—no doubt about it. From what little I knew, Wounded Knee was pretty much a symbol for all the bad things the white men had done to the Indians. I'd ask Joe Quint. I was going to be tied up at Zane's project the rest of the day, but I'd set aside time tomorrow to pay Joe a visit at the Plymouth County Hilton.

I stopped at Sever Street house to call Flagg. I wanted to tell him there were holes in the state's case against Quint and to ask him to lean on his friend to be more cooperative. Flagg's answering service said he was unavailable. I told the operator it was urgent and gave her my name.

"Oh, Mr. Socarides. I'm sorry. Mr. Flagg is in Europe. I can have him call you."

I asked if Flagg could call me in Plymouth around six and gave her the number. Then I drove out to the archaeological site. Eileen and Rick were chipping away in individual test pits.

Norma and Dil sifted soil. I volunteered to help, and Eileen showed me how to record data.

Zane showed up about an hour later. He was furious. The underwater camera wouldn't be available until the next day. He calmed down after I offered to draw him a diagram of the cave and sketched out what I remembered of the wall art. Around four o'clock, we called it a day and headed back to the house. We hit the showers and changed. Eileen stuck a Heineken' in my hand and pointed me to the veranda while she prepared dinner. I lounged in an Adirondack chair, sipping my beer, and looked out at the hazy harbor.

The smell of cooking food reminded me of dinner which reminded me of Kojak. I went inside to check with the neighbor I'd asked to cat-sit and to give her my Plymouth number. She was glad I called because my sister had been trying to reach me for hours. I dialed my parents' house in Lowell, where my sister Chloe lives. My mother answered.

"Hi, Ma," I said. "Chloe called. Do you know why?"

"Yes, *Aris*totle. I tell her to call, see if you are sick."

"I'm fine. Why would you think I was sick?"

"Yesterday was your father's name day. You promised to come for dinner."

Damn. I'd been so tied up with Eileen's project I'd forgotten about Pop. A name day commemorates the birthday of the saint you were named after. It's even more important than your *own* birthday."

"I'm sorry, Ma. I forgot." It was always best to tell truth. My mother knew when I was lying.

"So, you come tomorrow?"

"I can't, Ma. I'm busy on an important case."

"More important than your father?"

"No, Ma. Look, I'll get up as soon as this is over. It shouldn't take more than a day or two."

She sighed heavily. "You must do what you have to do, Aristotle," she said, using a tone that implied she didn't believe a word she was saying. "Come see us when you have time for the family."

My mother wrote the book on quiet rebukes. No yelling. No histrionics. Simply a dagger of guilt slipped between the ribs. I needed some air. I walked down to the harbor and sat on a bench in the little park near Plymouth Rock. I always seem to head for water when I'm in the mood for self-pitying introspective analysis. The sea is my shrink. It never interrupts or makes judgments. Best of all, it never sends me a bill.

Fourteen

To UNDERSTAND WHY a six-foot-one ex-marine who saw combat in Vietnam and on the streets as a Boston cop lets a little old Greek lady push him around, you have to know something about my mother. Slim and dignified, her pepper-and-salt hair pinned back in a neat bun, darkly dressed in a perpetual state of mourning for her endless supply of dying relatives, her features seem to have been chiseled from the mountains of her native Crete. More than anyone, my mother passed on the black and white sense of justice that has gotten me into trouble in a world where values are often so many shades of gray.

My mother's drive moved the family from endless hot hours toiling over a pizza shop oven to the wholesale trade. My father's shrewd Athenian business sense made Parthenon into the most successful frozen pizza company in New England.

Success had its costs. My brother George, sister Chloe and I only saw Pop on Sundays. The family routine never varied. Breakfast at a friend's restaurant, church, a walk in the park, then Pop was off to the coffee house for poker and strong coffee with his buddies, while Mom prepared dinner.

Last month Pop had a heart attack. I drove to Lowell as soon as I heard about it.

They had Pop in the Intensive Care Unit. Chloe was sitting near the nurse's station. Still dressed in his flour-dusted bakery whites, George paced the floor as if he were trying to wear a hole in the tile. Chloe jumped up from her chair, wrapped her arms around me, and buried her head against my shoulder.

"Oh, Soc!" she said. "I'm so glad you're here."

George stopped his pacing, and looked at me with sheer disgust. I went over to George. He gave me a quick limp handshake and went back to his pacing.

"How's Pop doing?" I asked, talking to his back.

"Not bad for somebody who looks like he's wired to a battery charger," George said over his shoulder.

I looked up and down the quiet hallway. "Where's Ma?"

"She's busy telling the doctors how to run the hospital," George added.

He was on the return leg of his circuit when I growled, "You got a problem, George?"

He wiped his flour-caked palms on his thighs. "Yeah. I got problems. I'm worried Pop might die. What that could do to Ma. I'm worried about the business going to hell. I've got more worries than I know what to do with, but I'm doing the best I can. Now my big brother, who doesn't give a damn enough about the family to come and visit once in a while, shows up, and my baby sister goes nuts, like he's the Lone Ranger riding in to save the day. What the hell does that make me? Tonto?"

George had about a pound of flour in his mustache. It was a badge of George's long hours running the family business, a job he wasn't crazy about. Martyr or not, George was a little too flip for my taste.

"I'm worried, too, George. I might be less worried if you stopped acting like a jerk and told me what the hell is going on."

Chloe charged over. My sister would give you the shirt off her back and ask if she could iron it first. But she's got a temper hotter than a jalapeño pepper. The idea that her two brothers were working out their sibling-rivalry problems while her father lay in the ICU was enough to set off the smoke detectors.

"I cannot *believe* this!" she shrilled. "Pop could be dying in there, and you two are fighting like a couple of spoiled little brats."

"Chloe, sweetheart," I said with exasperation, "I've been here five minutes, and nobody's told me one thing about Pop."

"Don't 'sweetheart' me, Aristotle Socarides. George is acting like a complete turkey, but he's right about you never coming up to see us." She was on the verge of tears again.

George smirked. "Hah!" he said smugly.

Chloe cut him down with a withering glare. George averted his eyes and threw his hands up in defeat. "I'm going out for some fresh air," he said. "*You* fill our big brother in." He stalked off toward the exit.

Chloe scowled. "He's going out to have a smoke. He thinks Ma doesn't know. She's just biding her time." Her gray eyes—my mother's eyes—were shiny with tears. She pulled a tissue out of her pocketbook and blew a trumpet solo with her nose. Half-laughing and half-crying, she said, "Isn't it wonderful how our family pulls together in times of crisis?"

A lump formed in my throat. I put my arm around her. "People get stupid in times of stress, Chloe. C'mon, tell me what happened."

We went over to the nurse's station and found a couple of chairs. "Pop was in the bakery. He was running around as usual, doing all the things he doesn't have to do any more because almost everything is automated. I was in the office doing the bookkeeping. Pop came out and sat down. His face was white as a sheet. He had pains in his chest. I called the rescue squad right away. It took them only a few minutes. They were coming in the door when he passed out. They brought him back with CPR.

"You may have saved his life, Chloe."

She dabbed at her eyes with a tissue. "Maybe."

"What are the doctors saying?"

"Heart 'episode.' Honestly, doctors must take a course in medical school on how to talk to people without telling them anything."

"Can I go in and see Pop?"

Chloe shook her head. "You'll have to wait. Ma's talking to the doctor now."

We heard the murmur of voices. My mother was coming down the hall with a doctor who was at least half a head taller than her. Far from being distraught, Ma, rather than the doctor, seemed in command. She was talking and the doctor was nodding. They looked like medical colleagues. I got up and went to meet them. Ma smiled and came over to kiss my cheek.

"*Ar*istotle. You come!" She turned to the doctor. "This is Aristotle, my oldest son. He comes from Cape Cod when he hears about Poppa. Now everything is going to be all right."

"I'm Dr. Ramsdell," the physician said.

We shook hands and I said, "How's my father doing?"

"I was just telling your mother here that he's a very lucky man. He suffered a heart attack, but in this case, it was just a warning."

"How strong a warning?"

"The best kind. He's still alive. Apparently, he's never had problems before; or if he has, he's never told anybody about them. The EKG shows erratic heart behavior. This has been building up. Your mother says your father works long days and never takes a vacation."

"I try to get him to rest, but he's stubborn, your father," my mother interjected. People in my family are always accusing other relatives of being stubborn. Ma was the last one who should talk. She comes from a people who have resisted every force, natural and man-made, that's ever been thrown at them. You couldn't dislodge her from the bakery with a stick of dynamite. Still, I thought it best to agree with her.

"He's been that way as long as I can remember, Doctor."

"Well he's going to have to change his lifestyle if he wants to *have* a life."

"Poppa is going to have a big rest," my mother said. "I am going to take care of him and feed him."

"Don't feed him *too* much, Mrs. Socarides. He could stand to lose a few pounds."

"Could we see my father?" I asked.

"He's under sedation now, but you can go in for a few minutes if you don't disturb him. I'd prefer no more than one person in the room at a time, if you don't mind."

"You go in, Soc," Chloe said. "I'll stay here with Ma and wait for George."

Pop lay on his back, the sheet drawn up under his pudgy chin. I pulled a chair close to the bedside and listened to his labored breathing, watching the lines on the monitor screen, thinking about the thin thread that life hangs by. He seemed so small, a roundish, wan lump under the sheets. I leaned closer. In the dim light, his skin looked washed out.

123

I sat there for five minutes, wondering where the years had gone. Wondering if there was any way to recapture them. Thinking about words never said. Missed opportunities. How I had pulled away from the family. The pain I had caused my parents. I had worked myself up into a near-orgy of enjoyable self-pity when the nurse arrived. She poked her head in the room and pointed to her wristwatch.

I adjusted the sheet around my father's neck, kissed his bald head, and went out into the hall. My mother told Chloe to go in next. George was sitting in a chair. He had a sheepish look on his face. Ma must have landed on him about his smoking.

"You're a good boy to come so far," my mother said.

"It's only a couple of hours, Ma."

A dark eyebrow arched. "That's what I tell you when I want you to come home for a visit."

"You're right, Ma. I should try to get home more often. I'm sorry."

"Well, I know you are busy now with the fishing. You come when you can."

I got an inspiration. "Look, Ma, with Pop out, do you want me to help around the bakery, maybe?"

George looked up and chortled. "Wanta bake some pizzas, Soc? Like they say about the Marines, it's not a job, it's an *adventure*."

My mother motioned for George to shut his trap. "George works very hard in the bakery. But sometimes he thinks he is the *only* one that works." She patted my cheek. "We call you if you can help," she said generously, knowing that if I tried working in the family business, I'd accidentally bake myself into a pepperoni pizza. "You come home and have something to eat. Maybe you stay the night in your old bedroom?"

I thought of the lonely drive back to Cape Cod. My mother and sister would fuss and putter over me, and make it clear that as elder brother, my opinion counted more than anyone's. I glanced at George. Behind all his bluster, he looked miserable. If I went home, I'd be the Prodigal Son, I'd be put in charge. I didn't deserve that, and neither did my brother.

"No thanks, Ma. I should get back tonight."

She nodded, but there was disappointment in her eyes.

She patted my cheek. "*Kala*, Aristotle. You must do what you must do." Chloe came out of Pop's room. Ma kissed me and went in. Chloe took my arm.

"You coming by the house?"

"I'd like to, but maybe it's not the best thing to do with George primed the way he is. It might be better for the family peace."

Color rose in her cheeks. "You're not staying because of *George?*"

"It's more complicated than that. I'm not staying because of Ma."

She looked over at George, who was standing near the nurse's station, hands stuck in his pockets, brooding. She nodded in understanding. I kissed Chloe good-bye and went over to George and shook his hand. His grip was strong and long. He looked me in the eye. There was pain in his face. His eyes were moist with tears.

"Soc, about what I said a while ago—"

I slapped his shoulder. "Don't worry, George. I apologize for losing it, too."

He heaved a deep sigh. "You know how it is sometimes."

I looked over at my mother, who was leaning on the counter telling the floor nurse how to do her job. "Hell, brother, I know how it is *all* the time."

I gave him a brotherly hug, told him to call me if there were any new developments, and left the hospital. It was a long drive home.

Dad recovered nicely and went back to work on a reduced schedule. My promises to rejoin the family were forgotten until my mother called about missing his name day bash. I did what I often do when confronted by guilt. I found a bar and stayed there until last call.

The house was quiet when I walked back to Sever Street under a starry sky. I crept upstairs to my room, pausing an instant to look longingly at Eileen's door. Then I went into my bedroom, got out of my clothes, and peeled back the cool sheets. Alone with my thoughts and weary from the exertions of the day, I slipped into a deep sleep.

Fifteen

"Soc. It's SEVEN o'clock. Breakfast is ready." Eileen's voice came through my bedroom door.

I rolled out of bed, pulled on shorts and a T-shirt, and followed the aroma of coffee downstairs. The crew was gathered at a long mahogany table in the living room. I sat down, returned the good mornings from the others, and buried my nose in a fresh cup of coffee. It had legs, the way I like it, and I said so. Eileen piled my plate high with pancakes and sausages. I had barely taken my first bite when the phone rang in the other room. Dil got up to answer it. He came back a minute later.

"It's for you, Soc."

I went into the parlor and put the phone to my ear. It was Flagg calling.

"Listen," Flagg's voice said.

Bells chimed in the background.

"Sounds like Big Ben."

"Righto, old chap."

"You're in *London?*"

"I'll be home later this week. Sorry I had to leave without saying good-bye. Duty called. They got me a seat on the Concorde and a hotel near Westminster. Not bad for a redskin from Gay Head. You got something for me?"

"I think we can break the case against Joe."

"You may have to sit on it for now," Flagg said after a pause. "Joe took a walk."

"He broke out of jail?"

"Depends on how you look at it."

"Aw jeez!" I groaned. "When did all this happen?"

"Yesterday. He made bail and was gone. The FBI was trailing him. Joe lost them."

"Our friend Rourke again?"

"One and the same. Mr. Rourke's not very happy."

"He's not the only one. I've busted my ass running around for Quint. What are we supposed to do now?"

"You sit tight. I twiddle my thumbs and eat greasy fish and chips. I should wrap up this assignment in a few days. Where are you talking from?"

"I'm staying in Plymouth. I'm doing a dive job for some archaeologists. It may have something to do with Joe's problems."

"Can you tell me about it?"

I glanced back at the dining room. The crew was finishing breakfast and would be tromping around the house in a few minutes.

"This isn't a good time or place."

"I got you. Try me later when you can talk."

"I'll call your answering service with a message."

"You do that. Got to go," Flagg said. And hung up.

Maybe I shouldn't have kidded Joe about his Indian name,

128

Running Deer. The guy was as unpredictable as the wind. First he refuses bail. Then he jumps it. Talk about the Vanishing American!

Eileen came into the parlor and said my pancakes were getting cold. I went back to the breakfast table. Dr. Zane was at the head of the table, pontificating.

"Archaeology has come full circle," he was saying. "For decades, archaeologists never left their libraries. They wouldn't *think* of getting their hands dirty digging into an old pile of rubble."

"Schliemann changed that at Troy," Norma said.

"Oh, yes, Schliemann did indeed." Dr. Zane speared a section of sausage with his fork. "He butchered Troy and Mycenae. He came up with gold and treasure and all the wrong conclusions. Had he not found Troy when he did, would anybody have been the worse off? If the sites were left undisturbed for another hundred years, until we could go in with modern scientific methods, would archaeology have suffered?" He looked over at me. "Soc, you seem to be a practical man. Now that you may have made the discovery of the century, you have the credentials to speak out. What do you think?"

I chewed a forkful of pancake. "I think the archaeologists who stayed in their libraries were smart. They didn't have to worry about greenhead flies and sunburn."

He beamed. "Aha, my assessment of your pragmatism was correct. In using the Socratic method, I have arrived at the truth. It doesn't matter if we don't dig up every inch of a site. When there is expertise and money lacking, we observe, we sample, and we go back to the lab and the computer. And today we take pictures." He pushed his plate away. "I have purposely lingered, although every molecule in my body is ready to explode, so this crew can go to work on full and relaxed stomachs.

But now I can stand it no more. If we don't get out there and photograph that cave so I can see what you have found, I will burst with curiosity." He stood up and shoved his chair back. "*Carpe diem*, my friends. Seize the day!" With that, he whisked out of the room.

I loaded a fresh air tank in the minivan and, with Eileen behind the wheel, we headed for the excavation site. Rick was already in his wet-suit bottoms. He was tinkering with a video camera that was protected by a cylindrical red-and-clear-plastic waterproof housing.

Dr. Zane removed a Nikonos V underwater still camera from its case and attached a Sea and Sea strobe unit. "We're going to need some still photos for publication. Think you can use this?" I looked over the settings and said I'd give it my best.

Ten minutes later Rick and I waddled like giant black ducks toward the stake marking the site and slid down the bank. Easing into the pond, we gave each other the high sign, waved to the others, and let the air out of our buoyancy compensators. We sank fins first, following the anchor line, then swam along the bottom a few yards, and up the slope to the rock shelter.

We plunged into the yawning mouth and swam to the back of the cave. Rick was first into the passageway. Jockeying ourselves and the camera equipment through the tunnel proved to be a challenge. We held the gear out in front and followed it around the twists and turns into the art gallery. Rick flicked on the video light and panned the camera slowly around to catch an overview. Then he started shooting individual drawings. I got into a few takes to give the artwork scale.

He wrapped up his work in a short time. I began shooting with the Nikonos. I sectioned off part of the wall in my viewfinder and hit the shutter release. Moved the camera over and did it again. A half hour went by quickly, and we were done. We squirmed through the passageway. Minutes later our heads popped out of the water into the bright sunshine.

I handed the camera to Dil. Norma helped me get my tank off. Eileen came over with a towel. "Dr. Zane wants to see the video right away, so we're calling it a day here."

Zane left immediately. I stripped my gear off and piled it into Eileen's van. When we got back to the house, Dr. Zane was fiddling with the VCR and calling down ancient curses on high technology. Dil helped him get the tape rolling. Soon we were seeing the pictographs float by in the dry comfort of the living room. With each close-up of a bird or deer came a chorus of oohs and aahs.

Throughout, Zane whispered, "Wonderful things, wonderful things."

They ran the video again. Having seen it all in the flesh, I went out on the veranda, crumpled into a wicker chair, and looked out over the rooftops to the *Mayflower II*. Maybe I was just spinning my wheels working on Zane's project. Damned if I could figure out the connection to Joe Quint. Joe was the only one who could shed some light on that, and he had flown the coop.

Quint puzzled the hell out of me. I was telling people that Joe was too smart to practically hand the cops the evidence to nail him for the murder and fire at Plimoth Plantation. For a smart guy, Joe Quint had done a dumb thing. He had run. It was like standing in front of Plymouth Rock with a sign that said: 'I'm Guilty as Hell!'

Eileen came out on the porch. She tousled my hair playfully, then put her hands on my shoulders and leaned over to brush my neck with warm lips.

"Congratulations, Soc. Dr. Zane thinks you and Rick

found paleo-Indian drawings going back to the Stone Age. This could be a very important discovery. He's going to get the still pictures developed and run them to Boston. We've got the rest of the day off. I was thinking we could pack a picnic lunch and go to the beach."

An afternoon spent watching Eileen soak up the sun in her bathing suit wouldn't be too hard to take with or without lunch. But I had promised Flagg I'd follow through on Joe Quint. I told Eileen we'd have to do it another time. I had an important matter to take care of.

"Maybe it's just as well," she said. She did a bad job of trying to hide her disappointment with a smile. "I've got some things to do in the lab."

She went up the stairs and I drifted back into the living room. Zane was talking excitedly on the phone. Dil and Norma were rewinding the video. I said I'd be back later in the day. I got into the pickup and drove out to Route 3 heading south. I crossed the Cape Cod Canal on the Bourne Bridge. Twenty minutes later, I turned off at Patty Hoagland's driveway. Two guys who looked like the Blues Brothers in their identical dark sunglasses sat in a black Ford sedan parked across from Patty's mailbox.

Patty was glad to see me. We went into the kitchen and sat at the kitchen table. "Are those men still out front?" she asked.

"If you're talking about two characters in a black Ford, the answer is yes, and I don't think they're bird watching."

"There are men with binoculars in the woods out back, too."

"Not everyone gets this kind of male attention."

"Not everyone wants it. I guess you've heard about Joe disappearing."

"Yes, a little while ago. Has anyone approached you?"

"Not yet." She grinned. "I called the town police and said I'd seen some suspicious men lurking in the neighborhood. They told me not to worry, that it was just workers from the state environmental department doing some sort of a survey. Do they really expect me to believe that? Do they really think Joe is stupid enough to come here?"

"Probably not. My guess is that these are federal cops. They may be trying to intimidate you so you'll be awed by the power and majesty of the government and cave in when they question you later on."

"Let them try," she said quietly.

The wolf lady was baring her fangs. The feds would find Patty Hoagland didn't intimidate easily.

"I was wondering," I said. "Did you have the chance to ask Joe about the auction?"

"No, I didn't. I'm sorry."

I told Patty about my visit to the auction house and my conversation with Renault. When I finished, she arched an eyebrow.

"Wounded Knee," she said softly. "Anything that came out of Wounded Knee would have been stolen by the cavalry-men who murdered those poor people. There are Native Americans alive today who are descended from some of the people who survived the massacre. They would consider it their property. Seeing those things sold at a public auction would certainly make Joe angry. *Very* angry."

"Angry enough to kill?"

"No, of *course* not. But angry enough to do something about it. That must be what all those calls were to museums and experts. Joe always made sure he prepared his groundwork before he struck. That's why he's been so successful in court fights."

"Only this time he was tossed in a cell before he got the chance to make his move. Do you know why he jumped bail?"

"No. It was a stupid thing for him to do."

"It was more than stupid. It's cut him off from anyone who can help him. The case against him has some holes in it. If Joe goes to trial, it's quite possible he can beat the charges. Will you tell him that?"

She smiled. "You're certainly not very subtle. You're assuming I can contact him."

"It was just a thought."

"How do I get by those watchdogs who've surrounded me?"

"I'm a firm believer that love will show the way. Have you considered smoke signals?"

"I might give them a try." She examined the melting cubes in her glass. "Assuming I *can* contact Joe, which I'm not promising, what would you want me to tell him?"

"That I think there's something fishy about the auction house. That he's got a chance of proving himself innocent if he wants to take this head-on. That he's not helping himself by being a fugitive."

She nodded gravely. "I'll see what I can do."

I gave her my number in Plymouth. "Just call here and ask for me. Don't leave your last name. The less people know about what we're doing, the better it is."

On the way out, Patty picked up a pair of binoculars from the fireplace mantel and handed them to me. "Look just to the right of that big oak tree."

I focused on the woody area she pointed to. Light flashed off glass or metal in the bushes. There was thick green growth on the ground.

"Those woods are loaded with poison ivy," she said.

"How about ticks?"

"They practically jump out of the grass onto you."

I gave back the binoculars. "I have the feeling the drug-stores are going to sell out of calamine lotion after today."

"By the way," she said, shaking my hand warmly. "What did you think of Peter, my brother?"

"There's a strong physical family resemblance, but that's where it ends."

"That's very diplomatic."

"It's also true."

I got in my truck and drove out to the end of the drive. Two black Fords were now parked in front. The driver's side door on one of the cars opened, and Rourke heaved his big body out. He plodded across the street, stuck his jaw in the pickup window and ran his eyes over the interior of the cab like twin searchlights.

"I don't have the Lindbergh baby if that's what you're looking for," I said.

He withdrew his head. "Naw. I was hoping to see a guy I thought was too bright to get involved with a bail jumper."

"You seem to have a problem hanging onto fugitives."

"It's nothing like the problem you're going to have if you don't butt out of this case. What were you doing in there?"

"I was talking to Patty Hoagland."

"What were you talking about?"

"We were talking about J. Edgar Hoover. Was he or wasn't he? Did he or didn't he?"

"Did he or didn't he what?"

"Look good in a taffeta dress?"

Rourke's face turned the color of a ripe plum. He glared hotly at me. I grinned. Then *he* grinned. I got nervous. I put the truck in gear. He stepped back. I pulled out onto the road.

135

I stopped off at a bar near the canal for a chicken-salad sandwich and a beer. While I waited for the lunch, I went to a pay phone and called my father at the bakery.

"Hi, Pop, how are you feeling?"

"Aristotle! I feel better now that you call."

My father has been in this country for forty years, but he still has an accent like an Athenian cabdriver.

"How is Ma doing?"

"Mama?" He rolled his eyes. "You have to *ask*, Aristotle? Mama is always Mama."

"You're right about that, Pop." I told him I was sorry I missed his name day.

"Don't worry, Aristotle. Sons and fathers go their own way, but they are never far apart."

"Pop, when you get better, you come to Cape Cod. The sea air will do you good."

"Sure, Aristotle, sure. But first I do some work before the bakery goes to hell. Don't tell Mama I said that."

"I won't."

Sixteen

I KILLED THE afternoon at the Plymouth library, reading "Bury My Heart at Wounded Knee," then headed over to the auction house.

Claude Renault sounded like a pimp pushing his low-end merchandise onto a reluctant john. Every piece of old junk he auctioned off was *gorgeous, shapely, warm,* or *big-chested.*

About two hundred well-heeled Rubes sat in metal folding chairs lined up in front of the auction house stage.

I leaned against a wall admiring Renault's salesmanship. When I talked to him, his voice didn't have a trace of an accent. Maybe a little New York around the edges. Now he dropped 'h's and rolled 'r's as if he had been possessed by the soul of a French boulevardier.

The overhead lights dimmed, a spotlight came on, kettledrums thundered, and the theme from *2001: A Space Odyssey,* blared from the PA system. A large lazy Susan built into a wall behind Renault rotated. Something that looked like a Victorian card table came into view. While the lights were low and attention was centered on the table, I ambled down a hallway next to the stage.

Past the restrooms was a door that had the words Employees Only stenciled onto a pane of frosted glass. I slipped a flat leather case out my pocket. Laid out neatly inside were some lock picks, miniature screwdrivers, a glass cutter, and a penlight. The Yale lock didn't stand a chance. I ducked into a darkened corridor, shut the door quickly behind me, and switched on the penlight.

Soon I was in the reception area. Betty, the receptionist, was back in the auction hall keeping tally on the bids. Behind her desk was an office. I stepped inside and almost gagged on the stench of musk cologne.

I rifled through the filing cabinets. The paperwork was routine; vouchers and bills having to do with overhead, payroll, and transportation costs. I checked the top of Renault's antique oak desk. He was neat, probably anally retentive. Then I used another pick to unlock the drawers. The only thing of interest were some kiddie-porn magazines. I went back to the reception area and sat at Betty's desk. Now what? A Compaq computer stared me in the face. Renault was holding a computer printout the day I saw him inventorying his stock. His auction records would be filed in his data base.

I found the On button and the screen glowed an indigo blue. I noodled around until a directory appeared. There were six categories. Beside the listing for auctions was a B. I pressed the B and the return key. The directory disappeared. In its place was another list of categories. By Date. By Name. By Category. By Seller. By Buyer.

I moved the cursor to the By Date listing, hit the F key for file and the R for retrieval. A column of dates appeared. I scrolled up until I found the auction I'd seen in the weekly newspaper and called for more info. What I got was basically a reprise of the auction ad.

Back to square one. I typed: AMERICANA, and hit retrieval.

Too broad. The listings were for folk art, like weathervanes and bird decoys. Try again. This time I typed NATIVE AMERICAN.

See INDIANS.

I typed INDIANS, wondering whether the computer knew I was incompetent and was just jerking my chain. A file jumped onto the screen. Renault said he rarely sold Indian stuff. But the screen listed dozens of offerings with hundreds of items in all. I scrolled up and found the auction date I wanted.

Bingo!

More than two dozen items were listed for sale under the title: NATIVE AMERICAN ARTIFACTS—WOUNDED KNEE. Next to each item was a description, date of origin, condition, the name of the seller, the buyer, and the sale price. As Renault had said, the seller was an estate. The sole buyer for all the items was a Boston company named Acquisitions Unlimited, Inc. I hit print, and a laser printer quietly clicked away.

I folded the printout and stuffed it in my pocket, then went back to the computer and scanned the other Indian sales one by one. In each instance, the seller was a private party from out of state. In every case, the buyer was Acquisitions Unlimited, Inc. I typed in Acquisitions Unlimited, Inc. and hit the retrieve button. NOT ON FILE.

Footsteps were coming down the hall. I turned off the computer and dashed into Renault's office. A light came on in the reception area. I dropped onto all fours and crawled behind Renault's big wooden desk. Metal file drawers opened and shut. A woman's voice was humming. Then cigarette smoke came my way. Shoes padded onto the carpeting of Renault's office. I scrunched deep into the desk's foot well. A woman's ankles were visible only inches away. Papers rustled overhead. I held my breath. The light went out. A second later, the outer office went dark.

After a few minutes, I crawled out from under the desk and rubbed my stiff knees. I took one last look around, then headed back to the auction gallery. I listened at the door with the frosted glass and opened it slowly. The drone of Renault's voice came from the hall at the far end of the building. The hallway was deserted. I slipped through and shut the door.

My hand was still on the knob when Betty stepped out of the ladies' room. She saw me. I smiled. She scowled.

"May I help you?" she said. It was clearly a challenge and not an offer.

"Headed toward the men's room," I said sheepishly. "Guess I walked right by it."

The men's-room sign was as obvious as a billboard. She gave me a cold stare. "I guess you did. That door leads to private offices. Can't you read?"

I moved my hand away from the knob. "Got a little confused back here. Thanks very much for your help."

I went into the men's room. High heels clicked on the tile floor and stopped just outside. She was standing there, thinking. Then I heard her move off. I cracked the door and peered out. Betty was at the Employees Only door. Satisfied that it was locked, she walked back to the auction hall. Minutes later, I followed. She was back at her table recording bids. I had to walk by her. I nodded. She studied me thoughtfully, running her tongue over the inside of her cheek.

Renault was working the crowd skillfully. A portrait that

could have been painted by John Singer Sargent was bringing in some healthy bids. I went back to my slot against the wall. Fifteen minutes later, I left the auction house and found a bar in Plymouth that wasn't any louder than six TV sets.

Over a cold beer, I reminded myself that the most complicated situation can be broken down and simplified. First I reduced the volume on the static that was confusing my brain. Then I jotted down in a notebook the most important recent events in the life and times of my reluctant client.

Joe Quint learns about the auction and goes ballistic. Joe is blamed for a murder. Joe gives Soc a hard time. Joe goes AWOL. I drew a square around this list and started another column. The cavalry wipes out the Indians at Wounded Knee. Somebody steals some souvenirs. The Wounded Knee stuff ends up in a private estate. The estate sells it to an entity called Acquisitions Unlimited, Inc. I enclosed this list in another rectangle and looked at my artwork.

In between the two boxes, I started yet another column. Heritage Auction Galleries. Claude Renault. Acquisitions Unlimited, Inc. I circled this stuff and drew lines connecting them to the two boxes. *Voilà!* Two separate series of events suddenly became part of an equation. Problem was, parts of the equation were missing. Flagg was in London and Joe Quint possibly hiding up a tree. I was on my own. I had another beer and played pinball until the boinks and buzzes gave me a headache.

I grabbed my Red Sox cap and left the stale smell of cigarette smoke and beer. I went down a narrow street to the harbor. The *Mayflower II* loomed in the darkness. I walked along the edge of the harbor, waiting for an attack of the smarts that never came.

Around ten o'clock I went back to the house. Eileen's car was gone. Dil and Norma were in the living room watching

Woody Allen in *Hannah and Her Sisters*. I liberated an Amstel from the refrigerator and joined them. After the movie, we sat around drinking beer and talked about The Three Stooges, how it was a shame when Curly died because the act just wasn't the same having three guys with funny hair.

"Where's the rest of the crew?" I asked.

"Rick disappears just about every night at nine," Dil said. "We suspect he's got a girlfriend. Eileen went up to Boston with Dr. Zane."

"How'd you hook up with the good doctor?"

"We worked with him in Arizona at his southwest office."

"I didn't realize he had another place."

"Oh, yes," Norma interjected. "In Tucson. It's his original office, in fact. Boston is a fairly new addition to his business."

"It sounds funny to hear archaeology called a business."

Dil pondered that. "I wouldn't recommend it to anyone who wants to get rich. But it's definitely changed since the days when the only way to make a buck at it was to teach. With the laws now in place, any government entity or individual who wants to build on a possible archaeological site has to hire a consultant. It's no different than bringing in an engineer to do an environmental-impact report."

"Zane pours a lot of the money he makes back into pure research," Norma added. "That's why we like working with him. You've heard him say he'd rather leave a site if the work can't be funded properly. But do you think he *really* wants to cover up a discovery so someone else can claim credit for it in the year 2525?"

"That's the reason he went bonkers over those pictographs," Dil said. "This could get him more consultant jobs to fund more research."

"Were you consulting with him in the Southwest?"

"Actually, we were involved in pure research through the University of Arizona. Have you ever heard the name Anasazi?"

"Wasn't he a pitcher with the old Chicago Cubs?"

"Maybe, but these Anasazi lived up in 'Four Corners' country, where Arizona meets Utah, Colorado, and New Mexico."

"And they made the most glorious pottery in the world," Norma said. "Patterns and colors you wouldn't believe."

"That's why the stuff is disappearing," Dil grumbled,

"People taking it for souvenirs?"

He nodded. "That's only part of it. Pothunters find the stuff. Then it goes into the pipeline. Some private collector pays major bucks, and it sits in his cellar."

Norma said sardonically, "Gee, that sounds like some museums we know."

"Okay, I agree. There must be thousands of pieces tucked in cardboard boxes in dusty museum basements, but at least the stuff is catalogued, and *maybe* the public will get the chance to see it someday."

"This may sound like a dumb question," I said, "but who's got the best claim to an artifact?"

"Depends on who you talk to," Dil said. "The Indians pretty much want everything you dig up. I can understand that when the tribe is still in existence, and you have people actually descended from those who made the stuff. But the Anasazi died out years ago. So who should we give it to? The Hopi? Or maybe the Navajo?"

"Dil and I have had this discussion before. We think if there are no lineal descendants, it should be made available to the greatest number of people possible. Probably through a museum."

"Which could be a problem with the rock art Rick and I found."

"Maybe that's not so bad. Who cares if it stays underground, where people can't spray-paint it or chip off sections to take home? Photos and videos should satisfy the curiosity of most people."

It was nearly midnight. "Any idea what Dr. Zane has planned for us tomorrow?"

"My guess is he'll want you and Rick to look around the cave for artifacts that can pinpoint the dates of occupancy. The pictographs are important, but they are meaningless unless we know when they were painted. We can do that if we find some tools, flints."

I yawned. "I'd better turn in. Thanks for the beer."

"No one said archaeology had to be completely dry," Dil said.

We went upstairs to our room. I looked longingly at Eileen's closed door. I shook my head and went into my room. It would be nice tomorrow to deal with the basic uncomplicated simplicity of rooting around in an underground cave.

As usual, I was wrong.

Seventeen

"A TOAST TO our underwater Indiana Jones!" Dr. Zane raised his glass of buttermilk.

Zane was holding court at the head of the table. "We celebrate an archaeological coup. You and young Master Rick may have made *the* find of the century in the Eastern Woodlands tradition." He turned to Eileen, who was sitting beside him. "Please explain to this sleepy-eyed gentleman that this is not merely the babbling of an over-the-hill bone collector."

"We stopped at Harvard and Boston University yesterday." Eileen said. "Dr. Zane showed the video to his colleagues."

"Green-eyed *vultures* would be a better term for them." Zane sniffed. "They were actually *verdant* with envy. I told them nothing beyond the video, of course." He turned a beady eye on me. "I can see by his face that our philosopher-diver is wondering why I would taunt others who labor in the same field. It is not sadism on my part, though God knows some of those stuffed shirts could do with some deflation. It is pure showmanship. Like Houdini, the longer I keep the audience in suspense, the greater will be their reaction when I produce hard evidence."

I spread some raspberry jam on an English muffin. "You mean the videotape isn't hard enough?"

"It is, very much so," Zane replied. "But in archaeology, it's not just *what* you find, but where and when you found it. Our task for today is to find artifacts that will tell us when this cave and art gallery were occupied." He clapped his hands for attention. "Now, please, we must be off, children. An early start means we can break before the noonday sun broils my scalp." He touched his peeling forehead.

We were on site by 8:30 A.M. A white sun was climbing into the pale sky. I switched my empty tank for a fresh one, and Rick and I dressed for our dive.

Dr. Zane came over and put his arm around my shoulders. "I have a favor to ask of you. Rick tells me that the still photographs you took yesterday didn't come out. No fault of yours, I'm sure. We've had the camera checked. Would you mind shooting another roll, as you did yesterday?"

I picked up the camera with the attached strobe light and said it would be no problem. Rick and I quickly went through the predive test ritual and hooked trowels and specimen bags to our belts. I strapped on my thigh scabbard and clipped a flashlight to my vest. I offered to go first and led the way into the water, down the anchor rope to the bottom, then up the face of the cliff to the cave entrance.

Inside the first chamber I stopped, pointed to the shaft entrance, tapped my watch, and showed Rick two hands, then one. Fifteen minutes should give us more than an adequate safety margin. Rick nodded. He stuck his trowel in the silt and pointed to his collection bag. He would dig in the main cave while I shot.

I swam into the tunnel and bonged my way around the curves. The claustrophobia that threatened to shut down all my systems the first time through wasn't as strong, but I was glad when the tunnel ended and I popped out into the picture chamber.

Slowly, I played the flashlight beam around the walls. One drawing caught my eye. I swam close for a better look at a crudely drawn stick figure of a man holding a bow. Next to him was a deer. The original outline, in black, was out of proportion. The artist had corrected it with red paint. The mistake gave the mute symbols and figures a humanity that I hadn't appreciated before.

In my imagination, a dusky-skinned man in a loincloth dipped makeshift brushes into shallow bowls of paint. Next to the drawings was a palm print. Signature? I covered the print with my own hand and connected with the long-dead artist. He was whispering in my ear: Here I am, remember me.

I swam back from the wall and steadied the camera. The handprint, the stick figure, and the deer appeared in my view finder. I pressed the shutter release. The room exploded in silver light. Moving the camera counterclockwise, I shot more pictures. I was familiar with the cave by now, and I worked fast, quickly using up the roll of thirty-six exposures.

Next, I explored the cave bottom and picked up some objects that might interest Zane. Time flew. I had gone over my self-imposed time limit. I glided to the shaft opening, took one last look at the cave art, then wiggled and bumped through the tunnel. I used short fin-kicks in the cramped space to move me around the curves and turns like an eel. I held the camera out in front of me in my right hand, the flashlight in my left. So it was the camera that caught the main force of what felt like the Berlin wall crashing down.

The tough plastic housing splintered. There was a grinding, gritty sound. The camera was pushed into my face mask, knocking it askew and breaking the rubber seal. Water poured into the mask and blinded me. I pulled back into the tunnel like a crab hiding in its shell. Not fast enough.

Something grazed my head. Red sparks flew; then darkness enfolded me. The black curtain descending over my eyes never lowered all the way. I could hear bubbles burbling from my regulator. I bit into the mouthpiece with almost enough force to crush it. Red-hot pliers pinched my right forearm, which had taken the full force of whatever hit me the first time. Instinctively, I reached for the pressure gauge at the end of its hose. It was a futile move. My mask was half off my face, and I didn't have light to read the gauge.

I twisted the mask into place, and cleared it by breathing through my nose. It refilled with water immediately. I took my glove off and felt the Plexiglas. Cracked. Okay, step two. I needed illumination. I groped ahead in the tunnel a few feet, but there was no sign of my flash. The ready light glowed like a ruby on the strobe. I pushed the test button. Dumb move. Brilliant light froze the tunnel walls. I was blinder than before. Precious moments were lost as I waited for the ghosts to clear from my retinas. I squeezed my eyes almost shut and held the pressure-gauge dial in front of me. I pressed the test button again. The lightning burst showed me that my air supply was at low ebb.

Holding the useless camera in front of me, I moved cautiously ahead in the darkness. The camera banged into a solid wall. I hit the strobe button. *Flash.* The way out was blocked by a yard-wide boulder wedged tightly in the opening. I pushed against the rock. It didn't budge. I tried using my shoulder. That didn't work either. The rock wasn't there before. Had I blundered into a side tunnel? Impossible. If the tunnel had branched off, I would have noticed it.

I ran my fingers blindly along the edge of the rock and felt a hairline space separating it from the tunnel walls. I probed the narrow opening with my trowel. The point was too dull to work into the seam. I pulled the knife from my thigh sheath, stuck the point in, and tried to move the rock. No dice. I jabbed the wall in frustration. Chips of gravel and dirt fell away. Maybe I could chop an opening around the rock. I needed a crowbar or a burglar's jimmy. All I had was this damn camera. Where was Rick? Was he trying to pry this thing off?

I ran my hand down the cylindrical strobe head. The strobe unit was supported by a flat piece of metal with a rubber grip at one end. I twisted the knurled knob at the bottom and detached the arm from the bracket holding it to the underside of the camera. Then I unscrewed the strobe head. The end was flat—not as incisive as the end of a crowbar, but the arm was about a foot and a half long and might offer some leverage.

I chipped more wall away from the boulder until there was space to insert the tip of the strobe arm. I put my weight against it and thought I felt the rock move, but I wasn't sure. My arm hurt like hell. I made myself stop, took ten even breaths, then jammed the makeshift lever in again.

Give me a lever long enough, and a fulcrum in the right place, and I can move the world, Archimedes had said. Too bad he didn't know Newton, who said for every action there is a reaction. When I pushed on the metal arm, the counterforce

149

moved me backwards. I couldn't bring the full muscle strength of my body into play. While I fiddled and diddled, air was being used up.

One of the first things you learn in dive school is how to remove your buoyancy compensator and put it back on underwater without drowning, so it was no big deal, except for the tight fit, to get mine off. I kept the regulator in my mouth and I pounded the strobe arm into the crack with the trowel handle. Then I removed my fins, bunched my body into a ball, and swiveled, so my feet were against the boulder.

I put my back against the tunnel floor, splayed my arms out for additional leverage, and heaved against the lever with all the strength in my body. *Ughh*. Nothing happened. I jammed the arm further in, and pushed once more.

The rock moved slightly.

I gave it a hard shove with my feet. An opening of about six inches appeared. I pushed until it was a foot wide, then eighteen inches. With the tank trailing by the regulator hose behind me, it was a squeeze. I wriggled, puffed and grunted.

Out!

Back once more in the main cave, I slipped the buoyancy vest on. I was operating blind. I removed the useless face mask and drew a diagram of the cave in my head. I swam to where the cave opening should be and hoped my head wouldn't bonk into a blank wall.

Light smeared the blackness. I swam toward the entrance. I was back into the pond. My hand reached for the sun-shimmered surface where two sets of legs dangled above my head. I popped up between Dil and Eileen like a jack-in-the-box.

They stared at me. "Soc." Eileen screamed, "thank God!" They helped me up the muddy bank. Norma and Dr. Zane grabbed my hands and pulled me onto the grass. I wiped the water out of my eyes and saw Rick standing a few yards away. His mouth curled around a deleted expletive. It lasted only a second. He pasted a phony grin on his face, bounded over and patted me on the back.

"Hey, man! Am I glad to see you."

I spit out some pond water. "What the hell happened down there?"

"Jeezus, I don't know. I was digging away. I think there was a cave-in. Rocks and stuff fell on my head. I thought I was done for. I dug myself out and went over to the shaft, but it was all plugged up, man. Tried to move the rocks, couldn't get any-where, and was losing my air. Figured we needed more divers. I came up. No spare tanks. We called the rescue squad to get a dive team in. We were going to come down again. How'd you get out?"

Rich had taken off his wet suit and air tank. He didn't look like someone who expected a dive team to arrive anytime soon. I wanted to tear his face off. Instead, I gritted my teeth and offered him my hand.

"I was lucky. You did the right thing, Rick. I appreciate it."

I took a few wobbly steps—and my knees turned to rubber. Dil and Norma grabbed me before I did a face plant and helped me to the truck. They got me out of my dive suit, and Eileen poured me a glass of lime Gatorade. Dr. Zane hovered around like a hummingbird.

The rescue squad arrived minutes later. Two EMTs piled out. I told them I was fine. They gave my head and arm a quick check and hustled me onto a stretcher. The doctor in the hos-pital emergency room said it didn't look like a concussion or a fracture. He cut away a patch of hair and put some gunk on the head bruise and battered arm. I sat on the examination table, thinking about Rick's story. If he were Pinocchio, his nose would be longer than his arm.

The doctor bandaged my head, gave me a little box of high-octane headache pills, and told me not to do any bungee jumping or my brains might fall out. He insisted that an orderly push me to the exit in a wheelchair. The EMTs were hanging around to see how things turned out. I thanked them and said I hoped they'd canceled the call for divers. They said not to worry. The divers wouldn't have been able to get to me for another hour.

Eileen drove me back to the Sever Street house. I didn't say much. Eileen was smart enough not to push the conversation. She kept checking me with sideways glances, almost as if she were afraid I'd disappear. I got out of my damp bathing suit and into a dry pair of shorts. She brought up some ice cubes in a Ziploc bag, bundled me into bed with my makeshift ice pack, covered me with a blanket, and pulled the shade down. She had to let the others at the excavation site know I was doing okay, but she'd be back shortly. I shut my eyes. When I opened them again, Eileen was in a Windsor chair a few feet from the bed, watching me.

"I thought you went out to the site," I said.

"I did. You must have dozed off. How do you feel?"

I pulled myself up on the pillow and lightly touched the bandage on my scalp. "I feel pretty good for somebody who had one foot in the grave and the other on a banana peel."

She leaned forward and took my hand, holding it so tightly that she crushed my fingers.

"I wish you wouldn't joke. I was so worried."

"Sorry. Near-death experiences always bring out the Henny Youngman in me."

"When Rick came out of the water and said you were

trapped in the cave, I had visions of Michael all over again."

Michael again. Screw him. What about Soc? Eileen's fixation on her baby brother was getting to me.

"Eileen, Michael didn't die in a diving accident. He died in an explosion. He died because he killed somebody and was trying to get away with it. He died because he was so damned obsessed with a dead ship that he couldn't let anyone or anything get in his way." It was a cruel thing to say, and I regretted it immediately. I get testy when somebody drops rocks on my head.

Eileen's face went pale. She jerked her hand back as if she'd grabbed a red-hot poker.

"You *bastard!*"

Eileen's anger was a relief. I was getting tired of her Florence Nightingale act.

"Do you want me to keep pretending, like you, that Michael was some street kid Father Flanagan could turn into a choirboy?"

Tears welled in her eyes. "No," she said hoarsely, "but you could show some human decency. For God's sake, Michael was a friend of yours."

"Michael was never a friend, Eileen. He was a client who hired me to do a job. And he was someone I liked, but Michael was a con man who worked people. He worked you and he worked me. And now he's dead, but he's still working us; still making you feel as you're the one who should be responsible for him forever. Let it go, Eileen."

She put her head in her hands, and her body was racked by deep sobs.

In the heat of our words, we had moved to within touching distance. I reached out with my hand, not thinking about it, feeling the burnished copper of her hair, weaving my fingers

153

through it, slipping my hand down to the soft warmth at the back of her neck, unconsciously drawing her closer.

She looked up, almost surprised at my gesture. I expected her to pull away, but that shows you how much I know about women. She put her hand on my arm, resting it easily, as if to insist that I keep it there. The remarkable blue eyes blinked away the tears. I could feel the fever heat coming from her body. She smelled of perfumed soap and outdoors. The Old Victorian Gentleman who occupies a room in the lodging house that is my brain was saying: "You cowardly bounder, you have made a lady weep." He was arguing with some guy with an Austrian accent who was saying, "*Ja*, a therapeutic catharsis is always difficult." I told both of them to shut up. I had made Eileen cry, and I didn't feel right about it.

"I'm sorry for saying those things, Eileen."

She uttered a sad little laugh. "You're right," she said. "I've played mama martyr for much too long."

Our knees touched. She moved her hand slowly along my arm, letting it slide behind my neck, so that our faces were only inches apart. I put my arm around her slim waist. We kissed like hungry travelers drinking at a fountain. She moved into me. I guided her onto the bed, and we slipped beneath the sheets.

Later, with her nude body next to mine, our naked thighs intertwined, the soft warmth of her breasts against my chest, I thought it was inevitable from the day I met Eileen that this would happen. But I wasn't sure it should have.

Eighteen

THAT NIGHT AT dinner, I told Dr. Zane I was getting out of the archeology business. He wasn't happy, but he said he understood.

Beetling his bushy brows, Zane said gravely, "It will be a blow to our operation, although I don't blame you for being nervous about the cave after nearly being killed."

I finished chewing a forkful of haddock Dil had cooked.

"Cave diving is always risky." I took a sip of a good California Chardonnay, pausing for effect. "Maybe this cave is under an Indian curse."

There was laughter around the table.

Zane's eyes widened behind his glasses. "Surely you don't believe—" he began. Noting my grin, he waggled his finger at me. "Ah, our diver-philosopher is toying with us."

While I had my grin plastered in place, I flashed it at Rick. He smirked and looked off into the distance. Rick tried to kill me. I was sure of it. The ceiling in the cave was rock-smooth. Nothing short of an earthquake would have shaken a piece loose with such precise timing. Rick waited for me to come up and dropped the boulder on my bean. Did Dr. Zane put him up to it? And if not Zane, who? And why?

Dr. Zane had launched into a exposition on the curse of King Tut. If the doctor was putting on an act, it was a damned good one. I gave up looking for clues to Zane's motives in his face and shifted my gaze to Eileen, who sat across the table. Her intense blue eyes said what I didn't have to be told. What we knew the second we climbed out from between sheets damp from our bodies. That the beginning was also the end. The electrical tension between us had masked deeper, more powerful emotions. We'd come together like two jungle cats in a quick, hot consummation. It was a coupling with passion, but no love—more like a test of wills. We did it because if we hadn't, we would always have wondered if a piece of our life was missing.

God, she was beautiful. Lifting my wine glass, I raised it in silent toast. Eileen smiled and did the same.

"Will you go back to fishing?" she said.

"Soon, I hope. Sam could use me on the *Millie D.*"

Norma tore herself away from Zane's dissertation. "We're going to miss you, Soc."

"Maybe we can get together for the Three Stooges all-nighter on New Year's Eve."

"No maybes about it," Dil added.

I promised to bring the beer. "If you'll excuse me, I'm going to get my stuff together. Thanks for dinner. The haddock was great, Dil." I got up from the table.

Zane said, "So soon?" He sighed heavily. "Well if you must, you must. Let me say again how grateful I am to you for your part in this discovery. I shall be sure to give you credit. I

156

want you to bill me for your services, and I'll reimburse you for diving equipment lost or damaged."

I thanked him and went around the table to shake hands. Rick looked relieved to see me go. Nobody likes to have a mistake staring him in the face. Eileen offered to help me with my things. She was up from the table before I could reply and followed me to my room. I packed my duffel, dropped it on the bed, and went over to the window. The lights of Plymouth Harbor glowed through a thin gauzy mist that had come in off Cape Cod Bay.

"Nice view. I'm going to miss it."

"Must you really go?" Eileen said. She was standing close to my side.

"Kojak gets lonely if I'm away for too long."

"It's not because of what happened here, in this room, is it?"

I tilted her chin up and kissed her lips lightly. "In a way. We'd always know it would never be better."

Eileen looked me in the eye. "Normally I would say you're laying your usual Greek blarney on me, but this time I think you're right."

"I know I am."

She gazed out the window. "We're alike, you know," she said almost sadly. "We both seem to be running from something."

"From what?"

"Ourselves, maybe. Guilt. Obligations. Childhood memories. Adult memories. Nothing. Everything. Do you think we'll ever stop running, you and me?"

Eileen was coming closer to describing me than I cared to know about. Geographically, I stayed pretty much in one place. But inside, I was constantly trying to escape everything on her list.

"Probably not. We'll just keep going until we drop. But what's wrong with that?"

She kissed me on the cheek and lifted my rucksack while I grabbed the duffel. We walked out to my truck in the warm summer air. She gave me her address in Cambridge. We embraced and kissed once more. Then I got in the pickup and drove to the bar where I played pinball the other night, had a couple of beers, and pumped more quarters into the machine. I didn't do much better than before. The beer washed the taste of Eileen out of my mouth, but her perfume still clung to my clothes. It would always cling to them.

I stayed at the bar until 8:45. Then I drove back up to Sever Street and parked in the shadows of a big maple tree. Dil and Norma said Rick left every night at 9:00. I was going to see if they were right.

At 9:01, Rick came out of the house and got into his red Mustang. He drove down the hill to Main Street, then headed north toward Kingston. I followed at a safe distance. I don't think I was surprised when I saw him turn off the road at Renault's auction emporium. I kept going another hundred feet and drove onto a fire lane. I left the truck and jogged back to the auction house. Lights were on in the office.

I plastered my back across the side of the building and inched forward to the nearest window. The blinds were down. Voices mumbled inside. I moved to the door. The voices were louder—angry at times—but they were still indecipherable. There was no point in hanging around. I went back to the truck and headed south south on Route 3. An hour later, the pickup's wheels sank into the familiar potholes of my driveway. It was good to be home.

I hustled my gear into the boathouse. Kojak was waiting in ambush. He launched himself at my knees. Life isn't complete until you've been mauled by a seventeen-pound Maine coon cat with a hunger gnawing in his gut. I fed him a whole can of low-ash food and poured him milk in a saucer as a treat.

I found a lone beer in the fridge, flopped into the mildewed splendor of my flowered sofa, and stared at the wall. Questions buzzed in my battered skull like honeybees around a flower. My scalp was still sore, but being back in familiar surroundings made it feel better.

I called my neighbor to tell her I was home and to thank her for taking care of Kojak. She said he was a very good and affectionate boy, especially around mealtime. Next I called Sam. I told him I was home, but that I couldn't go fishing just yet. He said that was all right, but the fishing was good, and he missed me. I said I missed fishing with him, too, and I meant it.

Sam gave me a fish-pier report. Who was highliner. What boats were having engine trouble. What the situation was on the new icemaker. He told me a stale joke he heard from the wharfinger. We agreed to get together at Elsie's the next morning.

I put the phone down and leaned back in the sofa, sipping my beer, listening to the bug chorus coming through the screen windows, the lap of the tide against the beach, pondering what my father had said.

Sons and fathers go their own way, but they are never far apart.

The file on Joe Quint was on the coffee table. I settled back on the sofa and opened it. There was something I remembered. Here it was. Joe's father still lived in Rhode Island. I got a road map out of the pickup. Charlestown was just over the

159

border from Massachusetts, a two-hour drive at most. I shut the lights off, kicked Kojak off my pillow, crawled into bed, and sighed contentedly.

Be it ever so humble.

Nineteen

OVER COFFEE AT Elsie's, Sam grumbled about the *Millie D.*'s engine acting up. Although he didn't come right out and say so, I could tell he wanted my help. We worked on the engine all morning. It was a nice break. A balky diesel doesn't snarl, threaten, or try to kill you.

Near midday we crawled out of the engine compartment, happily covered with grease and oil. The problem was electrical. I suspected Sam knew it all along. He took the fuel lines apart so he could keep me around while he unloaded the latest gossip Millie had picked up at her town-hall job. I escaped just before noon and went home.

The phone rang as I was toweling myself dry from the shower.

"Hi, Soc, it's your favorite Native American land developer," Peter Hoagland said. "How about getting together for lunch?"

Mashpee was a slight detour from where I was heading, but I had to eat somewhere, and Peter might have new information. I said I'd be glad to meet him, and he gave me directions to a place in Mashpee Village. I put on a blue oxford button-down shirt, khakis, and Topsiders. My preppie disguise.

Around one o'clock, I pulled up in front of a long cinder-block and brick building in the heart of Mashpee. There was a motel on the second floor, and the first level housed a strip joint, a real-estate office, gift shop, and a coffee shop. It was definitely not upscale, like the shopping center built like a fake New England village not far away on Route 28, but it had an honest charm to it.

Peter must have just told a very funny story because the customers in the coffee shop were roaring with laughter when I came in. He greeted me with his Ipana smile and viselike hand-shake and sat us at a table where we ordered sandwiches.

"Glad you could make it," Peter said.

"How's your shopping complex going?"

"Fine. I've lined up the subs and lit a pile of money under their asses. It's mostly a question of permits now. You need a permit just to sneeze these days."

"Good luck. Heard anything new about Joe?"

"Hell, I was going to ask *you* that question. How about Pal Joey? Disappearing like that."

"I think it's dumb. It makes him look guilty as hell."

"I agree. Any idea where he is?"

"Nope. You're closer to him, through Patty, than I am. I was hoping you'd know."

"Patty wouldn't tell me if her life depended on it. I thought where he was your client—well, what the hell. How's your in-vestigation coming?"

"Slow. A few leads. You got anything that might help?"

"Naw, I've been up to my ears in blueprints. This is the first time I've had to catch up with the town news. Pretty dull

162

this time of year. Everyone works at six jobs."

We talked about business, about the weather, about the tourists, and we even managed to talk a little more about Joe. The BLT wasn't bad, and it was entertaining to watch Peter work his charm; but when I shook hands and said good-bye, I wondered why he had asked me to lunch. I hadn't told him anything I couldn't have said over the phone.

I headed off-Cape, picked up Interstate I-95 on the mainland side of the canal, passed through New Bedford and Fall River, and was in Providence an hour later. Charlestown, R.I. is almost a straight shot south from the strip malls and fast-food joints around Providence to the hay silos, woods, and the rocky beaches along Block Island Sound.

Around four o'clock, I pulled off the road at a sign that had an ear of corn carved on it. Below the corn were the words: Narragansett Indian Longhouse. Two men were talking in front of the longhouse—actually a trailer on a permanent foundation. I asked where I could find Elwood Quint. They gave me directions to Elwood's place off the Indian Church Road.

The church road was an isolated, winding meander through tall, shaded stands of pine. At a battered and weed-grown aluminum mailbox with the letters Qui t painted on it, I turned onto a dusty dirt driveway that led to a clapboard house of Chinese-restaurant red.

An ancient golden retriever staggered upright and limped over to greet me with a black-lipped grin. On the front porch, a man in a rocking chair watched a television set balanced on a barnacle-encrusted lobster pot. The TV was connected to a series of linked extension cords that ran into the house through a window.

With the retriever dogging my footsteps, I went up to the

163

man. "Excuse me, are you Elwood Quint?" I had to raise my voice over the noise of the TV.

He turned, and Joe Quint looked at me. Joe as he'd be in twenty-five years. His long white hair was tucked under a Cleveland Indians baseball cap, and his skin was like baked apples. He had the same watchful eyes and rambling nose. The mouth was wide and thin-lipped, but friendlier, not cynical like Joe's. He had on a black Hard Rock Café T-shirt, shorts, and red high-top Keds.

Not saying a word, the old man pointed to a rickety wooden chair next to his. The dog flopped down by my feet, sighed wearily, and fell asleep. Geraldo Rivera was interviewing a panel of dwarves. The color was off-kilter, and Geraldo's face was lime green. It didn't look bad on him. The program was ending. The old guy clicked the TV off before I could find out what the dwarves' problem was.

"Do you ever watch Geraldo?" the old man said softly, his voice like wind rustling through the trees.

"I prefer Oprah. She looks like she'd be fun to party with. Geraldo impresses me as a guy who'd run up a big bar bill and stick you with it."

Nodding heavily, with ponderous seriousness, as if we were discussing the mystical roots of gnosticism, he said, "I agree. Oprah seems to be a much more feeling person. I get the impression that this young man is interested only in sensationalism."

"Maybe someday *Quiz Kids* will make a comeback."

"Yes, that would be nice. I liked *Truth or Consequences*, too. But anything that makes the time pass while you're doing busywork is good."

A pink plastic bowl full of string beans was balanced on bony knees that stuck out of baggy tan cutoffs. He snapped the ends off a bean and tossed it into an aluminum colander at his feet. His thick-knuckled hands were heavily veined with age, but his movement was sure and deft. He offered me a bunch of green beans. "Want to snap a few?"

"Why not?" After a few tries, I was into the rhythm. The beans went snap-plunk, snap-plunk into the colander.

Time passed. The old man said, "Why are you looking for Elwood Quint?"

"I'd like to speak to his son Joe. I thought Mr. Quint might be able to tell me where he is."

He gave me another handful of beans. "You're not too bad at this. Have you done it before?"

"Years ago, for my mother."

He nodded. More snap-plunks. "Are you a policeman?"

I took out a business card and handed it to him. He held it close to his eyes. His lips formed silent words. "You have a long and interesting name."

"Thank you. Some people can't pronounce it, so they just call me Soc."

He studied the card again and looked over at my truck. His lips puckered. "Detective work doesn't pay much, does it, Soc?"

I glanced at the GMC with its streaky green paint and fiberglass patches. "No, it doesn't. I'm a fisherman, too. That doesn't pay much, either."

"I used to be a fisherman. Lobsters mostly. Never made much money, but I liked it." He extended his hand. "I'm Elwood Quint."

"I had an idea you were. You and Joe look a lot alike."

"People have said that. It's too bad, because his mother was much better looking. Small nose and lips, big black eyes. She had some cancer and died a few years ago."

165

"I'm sorry to hear that."

"Thank you." He handed me more beans. "Why do you want to see Joe?"

"You knew Joe was in trouble."

"Yes, a shame."

"A friend who thinks the same thing hired me to help Joe. I had some things to tell Joe and questions to ask him."

The grin that crossed Elwood's face revealed two missing teeth. "Then you're a friend, too."

"I met Joe only once."

"That's all right. You're a friend if you want to help him. Want more beans? You're doing real good."

I reached for another handful.

"The police were here," Elwood said. "The town cops came by and said they were looking for Joe in Massachusetts. Then the FBI visited me."

"A man named Rourke?"

"Yes. Do you know him?"

"We've met."

Elwood shook his head sadly. "He's not a happy man. Maybe he should be in another line of work, but of course, that's his business. I told them Joe wasn't here. Hadn't heard from him. I don't think Mr. Rourke believed me. You came all the way from Massachusetts?"

"Cape Cod. It's only a couple of hours' drive."

"Nice place. I fished off there years ago. We put into Provincetown." He finished the last of the beans. "Thank you."

"You're welcome." I looked around. "Is this where Joe grew up?"

"Oh, no. We had a better house in the town. Joe was raised there. After his mother died, I sold it and moved out here to the woods where it's quiet. Just me and Nugget. Two old

166

dogs." He raised a snowy eyebrow. "You met Joe. You must know he wouldn't be foolish enough to come home where the police would be sure to look."

I nodded. "That's true. I didn't think he'd be here."

"Then why did you come?"

"It's something my father said. Sons and fathers go their own way, but they are never far apart."

"He's right. They both love the same woman. That drives them apart and binds them together. Would you like some Mountain Dew? I have some cold."

It was hot and the dark pines around the house cut off the breeze. I said it would be nice to have something cold to drink. He took the beans inside and came out a minute later with two Flintstone jelly glasses.

"Your father sounds like a wise man," he said. "He would tell you that a father knows his son. Joe could never have killed that man like they say. He never liked being a soldier."

"Somebody is trying to hurt Joe. I want to know who it is. I thought if I knew more about Joe, I would know who his enemies are."

Elwood stared off at the pines bordering his property. "Do you know anything about the Narragansett?"

"Only that there's a beer by that name."

"Oh, yes. I don't drink myself, but some people like it." He reached into the lobster pot for a tobacco pouch and a pack of papers and rolled himself a cigarette. He offered me one, which I declined, and lit up.

"Like all the Indian tribes, we welcomed the English. We thought maybe they were like the Asian boat people after Vietnam. We didn't know they were the biggest land thieves in the world. Bad-tempered, too. We ended up fighting them. They killed King Philip just up the road from here. We lost because we couldn't agree on anything, and it's the same today. There are maybe two thousand of us left in our tribe, but even now we fight among ourselves. The traditional faction on the reservation says it is in charge. The progressives at town hall say they are running things. The federal government recognizes the people in town hall."

"Where do you stand?"

"I'm the tribal medicine man. Do you know what that is?"

"You cure sick people?"

"No, that's a witch doctor."

"Sorry."

"It's an honest mistake. People make it all the time. Medicine man doesn't pay as well. My name is Tall Elm. I was tall for my day. Now I've shrunk. It happens to old people. Never to trees."

"What does the medicine man do?"

"Well, there's no job description, but I'm supposed to be the spiritual leader. Kind of a counselor. Man's laws and the natural laws are always in conflict with each other. That's why society is all mixed up. This makes people crazy in the head, only they don't know why. I tell people stories so they'll be able to figure out where they stand. Then it's up to them to decide what they should do."

"Does it work?"

"Sometimes. But if it doesn't, you're not broke, like you'd be with a psychiatrist."

"I'd like to hear one of your stories, if you don't mind."

"Sure, I've been telling this one a lot lately. One lonely night an Indian woman answers a knock at her door. A sailor stands there dripping wet. He asks if he can come in and warm himself by the fire. She can see the fire through his legs, but she says nothing. He asks if she wants any money, and she says yes. He tells her to go outside and dig behind her house. But each time she goes to dig, her children cry out. The next morning, she finds out that somebody else dug up the treasure. Then she knows that the sailor was really the devil tempting her to see if she cared more for gold than for her children."

"Good story."

"I don't think they'll make a movie out of it, but it gets the point across."

"Which is?"

'I can show you easily enough if you have an hour or two."

"I'm in no hurry."

He finished his drink. "Good, then. I'll feed Nugget and change my clothes into something more presentable."

When he came out a few minutes later, Elwood looked like a different man. He had pinned his silver hair back into a ponytail and exchanged his T-shirt and cutoffs for a turquoise western-style embroidered shirt and navy blue pants. He still wore his red high-tops. We got into my truck and he directed me onto Route 1, the old Boston Post Road. We crossed the state line into Connecticut and picked up Route 2 West, a two-lane country road that wound through woods and farmland. Elwood told me to follow the signs that said Mashantucket Pequot Reservation.

Gradually, traffic became heavier, and we moved at a crawl. Work crews had torn up the road and blocked one of the lanes. There was dust and diesel fumes, the rattle of jackhammers. We rounded a curve. "Wow!" I said softly. Half a mile away I saw what looked like the *QEII* rising above the trees.

Elwood gave me a sly grin. "That's the new tourist tepee the Pequot built. Luxury hotel."

The traffic flowed in starts and stops into a series of parking lots. We left the truck and joined hundreds of people head-

169

ing toward a sprawling one-story sandstone building. Arrow Line shuttle buses with Have a Nice Day messages and smiley faces on the front were dropping people off from the outlying lots. We walked up the front stairway into a raucous metal clanking din that came from the hundreds of slot machines. People fed coins from oversized paper cups into the machines, staring at the payoff windows in that dead-eyed glaze that comes from playing the slots.

"Welcome to Foxwoods," Elwood said. "Got a quarter?"

He popped the coin into the nearest slot. No payoff. He shrugged. "I never win at these things. C'mon."

We strolled past the roulette tables, blackjack and keno, across acres of gaming space to the bingo parlor. From everywhere came the unbroken clank and jangle of coins and machines. The casino was done in purple and green. A vaguely Indian basket design was repeated in the uniforms of the table handlers and the security people.

A couple of leggy blonde cocktail waitresses went by. They were wearing fringed imitation buckskin miniskirts. We walked to the atrium in the center of the casino, near a fake waterfall.

"Did we take a wrong turn and end up in Las Vegas?"

"This is only the start," Elwood said. "That hotel next door has three hundred–some rooms. There will be golf courses. Place for the helicopters to come in. Little train to run people around. They get ten thousand people a day here. What do you think of it?"

I thought about all the money coming out of all those pockets. "I think I need some fresh air."

We went outside and got back in the pickup. Elwood showed me the Pequot community center. He took me past the new houses, the tribal council hall, the tennis courts, the basketball courts, and the medical center. We checked out the site of the Indian museum and research center. Dark-skinned children played hoops at a new basketball court.

"The casino brings in more than four hundred million dollars a year, I've heard. Most profitable casino in the world. They're buying back land for the reservation. Kids all have their college paid for," Elwood noted. "Everyone in the tribe is becoming rich. The local non-Indians like it because it gives them work. The Narragansett—my tribe—sees this, and they want a casino, too."

"Is that bad?"

"Some say no. They say it's bringing the tribe together, people coming back from other parts of the country who couldn't afford to live here on the reservation before. Money's buying more reservation land. All this good stuff for the tribe. They say it's wagering like the Pequot have always done. Indians invented the shell game. They've got electric machines now. No big deal."

"But you think different."

"I'm a medicine man. I don't get paid to think." He smirked. "I don't get paid." We jounced over a dirt service road, dodging a couple of huge earthmovers. Elwood waved his hand. "Some people say all this—the traffic and the roads and the money—that it will hurt the culture."

"Do you agree?"

"I don't think culture's the problem. The Pequot were on their way out. Getting assimilated. Our culture was hurt long time ago, Soc. My family name used to be Quinit. They changed it because they thought it sounded more white, and the white man's ways were best because he always seemed to come out on top. I thought that way for a long time."

"Now you have doubts."

"If a casino is built in my backyard, poor people will become very rich. The question is, will they be rich in their pockets, but poor in spirit?"

"Like that story you told me about the woman and the stranger."

"That's right. Remember, though, it's just a story. I could tell it again and have the woman dig up the treasure. Go back and buy her children new clothes. What they call a Hollywood ending, I think."

"What would be so wrong with that?"

He shrugged an old man's shrug. "I know what you're saying. If the Indian can't be all red or all white, he might as well be all rich."

"You said it yourself. The tribe was losing its identity."

"Yes, and I still think spiritual poverty is a shame. But that's not what worries me. Tell me what you saw back there. Think like a fisherman reading the ocean."

"I saw slot machines and blackjack tables. Hundreds of people. None of them smiling. I saw a couple of Indians sitting around watching it all. I saw a lot of money, most of it going to the house."

He nodded. "Think of the money as water, a stream or a brook, maybe, running through a dry land. The one who controls this water controls the lives of those who must drink."

"You're saying money is power, Elwood. That's nothing new."

"It is for us Indians," Elwood said. "And we have to learn how to handle it."

"Isn't this a chance for the Indians to take something back from the white man?"

"Oh yes. That's the reasoning in my tribe. They want to build a place like Foxwoods. They got some English people in with their money. You see ten thousand people a day at Fox-woods. We're twenty miles away. We're looking at fifteen thousand a day."

I whistled. "That's a lot of wampum."

"Yes, but it worried Joe a lot. This thing—the gambling—it's splitting tribes across the country. The traditionalists and the progressives have been fighting each other. Should there be gambling or not? Who gets to count the money?"

"Joe was against gambling?"

"Some people think so. But Joe wants the best for all the tribes. If gaming brings them prosperity, that could be a good thing. There's so little for us now. But he is afraid that it would be run by the few, maybe with outsiders. He wanted it under strict tribal control. It works okay with the Pequot. Maybe it would be okay with our tribe. But he saw what happened with the Mohawk up in New York. They'd been fighting for years over who's got redder skin. Then big money comes in. Outsiders. People get killed. Joe doesn't want that for other tribes."

"How did Joe's views go down with the people who want the casino now?"

"There's a split in the tribe. Joe's been losing friends."

"And making enemies?"

"No enemies in our tribe. We're not like that. Most people know Joe from the time he was a kid. Just bad feelings. But Joe's been talking around the country. He's got a big mouth like me. Makes people mad. They think he's a spoiler. We got crazies just like the white man. The money thing again. Want to come by for fresh bean supper? You helped snap. Did a good job."

I accepted Elwood's invitation. We drove into Ledyard Center, a sleepy village on the edge of the reservation, and headed south to pick up Route 1 East. Joe boiled up the beans and mixed them with tomatoes, peppers, and onions, binding the mixture together with a secret sauce he found on the back of a label.

We talked about fishing and got back to the subject of Joe. Did he have any idea where I could find his son? I asked again. Elwood said, don't worry. Joe would find me. He gave me an apple and a can of Mountain Dew for the ride back to Cape Cod.

The radio was tuned to a soft-rock station out of Providence, but I didn't hear it. The jangle of slot machines and video poker games still echoed in my ears. I laid out the facts. Joe was in a mess. Joe had dug his heels in on Indian gaming houses. Did one affect the other? A typical Socarides syllogism. No conclusion. Just more questions.

I got home around eleven o'clock. By then I had pushed thoughts of Joe Quint out of my mind. All I could think of was crashing onto my bed.

But I'd have to wait. I had to entertain some unexpected company.

Twenty

MY BUTT WAS numb, my legs stiff, and my eyes bleary from the boring highway drive. Weariness dulled my edge. I was alert enough to notice that the floor lamp didn't go on at the flick of a wall switch. And that the living room smelled rankly of nervous sweat. My brain synapses were processing this information, trying to bring together cause and effect, when an arm snaked around my neck and closed on my windpipe.

Somebody breathed stale onions on my neck. Amateur move. He telegraphed where his face was. I snapped my head back, felt the sickening crunch of cartilage, and heard a yell of pain. The arm slithered off my neck. I crouched low and shot my elbow back. A pig grunted in the darkness.

Two shadows closed in on me, moving fast. Head down, I played battering ram and took the figure out on the right. Then I drove a short, hard uppercut into the mid-section of the guy on my left. He jumped back, and my knuckles grazed his ribs. Hot needles of pain jabbed into my elbow, still sore from the cave adventure. I tried a left hook, but it caught air and left me off-balance.

A fourth figure lunged at me, grabbed my hair, tried to introduce my face to his knee. I crossed my arms and ducked. The knee slammed into my wrists. I got a crab grip on his private parts and twisted. He bellowed like a castrated bull. Then what felt like the entire line of the New England Patriots jumped on my back.

With a ton of beef pressing on my shoulder blades, my legs turned to wet noodles. Somebody tried to hammer my nose into the floor. I curled into a fetal position, expecting kicks. I wasn't disappointed.

A guttural growl I didn't understand, and the kicking stopped. Metal, cold and hard, pressed against my neck.

"Get up, asshole, and do it slow." The voice was hoarse and panting. Onion Breath again.

The gun jabbed painfully into the soft flesh under my ear. Someone shoved me into the sofa. I never saw the open hand that came out of the dark. The slap was like a thunderclap. Galaxies wheeled in front of my eyes. There was the salty taste of blood in my mouth.

"That's for busting my nose," Onion Breath said. "You going to behave, or do I give you another one?"

I massaged my stinging cheek. I could get to dislike these guys. "Put that gun down and I'll do more than bust your nose." I had more adrenaline than good sense.

Another shadow moved in between me and the window. Five to one. Not bad odds—for the Terminator. The silhouette stood out against the silver moonlight streaming in from the bay. The face was in shadow, but I could see the gleam of white teeth. Long hair was tied back in a ponytail.

The shadow chuckled. "He's just trying to piss you off so you'll do something stupid."

"He broke my fucking ribs!" someone said.

"So what. He almost tore my nuts off!"

Onion Breath put his hand to his face and mumbled something about his nose again.

The silhouette said, "You didn't give the boys a very nice greeting." It was a deep voice, mellow to the point of sounding stoned.

"The boys didn't introduce themselves. Who are you?"

"We'll sign the guest book on the way out. First we talk."

"Tell your friend to get his gun out of my ear. Then we'll talk."

The chuckler said something in that language again. The gun lifted off my neck. "That better?" he said, like a mother pulling a splinter out of a kid's hand.

I touched my head to make sure it was still on my shoulders. It was. "You and your friends are harboring a lot of aggression. Maybe you should see a good shrink."

"Maybe you should listen to what I've got to say because you won't live very long if you don't."

I flashed on Kojak's being the biggest cat in the kitty orphanage and clamped a lid on my mouth. "I'm listening."

"Good. Now first, where is Joe Quint?"

Quint again. Was there anyone who *wasn't* out for his skin? The guy attracted ill-meaning people the way wasps home in on a Popsicle.

"I don't know."

"He's your client, and you don't know?"

"Quint doesn't entirely trust me. He thinks I'm a sleazy private eye."

There was a chuckle. "And are you sleazy?"

"I like to think I'm practical."

"How does ten thousand dollars of practical sound?"

"What do I have to do for it?"

"Tell us where we can find Quint."

"Now you're making me feel *really* bad."

"You *still* say you don't know where he is?" The voice had a dangerous mix of skepticism and impatience.

"Look around this place. Check out that old wreck of a truck I drive. Tell me I couldn't use ten grand to do a little interior decorating."

There was a pause. He was thinking. He chuckled. "You've convinced me. But you can still earn that ten thousand."

"How will I get in touch with you?"

"We'll find you. Just stay by the phone in case Joe calls. One other thing. Except for our deal, you're out of this. You tell us where he is, you get your reward. Stay in and you're dead. That's your reward, too."

He let the warning sink in. I licked the blood off my lips. My tough-guy act wasn't convincing anybody, not even me. *Especially* me. It would be dumb to say they weren't scaring me, because they were. I had to be careful here. If I caved in too quickly and said, "Okay, I'm off the Quint case," they wouldn't believe me. And if I said, "You guys can't push me around," they'd kill me.

"Like I said, I'm not putting my ass on the line for Quint."

"You're showing good sense," the chuckler said quietly. "But I want you to know that if you jerk us around, we'll come back and we'll kill you. It's as simple as that."

Headlights brushed the front window. Tires crunched in the clamshell driveway.

"Someone's coming," one of the guys said.

They melted into the darkness.

"Sorry, friend, but we have to go. Here's something so you'll remember we were here," the chuckler said. He spoke again in the language.

Someone grabbed me by the hair, pulled me forward, kneed me in the gut. I was on my hands and knees decorating my rug with my dinner when I heard voices over the sound of my retching.

The living-room lamp went on. Through watery eyes, I saw dungareed legs ending in two sets of boots. Hands lifted me onto the sofa. I wiped my eyes. Tommy and Ed, the Indians I met at Patty Hoagland's house, were bending over me.

"You okay?" the big one asked. He had the sad eyes of a mourner at a wake.

I felt my tender stomach muscles and tried to look on the bright side. A few inches higher, and the knee would have turned my beautiful nose into a shiitake mushroom. Lower, and I'd be singing in the Vienna Boys Choir.

Ed, the shorter man, came out of the bathroom with a cold wet washcloth. I put it on my forehead. Somehow this helped my stomach. Then I pressed the washcloth gently against my stinging lip. When I removed it, there was a dark stain on the terry cloth. Mention Joe Quint's name, and wham! The ceiling falls on you. It reminded me of the old vaudeville sketch where the crazy guy beats up on Lou Costello whenever he hears the name Niagara Falls, where the nut's wife jilted him.

Slowly I turned . . . step by step . . .

"You better?" Ed asked.

"Yeah, I'll be okay. How do I look?" My voice sounded as if I were talking through a burlap bag.

"Like a herd of buffalo trampled on your face," Tommy said. "Your lip is cut and your face looks like a cow pie. Your clothes got a lot of blood on them, but it don't look like it's all yours."

"What happened?" Ed asked. "The front door was open. We came in, and you were puking on the floor."

"I got home a little while ago, and a wrecking squad was waiting for me."

Ed said "Huh?"

"Five guys worked me over. Then they left in a hurry."

Tommy squinted toward the kitchen. The door was wide open. Night bugs invited themselves in and buzzed hotly around the inside of the lampshade. "They must have heard us coming in and run out the back."

I hitched myself up a few inches on the sofa. "While you reconstruct the crime, Tommy, maybe Ed could look in the cupboard over the sink. There's a bottle of ouzo I keep for medicinal purposes, if you don't mind."

Ed nodded and shuffled off to the kitchen.

"You have any idea who they were?" Tommy asked.

"Hell, I barely know who *you* are."

"My name's Tommy Slow Bear. That's Ed Two Knives."

"Pleased to meet you." I pressed the wet cloth against my skin. It felt good. "I never saw their faces. They kept the lights off. One of them was talking a language I didn't recognize. The others seemed to understand him."

Ed frowned and said something to me. For all the sense I could make of it, it might have been Esperanto. "Sound like that?" he asked in English.

"Could be. What is it?"

His granite face grew even stonier. "Mohawk."

His pal came back from the kitchen with a bottle and tumbler. He poured half a glass of ouzo and handed it to me. I took the bottle from him and filled the glass. Then I swallowed the

180

kind of gulp it isn't usually smart to do with ouzo. The sweet licorice firewater burned my throat and the inside of my mouth. I coughed, but at least felt alive.

Kojak came out of the bedroom and yawned. He'd slept through the whole thing. He looked at the strangers in the house, and went into the kitchen to check out his bowl.

I narrowed my eyes. "They're Mohawk, you're Mohawk. Forgive me for implying that all you folks look alike, but normally I don't see too many Indians in my living room. How do I know you're not with the bunch that just left?"

"You *don't* know," Tommy said. "But you're too smart to believe that."

I ran my eyes over his face and that of his friend. Their clothes were neat and their faces unmarked, unlike somebody who'd just been brawling with a crazed Greek.

I took another equally satisfying swig of ouzo. "If I were *smart*, people wouldn't be using my head for a lacrosse ball. In the past few days, I've had a case of the dumbs."

"What did they want?" Ed asked.

"They wanted me to tell them where to find Joe Quint."

"What did you say?"

"I told them I didn't know where he is."

"They *believed* you?"

"When I turned down their ten-thousand-dollar reward, they believed me. They wanted me to pull out of the Joe Quint case. I told them I would."

"You *mean* that?" Tommy said.

I made a painful attempt to grin. "I lie a lot." I sat up in the sofa, took the washcloth off my head, and pressed it against my mouth again. "Now let me ask a few questions," I said. "Who *were* those guys?"

181

They exchanged glances. Ed said, "They were Warrior Society."

"Well, that's a relief. Hell, for a minute there, I thought they were Shriners. What's the Warrior Society?"

"A bunch of guys who think they own the world," Tommy said.

"How'd they know I was working for Joe Quint?"

"I'd like to know that myself," Tommy said.

"Why do they want me out of the case? I don't know anything that could hurt them."

"Maybe they think you do. That's the same thing."

"You said they were Mohawk. That's upstate New York. They're a long way off the reservation. Which reminds me. Where do *you* come from?"

"New York." He smiled. "We're Warrior Society, too." He must have seen my hand bunch into a fist because he raised his palm in a gesture of peace. "Don't worry, we're not the same as them."

We eyeballed each other for a moment. "Those guys told me why *they* were here. Now it's your turn. Explain."

He nodded slowly. "Joe heard you were looking for him."

"Every cop in Massachusetts is looking for him. That's nothing new."

"This is. Joe wants to see you."

I looked around at the overturned furniture. "As you can see, my front door is always open."

"Not here. We'll tell you when and where." He picked the phone off the floor and replaced it on the table. "Your phone may be bugged. We're pretty sure the FBI's tapped into Patty's line. You might want to be careful who you talk to." He handed me a slip of paper with a telephone number on it. "Call eight A.M. sharp from a pay phone. We'll give you directions then. Any questions?"

"Lots of them, but most can keep til I see Joe. We're not exactly blood brothers. How come he thinks he can trust me?"

"He doesn't. But Patty says it's better to take a chance with new friends than with old enemies. You saved his ass when he was running from the FBI at the powwow. There's that, too." He reached out, patted my cheek lightly, and grinned. "From the look of your face, *you* could use some friends."

After they left I went into the bathroom and ducked my head under the cold water. The bandage had come loose from the bruise on my scalp, so I replaced it with another. I looked at my reflection in the mirror and decided I didn't look any worse than somebody who tried to push his face through a brick wall.

Tommy Slow Bear said I might need some friends. The swollen mouth on the battered mess in the mirror was telling me silently that he spoke like heap big straight arrow.

Twenty-One

AT 8:00 SHARP the next morning, I was at a pay phone outside a gas station calling the number Tommy Slow Bear gave me. The phone rang once, Tommy's voice came on.

"This you?" he said.

"Yeah, this you?"

"Be at the old Wampanoag meetinghouse off Route 28 in one hour."

Click. Ma Bell didn't make any money off *that* conversation.

I leaned against the pay phone and wondered why my parents never told me about the insanity that ran through our family. I'd just told Slow Bear I'd meet his friend Running Deer who was being hunted by the cops, the FBI, and a group of Indians with an attitude.

It was scary how quickly this kind of thing had become perfectly normal since John Flagg had bought me a hot dog at the powwow. My day wasn't complete unless I had a fresh bump or bruise on my face, and a fist, foot, gun, or boulder denting my aching cranium. Reality-check time. I walked to the highway berm. Out-of-state cars zoomed past, loaded like pack mules with bikes, surfboards, and windsurfers. The hot exhaust fumes cleared my head. I got behind the wheel of my pickup, merged with the vacation traffic, and pointed my nose west, toward Indian country.

The blue Ford Ranger with New York tags I had seen outside Patty's place was parked near the Wampanoag meeting-house, a little white building set in an old cemetery off Route 28. Ed was behind the wheel. He waved at me to follow. We went along Route 28 for a few miles, then headed south to Nantucket Sound. The low grass-covered dunes along the back of the beach were veiled by a chowder-thick fog. The wet air was keeping the sunscreen crowd home. A few cars with fishing-pole racks on their roofs were parked in the lot. A noisy gang of gulls fought over a crab shell like shoppers at a Filene's Basement sale. Otherwise, all was quiet.

Two ectoplasmic fog ghosts floated through an opening in the dunes and solidified into Joe Quint and Tommy. Tommy and Ed carried walkie-talkies. Ed got in the Ranger and took off. Tommy walked along the access road and took up a post around a hundred feet away.

For a man on the run, Joe looked relaxed. He wore the same T-shirt and jeans he'd had on in jail. He'd added punk sunglasses and a black felt wide-brimmed western-style hat, the same one I'd seen in his news pictures. The high crown was encircled by a silver-and-turquoise concho chain with a feather stuck in it. I was glad Quint was keeping a low profile.

He came over and flashed his cocky grin. "How's it going, paleface?"

"I like your hat," I said. "Is it Navajo?"

"Naw, it's Hopi. It's sort of my trademark. You got problems with it?"

"Hell, no. I think it makes you look taller." I glanced up the access road at Tommy, who was pacing back and forth. "I've got problems with this meeting place, though. This is a dead end."

"So what?"

"So, if anybody you don't want to see comes down that road, you're dead. And that's the end."

Quint looked as if he wanted to stuff a sock in my mouth.

"That's the difference between Marines and Airborne. You like to improvise. I plan. I've got a boat in the river. Ed's up by the traffic circle. He sees anything, he calls Tommy, who tells me. I get in my boat and buzz off. I may even do some fishing. So what's happening? Patty said you wanted to see me."

"My private-eye handbook says clients should be kept up to date on the status of their case."

"See what it says about people who *aren't* your clients, Socarides. It was Flagg's idea to hire you. I told him, and I'm telling you again; I don't need your help."

"You may be right," I said. "You probably changed your own diapers as a baby, too. But here's the situation. Everybody except F Troop is on your tail. The cops want you, the FBI wants you, and a bunch of hard guys called the Warrior Society want you so badly, they'll pay ten grand for your head and stomp on anybody who gets in their way. You can't show your face in public unless you've got some pals with walkie-talkies keeping watch and an escape boat gassed up and running. So tell me again how you don't need help."

186

Quint's eyes darted over my shoulder. Three white stretch limos followed by a dozen cars were cruising slowly toward us on the access road. He tensed as if he were going to run for it. Tommy waved that everything was okay.

The limos parked next to where we were standing. The uniformed driver opened the door of the first limo, which was decorated with pink and blue crepe paper, and helped a pretty young woman get out. She was dressed in a white dress whose empire waist emphasized her healthy bust. A garland of yellow and white daisies wreathed her long blond hair. She was followed by four young women, carrying daisy bouquets, who were dressed in white blouses and long green skirts. A handsome dark-haired guy emerged from the second limo. He wore avocado slacks, a white gypsy shirt, and a green vest embroidered with daisies. The other guys in the limo had the same outfit, but their vests were plain, except for daisy boutonnieres.

Two middle-aged couples got out of the third limo. The women dabbed at their eyes with lace hankies. The men looked as if they could use a stiff drink. A couple of dozen people dressed to the nines got out of the other cars and milled around us in a happy clucking, chuckling, smiling, laughing confusion. Finally, a bubble-cheeked minister wearing a green-and-daisy vestment over his black robe arrived and, like a sheep dog, herded people into a rough order at the edge of the dunes.

Reassured that the wedding party wasn't an invasion by the Warrior Society in disguise, Quint took a bag of tobacco and pack of papers out of his pocket and rolled a butt the effortless way I'd seen Elwood do it.

"I hate weddings," he said. He lit the cigarette, savored a puff, and gave me a curious look. "The boys said you're staying with my case even though the Warrior Society bribed you and threatened you if you stayed in. What's in this for you, Soc?"

"Nothing but my usual low daily rate and the chance to do Flagg a favor."

"It's your funeral." He spit a few stray tobacco shreds off his lips. "What do you want from me?"

"The whole story, without the forked tongue."

Joe stared at me a moment from behind the punk shades. Then he said, "Okay, you want the story. Here it is. I was visiting Patty on the Cape. Taking a break from all legal crap. Picnics and sailing, getting to know Patty again. Then one day I got a call from a friend. He said I might be interested in an auction in Plymouth. I went up to take a look. They were selling off Indian artifacts. I talked to the guy who ran the place."

"Claude Renault."

"That's right," Joe said, "Do you know him?"

"Patty told me you had a problem with an auction house near Plymouth. I tracked Renault down and talked to him."

"Lucky you! What did you think of him?"

"If he were any oilier he'd qualify as a toxic-waste dump."

"My impression, too. A real sleazoid. The artifacts were from Wounded Knee. Do you know anything about Wounded Knee?"

"Just what I've read. Refresh my memory."

"Back in December of 1890, three hundred Sioux were running from the U.S. cavalry. Mostly women and children. The cavalry found them at Wounded Knee Creek, South Dakota and took a couple of guns away. There was a fracas, someone fired a shot, and the cavalry wiped out most of the Indians —massacred them. The name's become a symbol to us. It meant the end of our freedom. That's why the guys from the American Indian Movement occupied the site back in the seventies and had the big shoot-out with the feds."

"Renault knew that?"

"He didn't care. I told Renault that stuff from Wounded Knee belonged to the descendants of the people who'd been killed there. I said selling it was like fencing stolen heirlooms. He said everything was documented and legal. That he wasn't in the business to give antiques away. I'd be welcome to bid at auction like anybody else."

"Was the sale legal?"

"I don't know. I tried to put a trace on the artifacts, but I didn't get anywhere. I went to the people at the state level. They suggested I go to the feds. Waste of time. The Bureau of Indian Affairs doesn't like me because I've whipped their ass in court. I decided to make some noise about the Indians being robbed. Maybe it would smoke Renault out."

"Did you really think that would happen?"

"No. I did it mostly because I was just plain frustrated."

"Did you know Renault sells a lot of old Indian stuff?"

"No," Quint said, "All I knew about was Wounded Knee. What have you got?"

I remembered the file I lifted from Renault's computer. The print-out was still in my truck. I fetched it from the pick-up and handed it to Quint. His frown deepened as he read it.

He rattled the paper at me. "Damn slimebucket! He's using his auction house to launder artifacts."

"Pretend for a minute I don't know what you're talking about."

"Certain kinds of old Indian goods are very valuable to a collector, so the pothunters have been digging up the whole Southwest. If you can find something on private land, you can sell it. No problem. But most of the good stuff is on public land, where it's illegal to dig without a tough permit to get."

189

"So the idea is to pass your goods off as coming from private land?"

"Uh-huh. Say you've dug up a hot item off federal land, something that will bring big bucks, like an Anasazi bowl. You don't just put an ad in the paper to sell it. So Renault salts his estate sales with batches of artifacts. Acquisitions Unlimited constantly outbids everybody. It's just a phony transaction, with no money passing hands. But now the artifact has a history of sale that makes it easier to get rid of. My guess is that Renault and Acquisitions are the same, and that they have a list of private collectors they deal with. Europe, Japan, who knows? Once the stuff is gone, it's gone forever. Nice little moneymaker for Renault."

"Nice enough for him to set you up on a blackmail charge?"

"All I know is I didn't kill that poor bastard at Plimoth Plantation."

The minister was walking over to us. "Gentlemen," he bubbled, "I am the Reverend Joseph Willet. I am about to join Ken and Daisy in holy matrimony. They saw you standing here and would be pleased if you would be witnesses to this wonderful miracle that is about to happen. They believe it would be good luck to have two strangers become one with our group."

The bride was watching us with a smile as innocent as a baby's. Joe eyed the wedding party. "I don't know," he mumbled. "We're sort of busy."

The Reverend Mr. Willet's clear blue eyes were fastened on Joe. "That's a lovely hat. You're not Navajo, by any chance, are you?"

Joe glowered at him. "No, I'm *not* Navajo. I'm a Narragansett."

"Oh, yes," the minister brightened. "Narragansett. When

190

I was a young man, I used to drink a beer by that name."

"Have a 'Gansett," I said helpfully.

The minister squeezed his fat chin with his fingers. "It was very cheap, as I remember," he said dreamily, as if the name brought back fond memories of theological-school bacchanals. "Well, will you accept our invitation?"

"We wouldn't want to impose," I said.

"No imposition. In fact, we'd be honored."

"Why don't you folks just go ahead?" I suggested. "We'll be done talking in a few minutes and would be glad to join the wedding party."

The minister beamed and signaled to a couple of bridesmaids who came over and stuffed daisies in my collar and behind my ears. They put so many daisies in Joe's hatband that he looked like a flowerpot.

Joe rolled his eyes. "Why'd you tell him we'd join the wedding?"

"It wouldn't have been friendly to refuse. Let's go back to Renault. He tells you to buzz off. You go to the authorities, and they say they can't help. You picket the plantation and Plymouth Rock and get your picture on the six-o'clock news. Renault knows you can't touch him legally. So why would he bother to try to neutralize you?"

"You tell me. You're the private cop."

"Something's missing. Patty said you made a number of long-distance calls around the country. What was that all about?"

"They were museums for the most part. Native American curators. Renault's brochure said the artifacts were all authenticated. I wondered who was doing the authenticating. There are only so many qualified people. I talked to most of them. They never heard of Renault."

191

Another blank. I looked off toward the beach. A bright sun was burning the fog off the dunes, but gray mists still clouded my brain.

"So who authenticated the artifacts?"

"Renault and I didn't get that far. The museums gave me the names of some private outfits that do that kind of thing." He ticked off a list. I made him go back to one name.

"Oh, sure. Northeast Archaeological Associates. I remember them because I thought it was funny they had an office in the Southwest with a name like that. They said I'd have to talk to the head man. I tried to get him a number of times at his Cambridge office, but he's been out in the field.

The brain fog blew away. "What was the head man's name?" I asked, already knowing the answer.

"Zane. Dr. Emery Zane."

Puzzle pieces were falling into place. Pothunters dig up illegal Indian goods on public land. Zane authenticates the stuff. Renault auctions it, always to the same outfit, which turns around and sells the goods—with a clean history now—to eager collectors.

Renault brushes Quint off as a harmless insect on their first encounter. Then Quint calls Zane's Southwest office. Renault hears about this and gets worried. He decides to ice Quint. Joe's publicity stunts give him an idea. Set a fire at Plimoth Plantation and blame it on Quint. I laid out my theory for Joe.

"That explains the fire, but what about the murder?" he said.

"Maybe a fire was all Renault had in mind. But his firebug gets surprised, and he whacks the maintenance man. All at once, the ante's been upped."

"You think Renault would go that far?"

I touched the shaved spot on my head. It still hurt. "I think he'd try to get rid of anyone who got in his way."

"Unbelievable! But it all makes a kind of crazy sense."

"There's one thing that doesn't. Why did you jump bail?"

"I didn't have any choice. I had to get out of jail in a hurry. After I talked to you, I learned there was a contract out on me inside."

"A contract, as in hit man?"

He nodded.

"This have anything to do with Renault?"

"Naw. Something else. Completely unrelated. The Warrior Society arranged it."

"Why would they want you dead?"

"They're working for some people who would like to shut my mouth for good."

"I now pronounce you husband and wife," the minister was saying. Ken and Daisy got into a clinch that looked as if they were starting their honeymoon early. Finally they came up for air, and the wedding party formed into a receiving line.

About the same time, Tommy ran toward us, waving his arms. "Joe!" he shouted. "Two fucking cars—"

Mr. Willet's mouth dropped as if he'd just seen an empty collection plate. Some of the younger people in the wedding group tried to hide their smiles. Tommy trotted over and lowered his voice to a stage whisper. "I just got a call from Ed. He says there's two cars full of guys in suits coming our way real fast."

"I think you'd better take that boat ride," I said.

Joe was way ahead of me. "Tell the preacher sorry, I had to go fishing." He broke for the dunes in that limping gait of his, leaving a trail of daisies behind him.

Tommy checked his watch. "They should be here in two minutes. We timed it. Joe can make it to his boat—no sweat."

Joe climbed to the crest of a dune, then reversed gears like a wind-up soldier. Now he was running back in our direction.

"Shit!" Tommy said in a high-pitched voice. "Shit!" he said again when his head swiveled and he looked in the other direction. Two dark blue Ford Fairlanes had made the turn onto the beach road and were coming our way fast.

Joe loped back, completely out of breath. "Damn it," he gasped. "Boat on the river . . . guys waiting to grab me."

Tommy was fixated on the cars coming down the road. He reached into a fanny pack. His hand closed on the gleaming metal of an automatic. "You want me to cover you while you break for it?"

"Bad idea, Tommy," I said quickly. "You wouldn't want any of these nice people to get hurt."

Joe pushed Tommy's hand back into the pack. The cars were closing.

"Take off your hat!" I snapped at Quint.

"Huh?"

I snatched the hat and plunked it on Tommy's head. "Running Deer, meet Running Deer," I said. "You go for the boat, Tommy. Take it out into the river nice and easy. If somebody tells you to stop, you stop. Do whatever they tell you to say. Keep your hands in the air so they don't get nervous and shoot you."

Quint caught my drift. "Drop your gun in that trash barrel and do as Soc says."

Finally Tommy was catching on. He got rid of the gun and headed toward the river.

The wedding-party cars had taken up all the nearest spaces, so the blue Fords had to park around a hundred feet away. That gave us a few seconds. I grabbed Joe's arm and pushed him behind some of the wedding guests. "Get in the reception line."

"What?"

"We're guests, remember? This is a special time for Ken and Daisy. Can you think of anything better to do?"

Quint glanced at the suits who poured out of the cars and spread across the parking lot like bloodhounds on the scent. "I hate weddings!" he muttered and took his place behind the other guests.

The suits had spotted Tommy running over the dunes and chased after him, leaving two men back at the cars. Agent Rourke took up the rear, barking orders.

Quint moved woodenly through the reception line. I made the best of it. I got to kiss Daisy and learned why Ken had her so long in a clinch. Her mother was a little heavier and grayer, but she was a knockout, too. She held my hand, asked how long I knew Ken's family, and gave me a lingering full-chested kiss that might have started trouble if her husband was sober enough to notice. I promised to save a dance for her at the reception. The father of the groom said I looked like somebody he met at an Aetna Insurance convention. I said I was with the Travelers, and that seemed to make him happy.

Joe and I stalled as long as we could, but we were running out of people to say congratulations and best wishes to, although Daisy's mother was throwing hot glances my way.

The happy crowd was moving toward the limos. We mingled in. "Now what?" Quint growled.

Quint couldn't get out of the parking lot without being seen by the men posted near the cars. It wouldn't take long for the others to figure out Tommy was an impostor. The wedding guests crowded around the first limo. Someone pressed a bag of bird seed into my hand. The bride and groom were making their way through a phalanx of hugs, kisses, and handshakes. I pulled the driver aside and pointed to Joe.

"This is the bride's uncle. Can he catch a ride up to his car?"

The young chauffeur looked at Joe's swarthy complexion, overgenerous nose, and long ponytailed hair and tried to reconcile it with the WASP good looks of the wedding couple and their party. I pressed a twenty in his hand.

"Anything for the family." He opened the passenger door for Joe to get in.

"Sorry you can't stay for the garter toss," I said.

"You catch it for me."

I closed the door. "Happy honeymoon!"

The bride and groom ducked into the back seat under showers of bird seed. With horns blaring, tin cans rattling, and crepe paper crackling, a JUST MARRIED sign tied to the bumper, the bride and groom, and Joe Quint, moved off to lead the noisy parade to the reception. They breezed easily by Rourke's two watchdogs who only gave them a glance.

The limo turned the corner onto the main road. I stood there alone, the empty bag in my hand. Rourke and his posse came thundering back over the dunes. He recognized me and came over. He was sweating with exertion, and his face was the color of cranberry sauce.

"*You*," he said. "Where the hell is Quint?"

"You seem to have a problem holding onto people."

Rourke did a pretty good imitation of a great white shark that's just found its dinner.

"Let me tell *you* something," he said with that scary grin of his. "I'm not the *only* one who's got a problem."

Twenty-Two

AGENT ROURKE WASN'T foaming at the mouth—not yet—it was only a matter of time. He paced back and forth between his desk and his office door. Every third pace, he stopped, spun on his heel, and jabbed his forefinger in my direction. Each jab was accompanied by a prediction that described my dimming prospects for a long and productive life. According to Rourke's gory monologues, I was drowning in a sea of troubles, more trouble than the Rosenbergs, Benedict Arnold, and Winnie Ruth Judd put together.

The forefinger came my way again, so close to my face it made me cross-eyed. Rourke had refined his attack into three themes: Bleeding-heart Liberal. Blundering Fool. Cop Gone Wrong.

Rogue cop–time again. "You make me sick, guys like you. You used to wear a badge; now you're on the outside. You've sold out. You're bent. You're a law unto yourself."

I jerked my thumb at the adjoining office. "If you look at the wallet you took away from me, you'll find that I'm duly licensed by the Commonwealth of Massachusetts as a private investigator."

He stuck his face so close to mine I could smell the last honey-glazed he had at Dunkin' Donuts. His eyes bulged like somebody with a thyroid condition. "I don't give a shit if you've got your mother's *picture* in the wallet. You've been obstructing justice from day one. That's against the law, my friend. License or no license, you're abetting a crime, and that's the way the federal government sees it."

"Since when is parking without a beach sticker a federal offense, Agent Rourke?"

"Don't give me that. There is a pattern here. This is not the first time you've gotten in our way. I haven't forgotten your interference at the powwow."

Rourke was clearly a guy who liked to pick at old scabs. "What is it you want, Agent Rourke?" I said wearily.

He dragged a chair around and sat in it the wrong way, resting his chin on the back so he looked like an oversized hand puppet. "I want you to tell me where Joe Quint is."

"I don't know where he is."

"Isn't he your client?"

"Joe doesn't think so. Ask him—when you find him."

Rourke cocked his head in thought. It must have penetrated his skull that the only thing he would get out of using the hard-ass approach with me was a case of high blood pressure. Who knows what goes on in the mind of a federal police officer? He took a dirty toothpick out of his pocket and cleaned his fingernails with it, then stuck the toothpick between his big teeth.

"Look, we're both coming from the same direction," he said like a hostage negotiator trying to talk a human bomb into taking his thumb off the switch. "I'm a cop. You used to be a cop."

"Before I became a law unto myself."

He brushed my answer aside. "You've been through an interrogation before. That was just shoptalk. Here's the pitch. We want to see Joe Quint back in custody, where he belongs. Or if he stays out on bail, we just want him to play by the rules."

"You weren't playing by the rules at the powwow. You came close to shooting him."

"C'mon, Socarides. How would you expect me to stop a fugitive? Send him a valentine?" Rourke gave me an alligator smile. "I had my gun out, sure, but I was going to fire it in the air. I'm FBI. I couldn't shoot John Dillinger if my life depended on it today. If the ACLU didn't get me, the Bureau would. I'd be up to my ass in hearings for the rest of my life. I was just trying to get Quint's attention."

"Even if I give you that, since when did a routine local murder case come under the FBI?"

He sat back in his chair. "We want Quint on something else."

Something Else again. Joe said the Warriors were after him over *Something Else*. "What are you talking about?"

"Obstructing justice. Aiding a felony after the fact. Suppressing evidence."

"In regard to what? Agent Rourke."

"In regard to none of your beeswax." He leaned forward again and looked closely at me. "What the hell happened to your head?"

"I was in a diving accident."

"Looks like you dove into a rockpile." He grinned pleasur-

199

ably at the image. "We should have taken a Polaroid when we brought you in so you couldn't claim police brutality later on. Heh-heh."

Heh-heh. Charming guy, Agent Rourke. "Quint told me you had a personal grudge against him. That what you're talking about?"

"Naw, I wasn't kidding about Bureau business, but Quint's right. It goes back a couple of years. A buddy went into an Indian reservation in New Mexico to serve an arrest warrant. Someone shot him. Didn't give him a chance."

"I'm sorry to hear about your friend, but Joe Quint wasn't the killer, was he?"

"Naw, he wasn't the killer. It was some other worm. Quint represented the guy in court. He got him off on a legal technicality."

"You've had Quint in your sights ever since?"

"C'mon, Socarides. I'm an FBI agent. I'm out here in the sticks. I can't go chasing some guy around the country just 'cause I don't like him. But when I heard the Bureau wanted him, and he shows up in my backyard, and he's charged with murder, I wanted in. I don't want him to slip away on a legal loophole."

"Did you ever consider the possibility Joe might be innocent?"

"Never crossed my mind. But say he *is* innocent—why did he jump bail?"

"Joe took to the bushes because he thinks someone had a contract out on to nail him in the house of correction."

"Shit! Did *he* tell you that?"

"You asked why he jumped bail. I've given you a reason."

"Okay, say he's telling the truth. We could protect him."

"You just told me you aren't bosom buddies. If you were Joe, would you put your trust in you?"

"He'd be given the same protection as anybody else."

"Don't try to con me, Rourke. I've been around too long."

"All right, we disagree. But it wouldn't hurt for Joe to talk to us. I'm asking you again. Will you tell us where he is?"

"I'm telling you again. I don't know."

He smacked his open palm against the side of the chair. I was glad my face wasn't on the receiving end. His hand was as big as a catcher's mitt. He got up and walked to the door. "I'm going to give you a little while to stew on this."

He slammed the door behind him. Silence. I looked around. I was on the second floor. If I tied some sheets together, I could shinny down them. But I didn't have sheets. I could start a fire in the wastebasket. They rush in, I run out. Big problem. No matches. Then again, Rourke had nothing on me. But, he could waste my time, and I didn't feel like sitting in a government office.

I picked up the phone on Rourke's desk and heard a dial tone. I dialed a weather number. It was going to be sunny and warm tomorrow. I looked at the closed door. Rourke was a horse's ass, but he was not a complete fool. I bet myself a six-pack of beer that a voice-activated tape recorder was hooked up to the extension. I thought a moment, then dialed Sam's number. Millie answered. She wanted to chat about something she'd heard at the town hall. Finally I got a word in edgewise. "I'm sorry, Millie, but this is rather urgent. Could I talk to Sam now?" She sounded a little miffed, but I could make it up to her later.

Sam came on. I dove in before he got talking. "Sam. I've got to make this quick. Listen carefully. I'm being held in the

FBI office in Hyannis. Please call Alan. See if he can do anything about getting me out. Got that?"

"Sure Soc, call Alan. But—"

"The FBI office in Hyannis. Remember. Got to go. 'Bye."

I got up and walked around. Looked out the window. Rattled the filing cabinets and desk drawers. Once a snoop always a snoop. They were locked. I listened at the door. I went back to my chair. After a while, Rourke came back and sat behind his desk. A second later, a stenographer with mouse-colored hair walked into the office, notepad and tape recorder in hand, and sat next to him. They both looked expectantly at me. Rourke gave me a wolverine grin.

"Okay," he said. "Who's this Sam?"

I looked at the phone, horrified. "You *heard* me?"

"Every word. Now, who's Sam?"

He had me cold. "I was talking to Sam the fisherman."

"Sam the fisherman." He winked knowingly at the stenographer. "Sounds like LCN, La Cosa Nostra. He with the mob at the Fulton Fish Market?"

"Sam moves a lot of stuff through Fulton."

"Interesting. What about Alan?"

"That's our D.C. connection."

"Christ, you guys are plugged in everywhere." He leaned forward onto his arms. "Where does Joe Quint figure in all this?"

"They've never met."

One of the other agents came in. "Sir, there's a phone call."

Rourke waved him away. "I'm busy now," he said, irritated. "What do you mean, they've never met?" he said to me.

"Sir, I really think you'd better take this call. It could be important."

Rourke got up from the chair and did a quick over-the-shoulder finger jab. "Don't go 'way."

The stenographer looked as if she had just been left alone with a child molester and scurried after him. She made sure she took the tape recorder with her. Five minutes later, Rourke came back. His angry eyes were in a battle with his smiling mouth over which should be in charge of his face.

"Pick up the phone!" he ordered.

I pointed to the telephone. He nodded. I picked it up and said hello.

"I'm fine, Senator," I said. "No, just a misunderstanding. Yes, see you in about two weeks. Oh, sure." I gave the phone to Rourke. "He wants to talk to you."

Rourke wrapped his hand around the phone and leaned his ear into it. The conversation from this end was pretty boring. Mostly yes, no, and finally, good-bye, sir. He hung up and glowered at me. "D.C. connection, huh?"

I put my palms together like a penitent and imagined a halo floating over my head.

"He's the chairman of the Senate Judiciary Committee, in case you've forgotten."

Rourke came around and brought his face so close to mine that our noses almost touched. In a hiss a boa constrictor might make just before it devours a naked mole rat, he said, "I don't know how you did it, or who this Sam character is, but the senator says he knows you. He also said that he voted favorably on the last budget increase for the FBI. He says he knows I have a job to do and understands my position thoroughly, but that I should let you go unless I have charges against you."

"The senator has always been a sensitive New Age kind of guy."

"Well I've got news for you *and* the senator. I was *going* to let you go anyhow. You're smelling up my office, You're nothing to me. Nothing." Rourke plunked my Red Sox cap on my head and pulled the visor down over my eyes. He strode to the door. "Get out before I throw you out."

Two agents and the stenographer stood in the other office. One agent handed over my wallet and the keys to the pickup truck. The other opened the door. Rourke followed to bid me fare-thee-well.

"I'm not through with you," he bellowed, his voice echoing in the hallway. "Senator or no senator, I'll have your ass in a sling."

I was in a hurry to leave, so a question that had been gnawing at the back of my mind didn't occur to me until the pickup was halfway out of the parking lot. How did the FBI know I was meeting Quint at the beach? I glanced up at the second floor. Rourke's bulky form filled his office window. Maybe I'd ask him another time.

The morning fog had burned off, and the sun slipped behind a layer of gray clouds that sent the temperature down and the humidity up. With the beach weather on hold, people drove around in their cars looking for something to do. I joined the traffic creeping along Main Street. There were too many traffic lights, too many signs, too many damned people. Patti Paige and her quaint little villages be damned.

The people come to Hyannis because they remembered it was where the Kennedys lived long ago in a dream. Jack and Jackie, and Caroline and John-John, in a whitewashed Camelot by the sea. You can still sail out of Hyannis harbor into the blue

204

waters of Nantucket Sound and escape from the crowds with the help of a passing zephyr. Or drive a few miles to the quiet north side of the Cape, past centuries-old captain's houses and Cape Cod cottages. But what people find in Hyannis is a mini-city full of strip malls, discount outlets, traffic jams, and fast-food outlets no different than the stuff they left back home in Paducah. If they take the back roads, the new generation of Kennedys can avoid the sneaker stores and mini-golf courses on the drive between their houses and the airport.

The sours had set in, big time. Nothing was right. My head hurt. My mouth hurt. Every time I turned a corner, I ran into a knuckle sandwich, a blunt object, or a threat. Every time I asked a question, I heard a lie. The little favor for Flagg had turned into a twenty-four-hour hangover. I needed a drink.

The bar across from the inner harbor was mobbed with people, kids mostly, who looked barely over the legal drinking age. I shouldered my way onto the deck and found a single seat at a small table. The sea breeze coming off the harbor cooled my brow, and the cold beer soothed the inner fires raging in my gut. I drank the beer and ordered another. The waitress was young, blond, tanned, and pleasant. She smiled at me with teeth whiter than Cool Whip. After a while, the kids at the next table didn't seem as vacuous. The music wasn't as irritating. Zen drinking. It works every time.

I started going through the rooms in the dusty mansion of my brain, straightening furniture, lifting the window shades to let the light in. There were dark cobwebby corners I couldn't reach with my broom. Like Joe's problem with the Warrior Society. They wanted to kill him. If everyone Joe irritated wanted to kill him, he'd be dead long ago. You could add my name to the suspect list. So why the Warriors? Renault went for Joe's throat because he was afraid he had something on him. Did the Warriors want Joe dead because he scared them, too? He was outnumbered and outgunned. Why would they be frightened?

The beer mug was empty. I threw some bills on the table and walked across the street to a pay phone at the marina. After a couple of rings, Patty Hoagland answered.

"It's your friendly private detective," I said.

"Yes." Not exactly an enthusiastic response, but I wasn't insulted. Patty thought her phone was bugged and she was probably right.

"I'd like to see you."

A pause. "All right. In about an hour. Do you remember where the eagle soared, the day we met?"

The Indian powwow. "Sounds good. See you there."

I hung up and sat on a bench, sweeping the pier with my eyes to see whether Rourke had a tail on me. An older couple strolled hand in hand along the line of charter boats and fishing trawlers. Younger couples walked around trying to tire out the kids so they could cuddle back at the motel while their off-spring slept. Fishermen came by, but they couldn't have faked the fatigue in their faces in a million years. Satisfied I wasn't being followed, I got in the pickup and set off toward Mashpee.

Patty's car was in the parking lot next to the powwow ball field. She signaled me with an on-off blink of her headlights, then drove down the street a half-mile and turned off at a little pond called the Flume. We stood by the pond, and I watched the road to see if we had company.

"It's all right," Patty said. "I made sure nobody followed me."

"Just being careful. Joe thought he was safe this morning, but the FBI crashed our beach party."

206

"Tommy said the FBI questioned him. He told them he didn't know what they were talking about, that he was just about to go fishing. They had to let him go."

"I can't figure how the feds knew about the meeting, unless they read it on a laundromat bulletin board."

"I don't know either. Outside of Tommy and Ed, I was the only one who knew."

"What about your brother Peter?"

"I wouldn't have told him. You met Peter. Do you think he could keep his mouth shut more than a minute?"

"I couldn't see Peter keeping quiet for a second."

"Do you have any suggestions on what Joe should do?"

"Short of digging up Clarence Darrow to be his lawyer, I don't know, and to be perfectly honest, I don't care. In my opinion, Joe is an egotistical motormouth. He's obnoxious, abrasive, and selfish. He's a rainy-day martyr, a phony and a hypocrite. Maybe he cares about the cause, and maybe he doesn't. I can't be sure. The only thing I *am* sure Joe Quint really gives a crap about is himself."

Patty didn't push me in the pond for running down her boyfriend. Instead, she started laughing, and didn't stop until tears came to her eyes. "You don't know how good it is to hear you say that. I've told Joe the same things myself. But I love him. That's why I couldn't understand why you wanted to help him."

"I'm a masochist no longer. Here's a message to take to Joe. I want him to tell me why the Warriors want his scalp. Otherwise, he can no longer claim the privilege of *not* being my client. I will go home. I will feed my cat, have a beer, and take a nap. Only if Cleveland plays the Sox will I have anything to do with Indians. I will not eat Indian pudding. I will not even ride in a Pontiac."

"I'm sure Joe will get the point. I'll try to arrange a meeting."

"Is he on Cape Cod?"

"I don't know where he is. I just call a number, and somebody relays my message."

We shook hands on it. Patty left first. I tailed her a couple of miles, but no one was following, so I headed back to the boathouse. I fed Kojak his low-ash food and ignored his reproach with steely resolve. I called Sam, thanked him again for calling the senator, and said I'd explain later. I went to the gin-mill I frequent and listened to a fascinating discussion on drywall. I came home and broiled some cod *Plaka* style with onions and tomatoes, and a splash of Rolling Rock beer. Now that I'd gone through the pretense of showing Kojak who was boss, I snuck him a piece of fish. I watched television and finally fell asleep on the sofa. All basically normal boring everyday things. Nobody broke into my house. Nobody hit me over the head.

That blissful state of affairs ended much too quickly. The phone woke me up. It was Joe Quint. He sounded tense.

"We've got to meet tonight," he said.

Tonight? I was groggy and irritable. "My office hours are over. Call me back in the morning."

"Soc, we've got to talk now. It's urgent."

Yeah. So. Sure. Right. Urgent. Joe Quint was getting to be a royal pain. I didn't care what I promised Flagg. My mind blanked out Joe's ramblings. Bleh, blah, blooey. I held the phone a couple of inches from my ear. I watched a sitcom. Bunch of people hanging around a sofa telling one-liners. Joe kept talking.

The word "kidnapped," broke through the canned laughter from the TV.

"What was that, Joe? Sorry, I didn't catch it."

"For God's sakes, haven't you been listening?" Quint said. "It's Patty. She's been kidnapped!"

Twenty-Three

THIRTY MINUTES LATER Joe and I sat in a booth at a country-and-western bar in Hyannis I like to go to because it's so far removed from the common Cape Cod stereotype. Joe had traded his Hopi hat in for a less-conspicuous baseball cap. His spit-in-your-face cockiness was gone. His wide brow had more furrows in it than a wheat field. Maybe he was smartening up, although I doubted it.

He was telling me about Patty's call. "They let her talk only a minute, so I'd know they really have her," Joe said. "Then Billy Big Oak came on the phone."

"Billy Big Oak?"

"Yeah. He was probably at your house the other night. Tall guy, talks in a real nice voice, but he'd cut your throat in a second."

The chuckler. "We've met."

"He said I've got twenty-four hours to come in, or they'd kill Patty."

"That's when you called me."

"I couldn't go to the cops because they'd grab me and wouldn't hear a word I said. You're a detective. You know how to find people."

"But I'm not your client."

"Damn it, Soc. That's *Patty* they're holding out there."

"She's not my client, either."

"Okay, okay, we'll *be* your fucking clients. *Now* will you do something?"

"Do you really think they'll kill Patty?"

He nodded grimly.

"You're saying your pals will kill somebody to get to you. That tells me they want you badder than a fish wants water. They know why. I don't. That leaves me at a disadvantage. While I get another beer, think about how you're going to connect the dots so I can see this pretty little picture, too."

I went up to the bar and ordered a beer and a Coke. Maybe it wasn't fair to let Joe stew in his worries about Patty, but I'd had enough smoke blown up my flue. When I got back to the table, Joe couldn't wait to tell me his story.

"Most of the stuff I do is *pro bono*, so I take outside work to pay the rent. A law-school buddy asked me to defend his client, a small-time racketeer. The feds were going to nail this guy's testicles to the wall. He had information to trade to the prosecution on a plea bargain. When he showed it to me, I told him I wanted it, screw the feds. We made a deal. I guarantee to get him off without the plea, and he gives me the information in lieu of legal fees, to do what I want with it. He was scared to death of going to jail, so he went for it. I was pretty sure they couldn't convict him because the prosecution had messed up on the evidence, but it was a damned slick defense, if I do say so."

"So he walked."

"Yeah, he walked. Unfortunately, my great legal work went to waste. His friends killed him a week after he hit the street."

"Sorry to hear that."

"You'd be the only one. They did society a favor. This guy would stick a pencil in your eye if you looked at him cross-eyed. With him gone, nobody knew I had the file."

"What was in it?"

"My ex-client was middle management. He'd graduated from the strong-arm stuff to number crunching. A lot of the projects the organization was working on came across his desk. This file dealt with one project in particular."

"What kind of project?"

"Part of the biggest transfer of money from one pocket to the other that this country has seen since World War II."

"What kind of money are we talking about?

"Billions," Joe said."

He let that sink in.

"No exaggeration?"

He shook his head.

"You're right," I said. "You and Patty are in deep trouble. Now tell me the whole story from the beginning. Omit nothing, and remember, we don't have much time."

"I can sum up the first three hundred years in a minute. The Pilgrims landed on Plymouth Rock. Half the population of Europe followed. They and their descendants have been screwing the Native American population ever since."

"Tell me something new, Joe."

"Okay, I will. In 1988, Congress passed a law called the Indian Gaming Regulatory Act. The law gives Indians the right to conduct gambling on reservation property. Some of the tribes jumped right into it."

"Like the Pequot tribe in Connecticut."

"I guess you *do* get over the Cape Cod Canal."

"Once in a while."

"So you know what a big success Foxwoods is. Other tribes, especially the dirt-poor ones, see the Pequot raking in money and they want a piece of the action. Tribes all over the country are jumping on the bandwagon."

"Like your tribe, the Narragansett."

Joe gave me a look that said maybe Flagg wasn't so dumb hiring me after all.

"Yeah," he said, "Like my tribe. But they're not the only ones. Flagg's tribe over in Martha's Vineyard is trying to build a casino. The law says it doesn't even have to be on reservation land. The Wampanoag can buy a few acres on the mainland near an airport or interstate highway, put it in trust, bring in investors who are drooling at the mouth, and build. Take New England alone. Six states. We're talking five casinos built or planned already."

"So this is the big money you're talking about? Indian casinos?"

"That's only *part* of it, Soc. Listen, I'll explain it the way my father would. First think of New England as a quiet pond. You've got your state lotteries and illegal backroom crap and poker games, but if you want some serious casino gambling, you've got to go to Vegas or Atlantic City. Okay, now imagine the federal gaming law is a rock. You throw it into the water. What do you get?"

"Ripples?"

"You've got it. The first ripples are the Indian casinos themselves. This creates a permissive atmosphere. Casino gambling becomes commonplace in bluenose Puritan New England. The states are strapped for cash now. They've about exhausted what their lotteries can do for them. The politicos are scared to death of raising taxes. They see the Indians bringing in millions and they say, 'Hey, we're in the gambling business with our lotteries, and we're supposed to supply the public with services, so let's give them a way to give us more of their money.' They start talking about legalizing gambling. Maybe video poker at first, then floating gambling casinos. The entrepreneurs want in, so the lobbyists work on their pet legislators. The bucks start to flow fast and furious."

"What if a state doesn't want Indian casinos?"

"Connecticut tried to stop the Pequot. But the Supreme Court ruled the Indians are entitled to *any* games the state allows. The state allowed blackjack and roulette for charities like all those Las Vegas nights the Elks have, and the bingo games the churches run. That opened the door for the Pequot. Say the states legalize video poker or keno, like some of them want to do. The Indians say, 'That's the same as slots, so we can run them in our houses, too.' "

"Sounds as if there's no stopping it."

"There is almost no way. The feds say a state has to negotiate in good faith. If there's an impasse, the tribe can appeal. If you've got a Secretary of the Interior who favors reservation gambling, like now, that appeal will be looked on kindly." He laughed evilly. "It shows what hypocrites the state governments are."

"How is that?"

"Take Connecticut, the death-on-gambling state. Some people in government started thinking how video poker games would be a logical extension of the lottery. They said the state alone should control where video poker games were put. The Pequot threatened to sue. Both sides were worried about casinos sprouting in other parts of the state, each for their own reasons. So they signed a deal. The state gave the Pequot the monopoly on the video machines. This kept a lid on potential competition. In return, the Indians give the state one hundred million dollars a year in return. Same thing's happening in Massachusetts. Attorney-General says casinos are a big mistake. Governor sees all that green."

"Okay, you've made your point. The Indians are scalping the white men and making them like it. That doesn't tell me why the Warriors are holding Patty for you."

"History lesson again. Back in the seventies, there was a lot of conflict on the reservations and struggles for rights. That's when AIM occupied Wounded Knee and Peltier got thrown in jail. A bunch of Canadian Mohawks staged a protest march in Ottawa in 1974. Mounties came in, beat them up and arrested them. One of the guys who got clubbed was at a sit-in in New York. It ended peacefully, but he promoted the Warrior idea."

"Which was?"

"He said it was stupid to leave yourselves open for a clubbing and arrest, to be humiliated and put in jail, and in the end, have your cause fail."

"How'd he suggest they prevent that from happening?"

"Simple. Get some guns and don't be afraid to use them."

"Did many people agree with him?"

"He got some of the young guys to go along. Over the next few years, there was fierce infighting within the Mohawk tribe. The elected chiefs who were supported financially by the feds battled for power with those who said they'd sold out. The clan mothers were trying to hold onto their turf. At the same time, the tribes were fighting the state over cigarette and gas sales on the reservation. State said pay taxes. Indians said no, it was a matter of sovereignty; Wounded Knee all over again. The Warriors sided with the tribe's commercial interests against the white man. At first, they were looked on as heroes."

"What changed that?"

"The usual thing. Money and the power it gives you. You had 'buttleggers' making smuggling runs to New York, outsiders getting their clutches in the business. The Warriors controlled a major portion of the butt traffic. The cigarette trade set the stage for storefront gambling casinos. Some of the reservation people didn't like what was happening. They felt the tribe was moving too fast, that the guys making money off vice were out of control, that it was dangerous to have armed vigilantes protecting quasi-legitimate enterprises, intimidating people who opposed them. They put up barricades to stop gamblers from coming in. The Warriors tore them down. The violence escalated. Cars wrecked, arson. Then gun battles. A cop was killed, then a couple of Mohawks."

"How did you get involved in this?"

"Remember the old expression, 'All chiefs and no Indians?' That's what this was. The tribe had no political mechanism where people could hash out their beefs in a back room without picking up a gun. I tried to set something up. It was a lost cause. The Warriors were only a symptom of the deeper problem."

"What problem is that?"

"The whole issue of Indian nationalism. The argument that Native Americans should have a moral right to be in charge of their own affairs loses its purity when you've got Warriors protecting vice dens like Mafia enforcers."

"Maybe I'm rubbing this in, Joe, but the Warriors are only a couple of degrees removed from the kind of activism that says Plymouth Rock should be pounded into rubble or Plimoth Plantation burned to the ground."

"I'll be the first to admit that my rhetoric gets overheated, Soc. But I use it mainly as a verbal club to beat people over the head and get their attention. I've *never* advocated violence, or suggested people start shooting. Sure, I've been militant, skirted the edge, but some Warriors started going beyond the pale."

"Shooting someone *isn't* beyond the pale?"

"Sure it is, but the shoot-outs were products of hot tempers and big money. Those aren't good reasons, but at least they are reasons. But how do you explain the Warrior Society sending three guys to Libya to accept a quarter of a million bucks from Qadaffi? Or one of their leaders saying that pacifist chiefs who won't take up arms are traitors and should be killed?"

"I don't know. How do you explain it?"

"You can't. Some of the Warriors started asking the same question you just did. They believed in the Warrior code, but saw it perverted by a small minority. Guys like Tommy and Ed had relatives and friends killed or threatened. They got worried about the fringe element and came to me for help."

"You're not a Mohawk. How did you get on the Warriors' hit list?"

"I advocated a go-slow approach on the gambling. I'm not crazy about the idea of casinos for a lot of reasons, but it can work if it's done right, the way they did it in Connecticut. I pushed for all-tribal vote on gambling, start with a clean slate, get rid of the existing gambling casinos that benefit a few people, and set it up so everybody in the tribe gets a slice of the pie. Some of the Warriors thought I was aligning myself with the traditionals, and maybe I was. When that happened, my effectiveness as a mediator went out the window."

217

"Let me get this straight. You were against moving too fast into gambling, so the Warriors kidnapped Patty and want to kill you?"

"No," he said. "It's something else."

Something Else again. "You haven't told me about the file. Does that have anything to do with what we've been talking about?"

"It's got *every*thing to do with it. You can debate all night if it makes any difference whether the tribes will lose or gain their culture by becoming instant millionaires. But the big problem I saw was outside interests—mainly organized crime —getting in on this."

"Has that happened?"

"There's been talk. Mob guys fronting companies that want to offer to finance big casino operations, but nothing solid. Up to now."

I could see where he was heading. "What's in the file, Joe?"

"What I suspected but couldn't prove. Definite links between the mob and major outfits fronting casino financing for one or more tribes. This stuff has been buried so deep, nobody knew about it. Not the reservations, not even the some of the front companies. Only my dead client. He kept good records. Names, places, and numbers."

My mouth went dry involuntarily. I took a sip of beer, but that didn't help much. "This file of yours. We're talking dynamite here, aren't we?"

"Nukes, Soc. Hundred-megatonners. If documentary proof got out that the Mafia was behind *any* Indian gaming houses, the feds would have to declare a moratorium. You'd see Congress set up hearings."

"The state attorney general would have ammo to fight the casinos, too."

"You're catching on, Soc. It goes right up the line. Money's been all over the place, greasing the skids for the gaming parlors, lobbying legislators who don't want gaming or financing candidates to run against them. All you need is a single mob fingerprint to put the kibosh on legalized gambling. This file's got dozens."

"One question. How come you're still alive?"

"Dumb luck, Soc. I knew I was sitting on on bombshell, so I zipped my mouth for a change. I had to verify the data. I put out feelers. Someone snitched. I think it was a government insider who works for the wise guys, but I can't prove it. That's why I'm even leery about the FBI. Why I wouldn't trust Rourke, even if he didn't have it in for me."

"What were you planning to do with the file?"

"You don't just pop a copy in an envelope and send it to *The New York Times*. There are too many prominent names involved. They'd run it through fifty lawyers before they decided to print. *If* they decided to print, eventually the story would be picked up by the TV networks."

"What's wrong with that?"

"Plenty. First of all, the outfits mentioned in the file would get their mouthpieces on the tube, saying the report was a bunch of crap. I'd have to be out there defending myself. Anyone who wanted to shut me up with, say, an accident, would know where to find me. I wanted a firestorm of publicity. I wanted to switch the attention from me to them."

"So why didn't you?"

"It takes time, Soc. I couldn't run off a hundred copies of this thing at the nearest Kopy Kat. I couldn't even trust my staff, and it would have been too dangerous to bring other people in. I had to do it myself, in between bopping all over the country to handle my regular caseload. By the time I got the plan into place, I was just plain exhausted. I came down to see Patty and to take a rest. Then I'd come out. Wham, bam, thank you, Sam."

"So while you were on vacation, you got arrested and thrown in jail."

"Yeah, Wounded Knee. That sonofabitch Renault."

"That sonofabitch may have saved your life. You were safer in jail than out on the street. Let me see if I've got this right. The bad guys know you've got the file. Before they can get to you, Renault makes his move, and you end up in jail. They line up a hit man on the inside. How'd you hear about that?"

"Tommy and Ed told me. I asked them to come down from New York and keep an eye on Patty."

"Okay, that's where I come in. The Warriors figure I might know where you are, so they pay me a visit. When that doesn't work, they snatch Patty so you'll come to them with the file. How's that sound?"

"About right. Trouble is, they don't want just the file. It dawns on them I've probably made copies, and I'm the only one who can say where they are."

"Does the FBI know about the file?"

"They know I'm onto something hot. They want a piece of it. I'm not convinced the Bureau is pure. Remember, there's big money here."

"Where's the file now?"

"The copies are in a safe place. The less you know, the better."

"Okay, let's simplify this. What we've got to do is find out where Patty is, keep you alive, and keep the file intact."

"That's simple?"

"Relatively speaking."

"You got any ideas?"

"Yeah. Let's get out of here. This music is giving me a headache." We went out into the damp summer night and got into my pickup.

"I saw Patty this afternoon. I asked her to get in touch with you. Did she?"

"Yeah, she called from a pay phone after she talked to you. She said you wanted to set up another meeting."

"She called you directly?"

"No. We've got a system. We work through a third party and use pay phones as much as we can. It takes time. I got the message later and had the relay person call her tonight. She wasn't home."

"Has anybody checked her house?"

"Tommy did. There was nothing amiss. No signs of break-in or struggle, so we started asking around. A friend said she'd been talking to Patty last night. Patty put her on call waiting, then came back and said she had to go out for an errand. Maybe around ten o'clock."

"Patty didn't tell her friend where she was going?"

He shook his head. "Next thing I know, the relay gets in touch with me. Says she talked to Patty, who wants me to go to a pay phone and wait. It's urgent. Patty comes on the phone and gives me Big Oak's message from the Warriors: either I come in with the file, or she goes out. Any thoughts?"

"Yeah, and I don't like any of them. They'll kill you and Patty after they get the file. Then they'll go after anybody they think knows about it. Me for instance."

"If I don't go in, they'll kill Patty anyway."

"Patty's friend said something about call waiting. Run that by me again. Step by step, as if you were doing a legal brief."

"Okay. Patty is talking on the phone to her friend. She says, 'I've got someone on call waiting.' She puts her friend on hold. She comes back a minute later. She sounds upset. She says she can't talk. She has to go out to do a quick errand."

"Ergo," I said.

"Ergo, what?"

"Ergo, whatever she heard in that call made her leave the house."

"That's right. She wouldn't interrupt a conversation just to go out and get quart of milk. If we knew who called, we might know where she went." Joe's face fell. "That's terrific—only how do we know who called her? It could have been anybody," he said glumly. "You got any ideas what we should do next?"

"Yeah, I've got an idea," I said. "But you're not going to like it. And neither am I."

Twenty-Four

AGENT ROURKE'S MOUSE-HAIRED assistant stared at the plastic bag in my hand with fearful eyes. I opened the bag to show her I wasn't carrying an AK-47, a hand grenade, or a vial of sulphuric acid.

"I'd like to see Agent Rourke," I said.

She grabbed her phone and punched the intercom button. Keeping her eyes locked on me, she murmured, "That *gentleman* you were questioning last night wants to see you."

A sound like a rottweiler that has treed a cat came through the closed door and over the intercom at the same time. The secretary said, "Yes, sir. No, sir. Yes, sir."

"Go right in," she told me, returning quickly to her work to avoid the risk of conversation.

Rourke stood palms flat on his blotter leaning the substantial weight of his upper body on his hands as if he were trying to push the desk into the floor. His head was lowered, and his eyes glared from under his brows like halogen headlights.

"What. The. Fuck. Do. You. Want?"

"I thought we might have a powwow."

It probably wasn't the best analogy. A muscle started working in Rourke's jaw. His neck flab rolled out over his collar like bread dough. "Like the *Wampanoag* powwow?"

"More like a powwow where people pass the peace pipe and talk about doing each other a favor."

"I don't need a fucking favor from you," he barked.

"Well, I need one from you."

Rourke was stubborn, uncouth, vulgar, and mean, but he wasn't stupid. He settled his bulk into his creaking chair. A triumphant gleam appeared in his eyes.

"Siddown," he said. I took a seat, slid the fifth of Jack Daniel's from the bag, and put it on the desk.

"Peace pipe," I offered. "You looked like a Tennessee-sipping-whiskey man."

He picked up the bottle, read the label with the exquisite care of an IRS auditor looking for phony deductions, and placed it directly in front of him.

"Wrong. I drink Johnnie Walker Red." He leaned back and folded his thick arms, staring at me like a butcher sizing up a side of beef. "You've got three minutes to tell me why I shouldn't throw you down the stairs, and you've already used up two of them."

"This will only take three seconds. Joe Quint is prepared to come in. No more chasing Joe all over the countryside. You can have him sitting in this chair tomorrow at this time."

His eyes narrowed suspiciously and he puckered up his mouth as if he'd just bitten into a particularly sour lemon. "Why the sudden change in heart?"

"Simple. You have something Quint wants."

"Like what?"

"First I have to know if you're interested. There's no use going any further unless you are."

Rourke eyed me a few seconds. Then he slid open a desk drawer and came up with two coffee-stained flowered mugs. He twisted the cap off the Jack Daniel's, poured the mugs half-full, and drank his down as if it were weak herbal tea. So much for Tennessee sippin' whiskey. He wiped his mouth with the back of his hand. "Okay, I'm interested. What does Quint want?"

"He wants to review last night's tapes from the bug you've got on Patty Hoagland's phone."

Rourke guffawed wetly. "What makes you think we bugged her house?"

"I would if I were in your place."

He tapped his fingers together and gazed out the window while his cop's mind probed for hidden traps. After a moment, he said, "Okay," almost genially. "Suppose I let you hear the tapes. What then?"

"Tomorrow morning Joe Quint walks into this office."

"Is Quint prepared to talk?"

"He said he will come in. You'll have to negotiate anything else. The file, for instance."

"What file?"

"The one the Bureau isn't sure exists. It encapsulates information Mr. Quint received from a former client, now deceased."

"How do I know he'll keep his side of the bargain?" Rourke said, doing his best not to salivate.

"You don't. He could change his mind and bolt for the hills again. But what have you got to lose?"

Rourke poured himself another half-mug. "You know,

you've been nothing but trouble since the day we met. You've attacked me bodily, hindered my investigation, and made a fool of me. You've been a thorn in my side, a mote in my eye, and a general pain in the ass."

"Nobody's perfect, Agent Rourke."

"Yeah." He grinned wolfishly. "Not even me. A go-by-the-book Bureau man would call in six lawyers and an accountant to get your little offer in writing. Now me, I'm different. It would give me great pleasure to tell you to take a hike, Joe Quint or no."

I leaned forward. "Yeah, you could do that. You could kick me out of your office, sit back, have another drink, and tell your buddies how you handled an uppity private eye. But if you do that, you'll lose any chance you had to get the file before any of those by-the-book guys and to bust the balls of the high-ups who stuck you in this backwater office. There's something else. While you're congratulating yourself for putting down a insignificant insect like me, somebody is going to die. Maybe two people. One of them will be Joe Quint. I can guarantee that."

The thick eyebrows drew down into a shallow V. "Are you shitting me?" he said quietly.

I shook my head.

Rourke ran his tongue over his lips. "Stay where you are." He got up and went into the front office, returning a minute later. We drank some more, me sipping and him gulping, and waited. Rourke drummed his fingers on the desk impatiently.

"While we're waiting," I said, "can you tell me how you knew Joe Quint was going to be at the powwow?"

Rourke shrugged and said, "A guy called in."

"How'd you know he was going to be at the beach?"

"Another tip. I'm not embarrassed to say so."

"Same guy?"

"We think maybe so." His phone rang. "Hold on." He picked it up, mumbled a few words, and turned back to me. "What time do you want to hear the tape from?"

"I called Patty early in the evening. Anything after that."

He mumbled some more and handed the phone over. I heard some clicks, then my voice from last night saying, "This is your friendly private detective," and Patty replying, "Yes."

I listened to the brief conversation. There were more calls and hang-ups. Then the conversation with her friend. I dug the phone into my ear, heard Patty ask her friend to hold while she answered call waiting. She said hello. A voice I knew answered. Quick talk back and forth. Patty's voice, nervous now, getting back to her friend, saying she had to go in a big hurry, that she'd call back. I listened to another run-by to be sure I heard correctly. Then I asked Rourke for a tape of the conversation and the loan of a tape player.

He gave his assistant some orders and a short while later she came into his office with a Panasonic recorder. I thanked Rourke, and said I'd see him in the morning.

"Socarides, you going into something where you're gonna need help?"

"Maybe."

"Say the word, and you get the full resources of the Bureau."

Getting Patty out alive would require delicate surgery, not a bunch of G-men in dark suits, mirrored shades, and ear radios running around the countryside. "Thanks for the offer. I'll let you know."

He stuck out his hand, and we shook on it. I knew that as soon as I left, he'd listen to the taped conversation and try to discipher why it was so important. I also knew his chances of making any sense of it were pretty slim.

* * *

"Hello." Patty's voice.

"Hello, Patty, this is Cousin Ed."

"Ed, how are you?"

"I'm fine, but I've got to see you. It's urgent. Aunt Sara's stomach is acting up again. I don't know what to do."

"All right." Tension now in Patty's voice. "I'll be right over."

"Good, I'll see you soon."

Joe Quint rewound the tape, played the conversation again, and clicked off the player. He stared into space.

"Let me guess," I said. "You were Aunt Sara."

He nodded. "Sometimes I was Uncle Fred, or Granny Hester. Each name was keyed to a meeting place."

"Cute. So Ed was saying that you were in trouble."

Quint smashed a fist into his palm. "I can't believe it! Ed's been working against us the whole time." He got up and paced the small living room of the cottage outside of Falmouth. Joe had been hiding there. It was the first time anyone—including Tommy—had seen it.

Tommy's long body was slouched in an easy chair. "My fault, Joe. I brought him into this."

"It's nobody's fault. He could have turned anytime after that. The question now is what we do about it." Quint looked at me expectantly.

I shrugged. "My guess is that Ed can lead you to Patty. Where is he now?"

Tommy rose from his chair slowly. "He's back at the place we're renting. I'll go talk to him."

Joe caught the menace in the quiet measured tone. "I don't want him hurt, Tommy. No rough stuff. He's got to help us find Patty."

228

A thin smile crossed Tommy's lips. "We're cousins. Like I said, I'll talk to him. That's all."

While we waited for Tommy, Joe paced a lot. I went outside and sat in the sun. Joe followed me and paced in the yard. About two hours after he left, Tommy came back with Ed. Leaving Ed in the truck, Tommy came over and said, "You got something that shows the state forest up in Plymouth?"

I dug through my glove compartment and came up with a state tourism map. Tommy spread it out on the grass and we gathered around. He pointed to the heavily wooded section between the Cape Cod Canal and Plymouth.

"Ed says there's a little pond almost in the state forest. Got a cottage on it. They're keeping Patty in it."

"What did he say when you told him we were onto him?" Joe asked.

"He denied it at first. Then he made up all sorts of excuses. All bogus. Ed's just a weak guy. I always had to protect him when we were kids."

"He could tell the Warrior Society we know where Patty is," Joe said.

"I said if he did that, Patty'd be dead. He didn't believe it. He said they just wanted something you had, and after they got it from you, they'd let Patty and you go. I said they'd kill you and Patty. Maybe him, too. That got his attention."

"What's he going to do now?"

"I told him the only reason I didn't kill him is 'cause we're cousins. But if he wants to keep breathing, he's gonna have to help get Patty out."

"He could still blow the whistle on this," Joe said, skeptically.

"I said if he did, I'd make sure the Warriors knew he talked, and that they'd probably kill him."

"Do you want to call in the cops?" I said to Joe. "It's up to you."

Tommy answered first. "Ed says they'll kill her if you do that. I believe him."

"No cops!" Joe snapped. "We can't take the chance."

"Okay," I said, "Then we'd better come up with a plan."

I told Tommy to bring Ed over. Then I patted the map down on the grass and weighted the corners with rocks. Like Sioux braves getting ready to steal horses from a Cheyenne village, we sat cross-legged around the map. We argued over what to do. A dozen schemes were discussed, and a dozen thrown out. After a hour, we hatched a strategy that wasn't half-bad.

There was only one major glitch in it. Tommy.

Twenty-Five

"THE PROBLEM IS, I don't know how to swim," Tommy was saying.

"Weren't you in the Navy?"

"On boats, I said. In the Coast Guard. You don't have to swim unless the boat sinks. Even then you've got life rafts and survival suits to keep you from sinking."

"You won't have to swim, Tommy," I said. "Just lie on the inflatable raft and paddle along."

Tommy looked as though he was being asked to stretch out naked on a bed of nails. "What if I fall off? If I'm drowning, do you think I'm going to be quiet about it? That's the idea, isn't it? We're supposed to be quiet."

The idea of drowning in soggy silence was Tommy's mother of all terrors. I tugged at my nose and studied the rough diagram on the kitchen table. We'd moved inside after it became apparent that rescuing Patty was going to be tougher than a game of Super Mario.

The amoebic drawing showed a pond at the edge of the

Miles Standish State Forest. Slade's Island, a pollywog-shaped peninsula, jutted off the shore, joined to the mainland by a thin neck of land. The heavy-lined X marked the location of the only cabin on the island.

Ed more-or-less volunteered the information in the simple diagram. He sat in the corner of Joe's kitchen like a large and melancholy mushroom. You couldn't blame Ed for being unhappy. He had betrayed Tommy, his best friend and cousin, and had been caught at it. He had lied to Joe. He had lured Patty to her possible death. Now he was switching sides again.

Joe still didn't trust him. In a voice as quiet and as menacing as a bayonet being sharpened, Joe said he might be tempted to kill Ed if anything happened to Patty. For all his mouthing off, Joe was not to be taken lightly. He was 101st Airborne in Vietnam. Anyone who jumps out of a plane into the nighttime jungle is no choirboy. He radiated hostility like a nuclear reactor in meltdown, and Ed could feel it.

"I know this is a pain, Ed, but we're going to have to go over this again," I said. "We make one little mistake, and Patty is in big trouble."

He dragged his chair over to the kitchen table and sat opposite me. Tommy and Joe hulked over our shoulders like cathedral gargoyles. Ed scowled at the map. "Same thing I told you before. The road goes in about a mile, and hits the pond. Then it splits, and both ends go around the pond and meet on the other side. Slade's Island is about in the middle, where they meet." He put his finger on the X. "The camp is right here on the point, up on a little hill. There's a set of stairs that goes down from the camp to the dock."

I drew my finger along the skinny land bridge between the island and the shore. "You said this dike connects the island to the mainland. How long and wide is it?"

"Couple of hundred yards long, maybe. It's wide enough for one car. There's a steep bank that goes down about ten feet to the water on the sides."

"How about the island itself? Is the camp out in the clear, or does it have trees around it?"

"It's open in front so people can look out on the pond. There's a little back and side yard, but mostly big pines."

"No other way to get to the cabin without getting your feet wet?" Tommy asked. I wondered if Tommy took baths; he was clearly an aquaphobe.

Ed stretched his arms wide. "Like I said, Tommy, the dike isn't much bigger than this. You'd have to be a snake to get past the guard."

"Any other cottages on the pond?" Joe asked.

"Nah. Whole pond is privately owned."

I handed Ed a soft lead pencil. "I want to be sure about the guards. I'd appreciate it if you could point them out again, Ed."

He nodded and drew a little circle where the dike met the mainland. "Last I knew, there was one guy here at the driveway." He circled the point. "Another guy sits here on the dock, in case somebody tries to get to the place by boat. He moves around the shore of the island, so you never know where he's going to be, but he spends most of his time in the little boathouse at the head of the dock, to get away from the sun and mosquitoes. The guards all carry walkie-talkies."

"What do they have for guns?" I asked.

"I've seen some pistols and a shotgun. They may have more. Probably."

"Who's in the house with Patty?"

"Big Oak and two others. He stays in the cottage with Patty. The others spell the guards."

"Draw a diagram of the house as you remember it." I gave him a clean sheet of paper.

Ed grumbled that he wasn't an artist and proceeded to prove his point. A combination living room and kitchen-bunkroom took up the front half of the cabin. There was an off-center front entrance and a side door that opened from the kitchen onto the porch. The rear half was cut up into a bathroom and two bedrooms. Patty was being kept in one of the bedrooms.

I gave the drawing to Joe. "Now that my three-pronged amphibious assault by flotation raft has been blown out of the water, would anyone like to suggest an alternative?"

Tommy looked at Joe. They both looked at Ed. Then all three looked at me. Joe shook his head. He looked worried. He had a right to be.

"C'mon guys," I prodded. "You're supposed to be good at stuff like this, skulking through the forest and setting up ambushes. How'd you ever beat Custer?"

"Custer was stupid," Joe said.

"We had him outnumbered, too." Tommy added. "Big Oak isn't going to fall for a dumb trap. He's ex–Green Beret."

"And I'm a Marine, you're Coast Guard, and Joe is One-hundred-and-first Airborne, which is made up of guys who chew nails to keep their teeth sharpened. The three of us ought to be a match for a green beanie and a few amateurs." The pep talk was as much for me as the others. It was years since Joe and I graduated from Uncle Sam's school for professional killers.

"I still like your idea, Soc," Joe said. "Maybe if Tommy doesn't want to do it, we can use Ed."

Ed looked as if he had just been informed that an eighteen-wheeler was bearing down on him. His eyes pleaded with

234

Tommy. "You said I didn't have to do any rough stuff, Tommy. I can't do it. Any one of those guys out there could eat me alive. No way," he said, his hands pushing back an invisible assailant. "No rough stuff."

Some warriors. "Okay," I said wearily. "Let's start over. Here's the situation. Problem one. Getting to the island. There are two ways. By land, over the dike. By water, across the pond. This has a slight advantage. It would be easier to get close without being seen. We come at the island from three points, take out the guard, then deal with the situation in the cabin. But with Tommy out of the action, that leaves only two of us against four guys on the island and one on the dike as backup. The odds aren't terrific."

Tommy shuffled his feet. "I'm a hunter. I can creep up on people real quiet," he said hopefully.

"That's no good until we're on the island," Joe shot back. "Soc's right. We've got to have three men come in by water."

"Joe, please don't make me go in water over my head. I'll lose it!"

Ed piped in and made everyone sure he didn't want *any* part of *any* plan. They squabbled like a flock of pigeons. This must be How the West Was Won. The White Man moved in while the Indians formed debating societies.

The lines blurred on the diagram in front of me, then became sharp again. "Aha!" I yelled. Six dark eyes stared at me.

"How deep is it here?" I tapped the area around the shoreline of the pond.

Ed frowned in thought. "Three or four feet, is my guess. I only been on the island once, at night, and I wasn't paying attention to the water."

Pointing my pencil at Tommy, so there would be no mistake, I said, "What if you followed the shoreline to the dike? The water is shallow. If you fell in, it would be only up to your waist."

Tommy wouldn't have been happy with anything deeper than a rain puddle. He was on the spot, though, and he knew it. "Yeah, I could handle three or four feet. If I fell in. I could hold onto the raft."

"You said you could be real quiet," I encouraged him. "It should be no problem, even if you come ashore in the middle of the dike, to follow the dike road to the rear of the cabin. You wait there. Joe and I come across the pond, we take care of the guard on the pier, and meet you behind the camp."

Tommy smiled. "Yeah, I like that." Joe clapped him on the back. Ed looked incredibly relieved.

Before anyone changed his mind, I said, "That was the easy part. Now we have to come up with an idea how to get Patty out of the cabin."

Joe leaned forward intently. "We've got two guns," he said.

"I went back and got mine at the beach after the FBI got through with me," Tommy said.

Click on. Freeze action. Tommy and Joe busting down the door, guns blazing. Click. Next frame. Patty and me caught in the cross fire. Bleeding bodies everywhere. Click off.

"I want your guns unloaded and in your holsters until I tell you otherwise," I said. "Keep the ammo in your pocket. That's the only way I'll do this deal. Otherwise, you're on your own, or call in the cops."

Joe said, "We'll do it your way, Soc."

"We'll need some stuff." I wrote out a list and handed it to Joe. "While you guys go shopping, Ed is going to show me the lay of the land."

Ed required some bullying on my part to get him into the truck. We headed off-Cape and crossed the Bourne Bridge, then after a few miles on Route 3, we left the highway. A narrow, windy back road took us through the silent pine barrens of the 14,000-acre Miles Standish State Forest between Plymouth and the Cape Cod Canal.

Every so often during the dry season, someone ignores Smokey the Bear, and the forest goes up in flames. There are still tall stands of oak and spruce trees around the kettle ponds the glaciers carved out back in the Ice Age, but most of what's been left after the forest fires are pitch pine and scrub oak, tough little trees that could survive a nuclear explosion and thrive on the sandy soil.

The road broke out of the forest and back into private woodland that bordered state property. Ed pointed to a wooden sign made from a broken oar. Painted on the paddle were the words SLADE'S POND. PRIVATE. An arrow aimed down a dirt road. "This is it," he said.

The road must have been cleared a long time ago with a single pass of a bulldozer. It was only inches wider than the truck, pocked with craters, studded with cobblestone boulders, and hemmed in on either side by a thick, inhospitable tangle of briars and poison ivy. It dipped and turned, and I held my breath at each blind curve, wondering what we'd do if we met a truckload of heavily armed Warriors coming the other way.

Ed must have been thinking the same thing. He kept muttering under his breath, "I don't like this. . . . I don't like this. . . ."

About three-quarters of a mile from the main road, according to the odometer, I spotted twin ruts heading into the woods at the right. I asked Ed how close we were to the pond. Not far, he said. I turned onto the track and drove about a hundred yards until I was sure the pickup couldn't be seen by anyone passing on the Slade's Pond Road.

As a slight precaution, we cut some branches and brushed out the tire tracks that might start someone thinking. I took a pair of binoculars and a compass from the truck. We walked toward the pond, treading quietly on the soft, sun-dappled, reddish brown pine-needle carpeting. The thickly grown boughs that blocked the sun kept the breeze out, and it was almost too hot to breathe. Clouds of thirsty gnats dove at our heads. We picked up our pace from a walk to a jog.

Ten minutes from the truck, we broke out of the woods onto a dirt road. Sweat poured off our faces and soaked our T-shirts.

Sunlight glinted through the trees on the other side of the road. The air had a smell of lily pads and rotting vegetation. We walked a few hundred feet until we came to a path, probably carved out through the years by the boots of intrepid fishermen, that cut through the thick undergrowth. The path descended until it came to a leafy clearing where someone had set up a campfire pit, then continued down a shallow bank to a narrow beach with sand the color of brown sugar.

Sheltered from view by the encircling trees and underbrush, we scoped out Slade's Pond. Ed was no Rembrandt, but he had a good eye for detail. The drawing he did was close to the real thing. The pond was almost perfectly round and about a half mile across. Directly opposite where we were hidden was Slade's Island. It jutted out into the pond for about one-eighth of a mile from the opposite shore.

Shading the lenses to prevent reflection, I focused on the cabin, which stood on a knoll—a rocky knob, really—around twenty-five feet above water level. The cabin was built of thick logs cleaned of their bark and painted mahogany, with green trim on the windows. A flagstone chimney towered over the dark red asphalt-shingle roof.

The front door was slightly off center, with a small regulation window on one side, and a preframed picture window to the right. A covered porch ran around three sides of the cabin. Thick woods closed in behind. In front, the yard was level for a few dozen feet, then sloped down a flat-rocked incline, broken here and there by knee-high berry bushes.

A narrow flight of stairs ran from the cabin to a boathouse that was sheathed in weathered gray planking and tar paper. The wide front doors were open. In front of the boathouse was a ramp, and next to the ramp was a rickety-looking dock that extended around thirty feet off the point of the island. A white-hulled Boston Whaler was tied up at the dock.

"Look," Ed whispered. "Over there." He'd been so still I'd almost forgotten he was with me. My eyes followed his pointing finger. A man was walking along the shore of the island to our left. He climbed onto the dock and walked out to the end, where he sat with his legs dangling over the water. I handed the binoculars to Ed.

"That's Nasty Jim. Mean bastard, but lazy as hell."

I took back the glasses and studied the guy on the dock. He flicked the butt he'd been smoking into the water and stared at it. Then he tucked a life preserver up against a piling and, using it for a pillow, stretched out for a siesta in the sun. I moved the glasses around the shoreline, then back to the cabin. There was no movement in the windows, but while I watched, the screen door opened. Two guys came out.

"Big Oak," Ed whispered.

They talked for a few minutes then split up. The taller of the two went back inside; the other disappeared in the direction of the dike. About ten minutes later, a fourth man came from the same direction and went into the house. Probably the dike sentry going off his shift.

I had seen enough. I tapped Ed's shoulder and pointed back the way we came. He didn't have to be encouraged. He took off through the woods like a startled doe. On the way back to the truck, I took my Swiss Army knife and cut swatches of bark off the trees exposing the white wood underneath. Ed glanced around nervously when I stopped. He almost jumped out of his skin every time an acorn fell. I thought he was going to have a heart attack when just as we passed under a tree a woodpecker did a *brrrrap* over our heads.

Before long, we were in the pickup, heading for the main road.

Ed was muttering something about the FBI. My ears perked up.

"What'd you say, Ed?"

"The stupid FBI."

"Why are they stupid?"

"They had Joe right in their hands—twice—but they blew it both times."

"I don't get you, Ed."

He folded his arms and stared straight ahead. "Never mind."

Things were starting to connect. "Did you have anything to do with tipping the FBI off about Joe?"

He shook his head, but said, "Yeah," at the same time. "I figured if the feds caught him, the Warriors couldn't touch him. Tommy and me would be in the clear. Nobody gets hurt."

Silence.

"You think it was a bad idea?" he said, looking for an answer, any answer.

"Actually, it wasn't a bad idea, Ed. Too bad it didn't work out."

That seemed to satisfy him. We didn't talk again. I was wondering which of the guys I'd just seen was the one whose teeth I'd rattled the night he jumped me at my house.

I'd find out soon enough.

Twenty-Six

At exactly 9:30 that night, I glanced at my Swatch. "Let's do it."

Like Agamemnon and his troops liberating Helen from ancient Troy, we set out to rescue Patty Hoagland. I talked tough, but it was obvious we weren't a SWAT team. Not even close. We were an over-the-hill paratrooper who was more mouth than muscle. An aquaphobic Mohawk. A reluctant turncoat. And a cut-rate private eye. I hoped Patty's life insurance was paid up. I had none to worry about.

Our rescue kit lay on the living-room floor. Three dark blue plastic rafts with little yellow smiling seahorses on them. (Tommy said that was all they had left at Bradlee's.) A roll of duct tape. A Louisville Slugger. A can of charcoal lighter fluid. Black shoe polish. Waterproof matches. Cutter insect repellant. Flashlights. We had cut rectangular patches off the white cotton curtains and taped them over the flashlights to dull their glow.

We had agreed to make our move on the cabin around

eleven o'clock. Originally, our plan was to go in when every-body was asleep. Then Ed mentioned there was a battery-operated TV set in the cabin. The TV would help drown out sounds if we got careless. For our plan to have a chance, people had to be up and around, although it wouldn't hurt to have them drowsy.

Joe rode with me in the GMC. Tommy and Ed were in their pickup. Around ten-thirty, the two-truck parade left the main road at the Slade's Pond sign, jounced along the ruts, and hooked a right to park under the canopy of pines. Ed slung the duffel bag holding our rescue gear over his shoulder. Tommy, Joe, and I tucked the rafts under our arms like three kids off to a day at the beach.

The rule was no lights except for an emergency. Walking through the pine grove at night was like sticking your head in a bag of coal dust. Roots caught our feet and branches whipped our faces. Mosquitoes and no-see-ums swarmed around our heads looking for spots we'd missed with the Cutter's.

"Jeezus!" someone bawled.

"What's wrong?" I whispered.

"I walked into a tree—that's what's wrong," Ed said. Maybe we had made a mistake wooing him away from the Warriors.

Joe growled at Ed to keep his mouth shut. "Tommy, you take the lead. The rest of us grab onto each other's shirts and go single file until we get out of here."

Tommy wasn't kidding about his woods sense. He led us through the maze of trees as if he could see in the thick black-ness. Within minutes, we broke out onto the dirt road that bordered the pond.

While Joe and Ed waited, Tommy and I took one raft and followed the road about a quarter of the way around the pond.

We went down another fisherman's path to the shore and stood at the water's edge looking at the hedgehog silhouette of Slade's Island.

A thumbnail moon hung in the star-sparkled sky. Yellow kerosene lights reflected into the still water from the cabin windows. Except for the hum of insects and the *ker-lunk* of lonely frogs, it was as still as a crypt. I brushed the comparison out of my mind and held the raft steady in the water. Tommy crawled on it and adjusted his body weight until he felt balanced.

"This is a very gutsy thing for you to do, Tommy."

"Thanks," he grunted. "Now push me the hell out of here before I change my mind."

I gave the raft a strong, even shove, and it skittered out about fifteen feet. Tommy dipped his hands into the pond and paddled gently. The insect chorus drowned out the quiet ripples his hands made. Once beyond the lily pads and pond grass, Tommy turned to the right, and like a giant water bug, moved along the edge of the pond until the night swallowed him.

With Tommy launched on his way, I rendezvoused with the others. We carried the remaining two rafts down the path Ed and I used on our spy mission earlier that day. Joe made some snide remarks when I smeared my face with shoe polish like an old-time minstrel. We sprayed insect repellant onto our skin and clothes. With the Louisville Slugger at my side, I crawled onto my raft. Joe took a waterproof bag with him. Ed pushed us off the narrow beach, and we started paddling.

With no wind or current, we quickly skimmed across the pond. About a hundred feet from the end of the dock, we veered to the left and moved toward the island. With the dock between us and the boathouse, we stopped and raised our heads like curious turtles. There were only the usual croaks and splashes you hear around a freshwater pond at night.

We started paddling again and slipped into the protecting shadows under the dock. Joe waited by a piling. I glided over to the Boston Whaler I had seen through the binoculars. I reached up and ran my hand past the steering wheel to the console. The key was in the ignition. I pushed off and tapped Joe's shoulder twice. The signal for okay. It was miserably hot and smelly under the dock. My sweat diluted the insect repellant, and the mosquitoes didn't seem to mind the taste of shoe polish.

Cigarette smoke. I tensed. Soft footfalls creaked on the old planking just overhead. *Pht.* A butt hissed into the water. The footsteps continued to the end of the dock and stopped. I let my breath out, slowly.

I whispered in Joe's ear. "Can you do a snake?"

"What?"

"Can you imitate a snake?"

"What kind of snake?"

"*Any* kind. Water moccasin. Copperhead. Cobra, if you want to. Just make a snake sound to distract the guard so I can jump him."

"I suppose so." He didn't sound convinced.

"I don't need Mel Blanc. Just a simple hiss will do."

From at the end of the dock, came a muttered curse, and a slap. I don't know if the guard nailed the mosquito, but quick footsteps thumped along the pier.

"Watch it—he's coming back," Joe said.

At the point the dock joined the shore, we quietly slipped off our rafts into about three feet of soupy water. Joe was on one side of the dock, and I was on the other. I hid behind a piling that was far too small. The guard came abreast.

Pssst.

Joe sounded like someone selling dirty pictures in an alley.

The guard stopped. He had his back to me. He was so close that I could have reached up and grabbed his ankle.

Pssst, pssst.

The main idea was to get the guard's attention without scaring the wits out of him. From that perspective, Joe succeeded. The guard's flashlight flicked on. He leaned over the pier. Joe slid under the dock and let out another *pssst*. The guard got down on one knee. I came up behind him, the Louisville Slugger in my hand. Water dripped off me and made noisy little patters. The guard turned. I slipped on the wet bank. He started to get up, and his hand dropped to his belt. Even as I fell, I brought the bat down between his neck and right shoulder. He grunted with pain, and the flashlight plopped into the water.

Joe was on the dock. He jumped onto the guard's back, dragged him facedown. I got my knees into his shoulders, but the bat had taken most of the fight out of him. A hunting knife appeared in Joe's hand. I thought he was going to cut the guy's throat. Instead, he wrapped duct tape around the guard's head, covering his mouth, and sliced it with a quick swipe of the sharp blade. We taped the guard's wrists and ankles tightly and tied him with his back against a piling. I took his walkie-talkie and tossed his gun into the pond.

Joe went to see whether Tommy had made it without falling off his raft. I hauled the Whaler around the end of the dock, away from the boathouse, and hid it in some bushes. Then I went back to the boathouse and chewed on my fingernails. The longer this thing went on, the greater the chance for a screwup. Someone might come to relieve the guard. The TV batteries could go dead. A call on the walkie-talkie. A million unwelcome possibilities danced around in my mind.

A sound like a choo-choo train came my way in the darkness. Joe huffed and puffed from exertion. "Tommy made it," he said between gasps. "Had trouble getting through the thick grass along the dike. That's what took him so long."

The guard we had tied up was awake, struggling against the bindings. He calmed down after I gave him a good top-to-bottom spraying with Cutter's. Then I followed Joe past the boathouse with the water lapping at our shoes. The cabin was on our left, curtains drawn across the windows.

Tommy was waiting in a small yard behind the cabin. The land dropped back sharply behind the building. The bedroom windows overhead were about ten feet off the ground. Tommy and I got down on our hands and knees, and Joe climbed on our shoulders. We hoisted him up so his face was level with a window. He scratched lightly against the screen and held the flashlight at his face so Patty would see him. He put his face close to the window for a few minutes, then whispered at us to let him down.

"Patty's okay," he said. "But the window's nailed shut. I told Patty to crawl under the bed in fifteen minutes and to stay there until we tell her to come out."

After a quick conference, Tommy disappeared like a ghost. He returned minutes later, smelling of lighter fluid. "It's done," he said. "Found some gasoline to help it along."

The three of us crept around the side of the cabin which was now on its slight rise to our right, skulked down behind some bushes, and watched the boathouse. We smelled smoke before we saw any flames. The fire broke through one wall and the roof at about the same time. The wood was old and dry. Soon, one side of the boathouse was totally enveloped.

Tommy kept his eyes glued on the cabin. He chafed like a kid whose mother won't look at his crayon drawing. "Christ!" he grunted. "Those bastards all asleep?"

Joe picked up on Tommy's annoyance. "Maybe we should knock on the door and tell them to look out the window."

More time passed. I was starting to worry. The plan hinged on drawing the bad guys out of the cabin. That meant they had to see the fire. Joe's suggestion wasn't sounding so crazy. Then someone inside the cabin shouted. The front door flew open, and three figures piled out onto the porch. Big Oak's voice thundered. "Check it out. I'll watch the girl."

Two figures ran toward the blazing boathouse. Greasy black smoke billowed skyward. The entire island was bathed in a rosy glow. Big Oak stepped back inside. Leaving Tommy to cover our rear, Joe and I crouched low and ran for the cabin. We vaulted onto the front porch and edged up to a window.

The curtains had been pulled aside, and we could see into the living room. A door that led off the living room was open. Big Oak was framed in the doorway, his back to us. He stood there a second, then knelt to look under the bed. Joe and I sprinted into the cabin and flanked the bedroom door. Joe had his gun out. I gripped my Louisville slugger. A booming laugh came from the bedroom. Big Oak had found Patty's hiding place.

Hauling Patty by a slim arm, he dragged her into the living room. This was the first time I had seen Big Oak close up in full light. I was sorry to say that his name fit him well. He was at least six-three, and his body looked as if it had been assembled from old tree stumps. He saw us, and the grin on his wide mouth vanished. He pulled Patty to his chest and wrapped his arm around her neck. I had no doubt that he could snap it like a twig. He advanced on Joe using her as a shield.

248

Joe hesitated, uncertain. Big Oak saw his opening. He threw Patty at Joe, who tried to grab her. But he lost his balance and they both tumbled to the floor. Big Oak was fast. He lunged for Joe and twisted the gun out of his hand. He swung around and pointed the ugly black eye of the muzzle at me. He smiled and tightened his finger on the trigger. He was only a few feet away and couldn't miss. My stomach muscles tightened involuntarily, as though they could stop a bullet at close range.

Click!

Big Oak couldn't have been more surprised if the gun turned into a cigarette lighter.

Click-click.

Sometimes forgetfulness pays off. I hadn't given Joe the okay to load his gun. While Big Oak was giving his trigger finger more exercise, Patty grabbed a fireplace poker and brought it down above Big Oak's elbow, so hard that even I winced. The gun thudded onto the floor and Big Oak doubled over with pain, clutching his arm.

I discovered that I was still holding the baseball bat. I swung it against his butt. Big Oak crashed forward and kissed the hardwood floor. *Timmberr!*

Joe gave Patty a hug that was the kind of melodramatic scene-closer that plays well at the end of Act Three. Patty was still holding the poker. I *knew* there was a wolf lady behind that calm exterior. I asked what her Indian name was.

"Peaceful Dove," she said, smiling.

"Talk about names when we get off this island," Quint said. "There are four more guys we gotta take care of."

He was right, of course. We were sitting ducks—or doves —in the cabin. He took Patty by the hand and headed out the door with me bringing up the rear. A man's body was stretched out on the ground near the cabin. My first thought was that they had gotten Tommy.

I rolled the guy over. He was a complete stranger. His head was bleeding from an ugly bruise, but he was still breathing. Tommy rose from behind a bush. He had his gun in his hand.

He grinned. "Works better without bullets."

The whole island was flooded by light from the blazing boathouse. I led the others past the front of the cabin, and we scrambled off the knoll toward the pond. The whaler was where I left it. We shoved the boat into a couple of feet of water. Patty got in, then Tommy and Joe. I pushed the boat out where the propeller wouldn't foul on vegetation and looked back.

The fire was a pretty piece of work. The old wood in the boathouse made dandy kindling. But it wasn't the pyrotechnics that interested me.

Figures were sprinting across the island in our direction. Muzzles sprouted red flowers. Then came the ugly *cuh-rak* of high-powered handguns. The bullets hit the water with a funny *Zoop . . . Zoop.*

The others pulled me aboard. I dove headfirst into the boat, scrambled into the seat behind the steering wheel, and turned the ignition key. Nothing happened. We were drifting back toward shore. Tommy and Joe found oars and started to pole us into deeper water. I kept fumbling with the starter. Nothing again. I hefted the gas tank. It was heavy and full.

Zoop! The water splashes were closer.

I lifted the cover on the motor to see if the spark-plug connection was loose. Did the same with the battery. Nope. I bent over the console. That's when I noticed the short red plastic coil dangling from the ignition key. A string of Greek curses flew off my tongue. The coil connects to an emergency switch

250

on the console. Unless the switch is popped out on its spring, the engine doesn't start. It's a safety measure, but this kill switch could get us killed.

I slipped the clip under the switch and hit the ignition again. The motor coughed and died. I pulled the choke partway out, tried again. The outboard sputtered and caught. I pushed the choke in before the motor stalled out and gave it the gas. It smoothed out.

Hoping Joe and Tommy had gotten us clear of the shallow water and weeds, I jammed the motor into reverse, spun the wheel, and shoved the throttle forward. The shovel-shaped bow lifted, and we raced across the water. Slade's Island and the pond around it were lit up as brightly as floods at a Hollywood premiere. The outboard's whine drowned out the gunshots, but bullets plopped into the pond around us like suicidal bees.

A fist-sized hunk of fiberglass flew off the transom inches from the outboard clamp. They say you can cut a Boston Whaler in half and it will still float, but I didn't want to test that right now.

"Keep your heads down!" I yelled, hunching low over the wheel, nervously aware there was nothing between the guns and my back but a few hundred yards of air.

I whipped the wheel left, then right, like a broken-field runner.

Pow! The unmistakable roar of a shotgun. Pellets slammed into the boat.

"Ow!" Tommy doubled over.

"You okay?" I shouted.

"Caught some lead in my shoulder," he yelled.

The shotgun thundered again, but we were moving out of range. The dark tree-lined opposite shore was approaching fast. I practically ran the boat into the woods, cutting the motor at the last second and yanking the outboard up on its swivel. I jumped into a couple of feet of water and held the bow while the others piled out.

Joe was hollering Ed's name and swearing in between.

"That little bastard double-crossed us," Joe screamed. Sometimes you shouldn't jump to conclusions. A flashlight wigwagged about fifty feet up the beach. Ed shouted, "Over here!"

Ed was waiting to lead us away from the pond. We ran across the road into the pine grove, our feet digging into the soft needles, breath coming hard. A dark stain spread across the back of Tommy's T-shirt, but he plugged on gamely without a complaint. Which was fine with me, because I was worried about Big Oak's little acorns driving around the pond and planting themselves where they could block Slade's Pond Road.

Ruby eyes winked through the trees. Tail-light reflectors. The trucks were parked pointing out. Patty and Joe got in my truck. Within minutes, we were pounding the life out of the shock absorbers. I thought I saw headlights once behind us, but it could have been my fevered imagination.

Our tires left the dirt and bit into the macadam, and I nailed the accelerator. The pickup lurched forward. And died.

I'd been putting a lot of miles on the old Jimmy with all my trips to Mashpee and Plymouth, and her faithful old heart just plum gave out. Luckily, the others were behind us. We piled into the back of their truck and sped off along the backroads. The breeze blowing in our faces felt good, but we were far from safe. The state forest is a big and lonely place. Big Oak could cut us down without waking up a single camper.

We made it through the forest without incident and found

a pay phone. I called Rourke and gave him a quick rundown. He said to meet him at the state police barracks. He'd have a doctor there for Tommy.

True to his word, Rourke was waiting at the barracks with a troop of suits and staties. I had to admit that, for a change, I was glad to see his big ugly face.

Twenty-Seven

ROURKE CALLED ME the next morning and told me to look out the front window. My pickup was in the driveway. The sun reflected dully off its faded green paint and fiberglass patches. Rourke said he got it fixed and had somebody drop it off, courtesy of the FBI. They had even waxed it. While I was in a good mood, he gave me the bad news. Big Oak and his band of Warriors had vanished. Rourke said the only people they found at the cabin were fire departments from Plymouth and Carver and half a dozen surrounding towns. I was happy to learn we didn't burn down the state forest.

"What next?" I said.

"Could be a problem if they're back on the reservation. Sovereign nation and all that. We send a squad in to apprehend them, and even the Indians who *don't* like the bastards will throw burning tires onto the interstate."

"So they've gotten away scot-free."

"Maybe not. I talked to your boy Quint a little while ago."

"Did you discuss a file he has in his possession?"

"Yeah. Just skimmed it. But from what Quint tells me, it's hot stuff. Maybe there's something in there to give Mr. Big Oak and his pals the sweats when it hits the headlines. That's *my* problem, though. You're out of it."

"Not quite, Agent Rourke."

"How's that?"

"Joe Quint is still up on murder charges. He can't go public with the casino file until he clears himself."

"Whaddya mean?"

"Joe might become a national media figure when the story hits the networks, but the legal guns the other guys are going to hire will try to demolish his credibility by pointing out he's a murder suspect and bail jumper."

"That's a tough one. Got any ideas?"

"A couple."

"Let's hear them."

I'd been thinking about the Quint case when Rourke called. I could continue to nibble around the edges, doing things by the book, chipping away at the wall of evidence against Joe until it crumbled. Or I could take the direct course, which would be unorthodox, contrary to accepted police procedure, and probably illegal. I looked out on the shimmering waters of Pleasant Bay, ran my fingers through Kojak's scruffy black coat, and decided that I didn't want to be away from home any more than necessary.

So when Rourke asked if I had any ideas, I was ready for him. I laid out my scheme. I'd figured Rourke to be a throwback, the kind of guy who hated paperwork, the bureaucracy and stuffed shirt agents. I was right.

"I like it," he said flatly.

We talked some more. Rourke made a few suggestions. He was chuckling when he hung up.

The boathouse smelled of mold, and spider squatter camps filled every corner, but God, it was good to be home! I was so glad to see Kojak I took him off the low-ash diet for one meal. I went to Elsie's for breakfast, then spent most of the day hanging around the fish pier. I was waiting on the dock when Sam came in on the *Millie D.* with a heavy load of cod and some haddock. I helped him offload and said I expected to be back at work within a day or two. He allowed as that was finestkind and invited me to his house for dinner.

Sam cooked chicken on the grille. Mildred boiled up corn on the cob and made a salad with lettuce, tomatoes, and onions fresh from her garden. As usual, Sam beat me at cribbage, but after a couple of games I excused myself and went back to the boathouse.

I called Rourke to make sure we were still on track. He was eager as a young pup. He said all the fun he'd had since he met me made up for those boring hours sitting in the Hyannis office. I said I'd see him later. I got in the truck and headed toward Plymouth. Before I left the boathouse, I chewed on a fresh garlic clove. It never hurts to give yourself an edge.

A few minutes before nine that night, Rick came out of the house on Sever Street and got into his Trooper. He'd just put the key in the ignition when I popped up in the backseat behind him.

"Hi, Rick," I said. "It's your old dive buddy, and this is a cocked speargun I've got pressed against your neck, so I'd appreciate it if you kept your hands on the steering wheel where I can see them."

"What the hell's going on?"

"We've got a lot to talk about."

"Sure, no problem. You don't need a speargun to talk to me."

"I'll think about that. After you answer a few questions."

"Hey, man, you can ask me all the questions you want."

"Good. Now tell me who you work for."

"I work for Doc Zane. You know—"

"*Hold* it." I put a lot of garlicky heft on the H and touched his neck just below the ear.

"Jeezus! Watch it with that thing!" I couldn't tell if he meant the spear or the garlic breath.

"Sorry, my hand shakes when people tell me lies. I'll rephrase the question. "You're working for Renault, aren't you?"

"Yeah, I work for him. So what? I do some moonlighting to pick up a few extra bucks. Is that a crime?"

"Depends on what kind of work it is, Rick. What do you do for Renault?"

"I help around the auction house. Get stuff ready to be sold."

"Does that include the Indian artifacts?"

"You know about that?" Wary now.

"I know about it, Rick. Now tell me, why did you try to kill me?"

"I didn't—"

The spear point tickled his neck.

"Hey, Rick, don't blow smoke up my flue. It's okay. I don't care. If I were mad about it, you'd be dead right now. I'm not interested in you. I want the big guy. It was Renault's idea, wasn't it?"

"He found out you were a detective."

"How did he know that?"

"Zane had a recording machine on the phone so he wouldn't have to take notes when he made his research calls. I cleared the machine in the house. I heard you talking to some guy. Told Renault about it."

"That tells me *how*. It doesn't tell me *why*. You don't kill somebody just because he's a detective."

"You don't *know* him. He's the biggest paranoid sonofabitch in the world. First you showed up on the dig, then you came to the auction house."

"There's got to be another reason."

"There is. Renault's secretary saw you hanging around the auction house one night and got suspicious. She checked her computer and found the printer on. Renault figured you got into the files. If that stuff got out, he'd be through. He didn't want to take any chances."

"It all goes back to the mess at Plimoth Plantation?"

"I don't know what you're talking about."

"We'll hold off on that for a minute. Where does Zane figure in all this?"

"Renault's been using him as a cover on the Indian goods. He didn't know anything about the rough stuff, but he was getting nervous and wanted to pull out. Renault told him no way. He sent me in to keep an eye on Zane, let him know he's being watched."

"You didn't seem too happy doing that."

"I got better things to do than dig ditches in the hot sun."

"What about Eileen and the others? Did they know what Zane was doing?"

"Naw, they're clean. The only thing they've got on their minds is that dumb project."

"Tell me about the night at the plantation."

Rick dug his heels in. "There's nothing to tell. I don't know a thing about it."

This was going to take more finesse than a couple of spear jabs.

"Before you go down that road, let me tell you where you stand, Rick. Mr. Renault was arrested about an hour ago. Even as we talk, the cops are asking him about the Indian stuff. They'll use that to segue into the Plantation murder. Their theory is that Renault engineered the deal at the plantation to blackmail Joe Quint and get him off his back."

"They can't prove that."

"Don't be too sure. They've got the motive. They know somebody else knew about the murder because they got a phone tip. They know you're a convicted car thief who could have ripped off Joe's car and brought it back. Renault is clean on the strong-arm stuff. Cops don't like not being able to throw people in jail. They'll want to nail somebody for the murder, and they won't care who. That leaves you. Here's the crazy thing, and you've been around long enough to know I'm not lying. They'll go easier on the guy who actually *did* the murder if they can use him to get at the guy who *planned* it."

I let that sink in, then went on.

"It comes down to the word of a businessman with no arrest record against a felon's. Before you know it, Renault's on the beach at Cancún, balancing a margarita on his belly, surrounded by babes for hire while you're in jail dodging guys who want you to be their sweet mama."

There was silence, except for the heavy sound of Rick's breathing.

"You're just a private cop, what can you do?" Spittle clogged his voice.

"A lot, Rickie boy. First, I can keep my mouth shut about you dropping a rock on my head. Then I can tell the DA what I know. I can say you've told me you'll testify against Renault. The whole story. I can recommend he go with murder two. Tell the jury you were abused as a kid, or that you were on steroids, and maybe you can get away with manslaughter."

"What do you want?"

"I want you to tell me what happened."

"And if I don't?"

"Nothing. I get out of this car and the next time you see me will be in court." I moved the speargun away. "Just picture Renault sunning that big fat body on the beach." I opened the door. "Kinda gross when you think about it." I started to get out of the car.

"Wait!" Rick said.

I got back in, leaving the door open partway.

"We got a deal if I talk?"

"We'll discuss it. Tell me about Plimoth Plantation."

"It was just supposed to be a fire. Renault wanted me to go in, burn down a building or two at the plantation, and we'd pin it on Quint. He'd be too busy defending himself to bother us."

"So you stole Joe's car?"

"It wasn't hard. We found out he was staying at his girl-friend's place. Renault dropped me off. I hot-wired the car and drove it to Plymouth. I was going to get the fire going, put the gas can in the car, then leave it. Renault would pick me up. We'd tip the cops off that Joe was the one."

"What happened with the guard?"

"It was an accident. He caught me setting the fire. Came out of nowhere. I just wanted to get the hell out of there. The bastard had a hatchet. He was an older guy, but he was strong. I grabbed the hatchet away and hit him. He went down. I ran back to the car. I forgot I still had the hatchet. I wiped the handle clean and left it in the car."

"Then Renault picked you up, and you went ahead and tipped off the cops as planned."

"That's right. Look, on that plea bargain, there's something else I can give you."

My mind was racing ahead, trying to figure if I had all the nails I needed to pound into Renault's coffin.

"We can talk about it later."

"There's no time."

"No time for what?"

"When Joe Quint jumped bail, Renault had another idea. This would finish Joe forever. He said if we destroyed this symbol, everyone in America would be so pissed off at Joe, he'd have to keep on running for the rest of his life." Rick was practically babbling.

"I'm not getting the whole picture here. What are you talking about?"

"Look, if this thing goes off I'm going to be in deep shit. You've got to guarantee a plea bargain."

I jabbed him in the neck. "Here's your plea bargain. I asked you what symbol. Talk."

"The *Mayflower*."

"What *about* the *Mayflower?*"

"I planted a bomb under the hull."

"When is it supposed to go off?"

He glanced at the dashboard clock. "In about fifteen minutes. I was on my way to the breakwater to watch the fireworks."

Fireworks! I sucked in my breath. "Where exactly is it?"

"About the middle of the ship. Near the keel. We had to use a big charge to do any damage, those timbers are thick."

A cellular phone was resting on my lap, transmitting every word out of Rick's mouth to a tape recorder. I picked it up. "Did you hear that?"

"Every frigging word," Rourke said. "We're coming in."

I was out of the car. Shadows materialized from behind bushes and houses. Rick was dragged from behind the wheel and handcuffed.

Rick was shouting as they stuffed him into a car: "Don't forget, we've got a deal on a plea bargain."

My pal the FBI man trotted over. "Jesus Christ!" he said, "Was that bastard serious about the bomb?"

"He was serious." I started toward my truck.

"I'll call in the bomb squad."

"You can call in the U.S. Marines if you want to, but they'll be picking up splinters."

"What the hell can *you* do?" he yelled.

It was a good question. To tell the truth, I didn't have the slightest idea.

Twenty-Eight

THE PICKUP'S ENGINE coughed like a heavy smoker and flooded in a soggy gargle. I counted to thirty and tried again. It was the longest half-minute I can remember. The engine sputtered and caught. I jammed the gearshift lever into first and snapped the clutch. The Jimmy surged forward in a series of bronco hops. But at least I was moving.

I pointed the pickup downhill toward the harbor. Finally the truck's lurching stopped, I blasted between Burial Hill and the county buildings, cut off a Ford Taurus whose driver leaned on his horn, shot onto Water Street, and left onto the state pier. The pickup wasn't made for slalom. The body wanted to leave the chassis. The tires were screaming, don't-*do*-that-to-us.

I stood on the brake pedal and brought the pickup to a screeching stop next to the *Mayflower II.* I flew out of the truck, vaulted the turnstile, ran up the metal gangway, and stopped. I couldn't *believe* what I saw.

There were *people* on the ship's decks. About fifty elderly men and women in tuxedos and party dresses sat at tables being served champagne by young men and women in Pilgrim costumes. The sign on my right explained it. *Mayflower* Descendants' Dinner.

A tall reed-thin woman with steel-wool hair got up from a table and came over. The last name on the ID tag pinned to the bosom of her white chiffon dress was the same as some carved into the Burial Hill gravestones. Starting just above my hairline, pausing at the gold earring and going down my sweaty Corona Beer T-shirt, past the rumpled tan shorts to the disreputable scuffed Nikes on my feet, she examined me as if I'd been left behind by the low tide. Her nostrils quivered slightly as she smelled Ellis Island in my background. It could have been the garlic.

"May I help you?" she inquired in a bloodless tone that told me she didn't really mean what she said.

"You've got to get these people off the ship." I tried to say it calmly.

A well-trimmed brow arched over one cold eye. "I beg your pardon. I don't even *know* who you are."

"I'll be glad to introduce myself as soon as you get these people off the *Mayflower.*"

She impaled me with a stubborn glare that would have made her ancestors proud. Sharpening the edges of each word with her tongue, she said, "Young man, you are interrupting a private party. If you don't leave immediately, I will call the police."

The people at the tables had stopped tippling. Their eyes were fixed on the confrontation, surely the most exciting thing that had happened in their lives lately. Lives, incidentally, that might end quite soon.

Heavy footsteps pounded up the gangway. Rourke.

264

"What the hell's going on?" he bellowed. "Who the hell are these people, and why aren't they off this boat?"

The woman shifted her attention to the new usurper "And *who* are *you?*" she said as imperiously as the caterpillar talking to Alice.

Rourke yanked out his wallet and held the badge high above his head in a Hail Mary. "You see this lady? It's an FBI badge. I want everybody off this goddamn boat now or you're all under arrest."

The woman stood her ground; her thin body seemed to expand around the ribs and shoulders like a cobra spreading its hood. "You have no jurisdiction over this gathering. Why should we do as you say?"

Rourke's face became a hard-sell commercial for blood-pressure pills. "*Why*, lady? Why? Because there's a fucking bomb on this boat, and if you and your friends don't haul your asses off right now, you will be blown to shit. That's why."

Rourke speaks as if he has a megaphone attached to his mouth. You had to hand it to him; he really knew how to get your attention.

I had hoped to prevent what followed. The silence was so thick, you could have cut it with a butter knife. Then came muttered echoes of the word. *Bomb.* Chairs tipped. Glasses shattered. There were frightened screams and yells. Wrinkled hands reached for canes and walkers.

Fear is a better tonic than Geritol. The old folks charged the gangway like settlers running for the fort in an Indian attack. Rourke and I helped a couple of the less firm, and the kids serving champagne put down their trays and took charge of the others. The steely-haired guardian of the *Mayflower* descendants was brushed off the ship onto the dock. A couple of Rourke's FBI suits dashed on board.

We stood amid the trashed remains of the cocktail party. "*Now* what?" he said.

I pulled off my T-shirt. "I'm going diving."

"You're crazy. Let them blow this thing to hell. They can always build a new one."

"There's still a chance." I yanked off my Nikes and stripped down to my shorts.

About thirty feet in front of the *Mayflower*'s bow was a floating pier where people who have boats anchored in the harbor leave their tenders.

I told Rourke about it. "Grab one of the boats tied up there. See if you can find something with an outboard motor that works. If not, anything with oars. If you can't find a key, look under the motor casing. Sometimes there's a spare key there. Then bring the boat over and tie the line to the shallop."

"Huh? What scallop?"

"The *shallop!* Here." I dragged him to the rail and pointed to the wooden sailboat moored about twenty feet away from the *Mayflower*. "*That's* a shallop. Have something that floats waiting for me there when I surface. Get the motor running if you can."

"Do as he says!" Rourke shouted at his trained seals. "And get everyone away from this thing in case it blows."

I held onto the rigging and climbed onto the rail where I stood for a second like Errol Flynn in a pirate movie. I glanced at my watch. Ten minutes had passed since Rick made his announcement. Not one second to spare. I jumped off the *Mayflower II* feet first.

The deck was at least fifteen feet off the surface. I plunged deep into the black harbor before I kicked my way to the surface spitting out gobs of oily water. I was between the *Mayflower* and the shallop. The bulging hull of the ship loomed above. Lights still blazed from the deck and masts.

I hyperventilated to build up the air supply in my lungs, then dove under the ship, wishing I hadn't glanced at the *Mayflower* diagram in the brochure so casually. Not that it would have made much difference. I couldn't see a damned thing. Using a sort of undersea braille, I guided myself by touch along the slimy, barnacle-encrusted bottom until I came to the massive keel.

I passed under the ship and came up on the other side, gasping for breath. This was madness! No way would I find the thing in the dark. The ship was just too big. I tried again, swimming upside down. The marine growth was thick on the hull, and it felt as if I were reaching into an octopus nest. Still no bomb. I surfaced, took a quick breath, then went back under again.

If I didn't find anything soon, I'd get myself out of the water, buy some popcorn, and watch the fireworks.

My groping hand touched the hard edge of an object that was neither wood nor seaweed. I explored it with my fingertips. It was about the size of a shoebox, rectangular, and wrapped in plastic.

My lungs were ready to burst. I could surface, but precious moments would be lost. I'd never find the bomb again. I felt around the packet. Rick had used a staple gun. I dug my fingers into the plastic, braced my feet against the hull, and pulled.

The plastic ripped and the package came free. Hugging it to my chest as if it were a newborn babe, I spun around, confused, saw the glare of lights above, and struck out in that direction. I popped up next to the shallop and filled my lungs with great sweet gulps of air.

An FBI guy was scanning the water for me. "There he is!" the man yelled.

Rourke came from the other side of the shallop and leaned over.

"Here's your boat, you crazy bastard!"

The FBI man hauled on a line, and an aluminum colored Quicksilver inflatable about six feet long floated near to where I could grab it. Treading water, I reached up and put the plastic-wrapped package carefully into the boat. Then, gingerly, I pulled myself in, careful not to tip the boat. An old Johnson 2 horsepower outboard was idling. Purple smoke billowed from its exhaust.

Pockettypockettypockettypock. . . .

"This is it?"

"The *QEII* was busy."

Rourke's reply was nearly lost in the popping of the motor as I goosed the throttle and grabbed the tiller, steering toward an open space between the pleasure boats anchored in the harbor.

Pockettypockettypockettypock . . .

We moved like a fly caught in molasses. The motor sounded on the verge of a stall. Slowly—all too slowly—the space increased between me and the *Mayflower II*. I looked back at the stubby little ship. It was still lit up for a party. I glanced at my watch, trying to remember where the big hand was when Rick told me about the bomb back there in his car. In the excitement, I had lost track of the time.

While I debated how far to push my luck, the inflatable crawled farther into the harbor. Blue and red police bubbles blinked on the state pier. I felt very lonely even though I had a bomb to keep me company.

A voice told me I'd better say, good-bye bomb. I set the tiller and, trying as gently and as smoothly as I possibly could, rolled off the boat into the water and started swimming to shore.

A motorboat was coming out to meet me. Rourke had found the harbor patrol. He and his man pulled me into the skiff. I wiped the salty water out of my eyes. The inflatable was a dark smudge against the harbor, but the sparkle of its wake was clear in the lights reflected from shore.

Something looked wrong. A second later, a spotlight beam from the pier picked out the inflatable, and I saw what it was.

The boat had changed course.

A dozen things could have happened. Maybe I hit the tiller accidentally when I went overboard, or the shift in weight threw off the direction. Maybe it was the current. Maybe it was just fate. The inflatable no longer held a straight course to the outer harbor, away from the shore and the anchored boats which might have people bunked out in them. It had turned to the right. It curved around the riprap protecting the small park that fronts on the harbor and was heading to shore.

The harbor squeezed into a funnellike cove here. And at the narrowest point of the funnel was the Plymouth Rock pavilion.

Pockettypockettypockettypock . . .

Rourke growled low with astonishment. "Holy shit! She's going to blow up the frigging rock!"

Pockettypockettypocketty . . .

The boat would slam into the pavilion like a torpedo. The old metal bars guarding the rock offered scant protection from an on-target explosion.

Pockettypocketty . . .

Fifty feet off and closing. A crab clawed at my gut. Headlines: Rock Is *Soc*ked. Every school kid in America would hate

269

me. Thanksgiving would be canceled. Even worse would be Joe Quint's reaction. I could see the sarcastic grin on his face.

"Ah jeez!" I said helplessly.

Pockettypo—

Kawump!

Dawn came early to Plymouth Harbor. A yellow-and-red star blossomed about twenty-five feet from the rock. The sunburst lit the boats at anchor and the blue trim on the *Mayflower*. It lit the faces of the people lined up on the state pier and the lovers in a tight clinch on a park bench. It lit the granite columns of the Plymouth Rock pavilion, which were drenched by the spray from the blast.

Water pattered down like rain. Waves rippled out from the spot where the inflatable had disintegrated and splashed against the protective bars.

"I'll be damned!" Rourke said. He slapped me on the back. "You did it. You saved their crummy old boat. You are one crazy mother!"

And for once, I had to agree with him.

Twenty-Nine

PETER HOAGLAND GAVE me his piano-key smile, sprang from his chair, and pumped my hand warmly. Peter was a likable guy. It was going to be tough pushing the down button on his elevator.

"Hey, Soc, good to see you. Have a seat. Back for another historical tour of the old Indian reservation?"

"I came by to give you a present." I dropped a 9-by-12-inch envelope onto his desk blotter.

"What a pal! What's this, a *Playboy* calendar? Hell, Soc, the year's half over."

"This is hotter then *Playboy* and *Penthouse* put together."

Peter gave a Groucho Marx hitch of his eyebrows and sucked on a nonexistent cigar. Then he rubbed his hands together, undid the clasp and slid out an inch-thick folder. Opening the folder carefully, he extracted the stack of white paper and put on a pair of dark-framed reading glasses that made him look like a Harvard grad student. He read the first page. Then the second. Then he leafed through the rest quickly and looked up.

"I'm disappointed, Soc. No centerfold girls." He pushed the file aside. "Guess I'll wait until they make this into a movie."

"You can find it at the video store. They called it *The Godfather*."

"No kidding. Don Corleone?"

"Something like that. Only with Indians."

Peter reached into his drawer for a fresh Havana, which he lit and looked at in the loving way cigar smokers do.

Still smiling, he said, "I've got the feeling you're trying to tell me something, Soc, so let's lay it on the table."

"Glad to. First let's talk about Patty."

"I'm always happy to discuss my loving sister."

"She's not very loving right now, Peter. She doesn't understand how her baby brother could set her up for a kidnapping."

"I don't know what you're talking about."

"Next you'll be telling me you don't know anything about the Warriors."

"Warriors. Is that the new town basketball team?"

"It won't fly, Peter. We checked. The cabin on Slade's Pond belongs to you. We had to burn down your boathouse when we got Patty out. Sorry about that."

His skin turned the color of cold ashes. "Look, Soc, you've gotta understand my position."

"I think I understand it pretty well." I looked around the well-appointed office. "You were in trouble. We checked that, too. All your investments, your developments; they're nothing but a financial house of cards."

"You have to go out on a limb in business, Soc. Sometimes you have to take a chance."

272

"You took too many. That was your problem. You're a compulsive gambler. Like a lot of gamblers who can't stop, you're a loser."

"I suppose you checked that, too."

I nodded. "Personally, I don't approve of credit-card snooping, but it does save a lot of legwork. We traced your trips to Vegas and Atlantic City. The long weekend in the Bahamas. The day trips to Foxwoods. The casinos keep good records on high rollers like you. They want you coming back again and again."

"Okay, so I like to gamble, I won't deny that."

"You like it too much. You went in the hole big-time. You borrowed against your investments, and when that well dried up, you went to the loan sharks. They sold your paper to the guys with the muscle to collect it, and you were in deep, deep trouble. Then Joe showed up to see Patty. He mentioned to you that he had some information having to do with the Indian gaming thing. He had this funny notion he could trust his best girl's little brother. It wasn't much, as Joe recalls, an offhand comment he made when he was relaxed, but it was just enough to get you thinking."

Peter's cigar had gone out. He put it into an ashtray. "I'm always thinking, Soc. That's how I make my living."

"You're a bright kid, Peter, I won't argue with that. You'd have to be smart to put this together. You thought Joe's thing might interest the guys you owed money to. You dangled it in front of them. They went for it. The word was out that there was a file, but nobody knew what happened to it. If you could get that information, you could sell it, liquidate your gambling debt, make a profit to boot, and live happily ever after."

"So why didn't I?"

"You tried like hell. You started spending more time at

Patty's house, doing work around the place so you could search it. Patty thought it was maybe a case of her little brother growing up, and she was pleased to see you, even though you disagreed on a lot of things."

"We're family, Soc. Sometimes families grow closer the older they get."

"That's touching, Peter, but the family reunions tapered off when you couldn't find the info. You'd already told the prospective buyers about the file. They were impatient. They sent in a renegade group from the Warrior Society to use a little persuasion on Joe, get the file, then take Joe out."

"I told you, Joe and I were like brothers. I'd never want any harm to come to him."

"I'll give you the benefit of the doubt. I don't think you knew you were getting into the big leagues. Fortunately, while the Warriors were getting ready to come down on Joe's head, he heard about an outfit up in Plymouth that was selling Indian artifacts illegally. He started raising hell, got hit with a phony murder charge, and was thrown in the slammer just when the Warriors were about to close in. His big mouth saved his life. Joe was where he couldn't be touched. But someone took a contract out on Joe in jail. He heard about it, bailed himself out, and disappeared."

"End of story?"

"Really only the beginning for me. I get hired to help Joe beat the murder rap. So I do what a private eye does. I go around knocking on doors, asking questions that sometimes get people mad. I turn up stuff that might help Joe, but I don't know at the time that he's in much bigger trouble than just a little old murder charge." I checked Peter's face for a sign that I was getting through to him, but it was smooth as glass.

"With the Warriors," he said.

"With the Warriors. They're angry as hell. They were all set to grab Joe, squeeze him til they got the file, then kill him and go home. Now they've got no Joe, no file. A little birdie named Peter Hoagland tells them I'm working on the case."

"You can't prove that."

"No, I can't. It was probably a coincidence that they dropped by my house the same day you call me for a lunch date and I mention I might have some leads on the case. They work me over. They're interrupted. They decide I'm probably just a dumb sleazeball gumshoe who doesn't know anything anyway, so they go back to the source. They kidnap Patty and get word to Joe that they'll let her go if he comes in with the file."

He squared the pages on his desk without looking at them. "Is this as big as they say?"

"Bigger."

"Names names?"

"More than you'll find in the Bible."

"How about figures?"

"Carried out to the cube root."

He brightened. "Hey, I get it. You want a piece of the action, right?"

"Wrong, and I'll tell you why in a second. But let me ask you a question. How much were you supposed to get if you turned this in?"

He told me. I laughed. "If only half the information in that file is true, every Indian casino in the country, past, present and future, is going to go under the microscope. You were lowballing it, Peter. You were thinking like a small-town real-estate developer. This thing was worth millions."

He frowned, as if the thought that he'd been trumped was tougher to take than accusations that he helped set up his sister to be kidnapped and his friend to be hit.

"Guess they outsmarted me on this."

"They outsmarted you on *everything*, Peter. But it really didn't matter much until you got Patty and Joe involved."

"They promised they'd just keep her overnight until Joe came in with the file. They'd let them go."

"They planned to kill them both, Peter, file or not. Then they would have come for you. They don't like loose ends."

He picked up the file. "Why are you giving me this now?"

"It's what you wanted. It's what you were willing to sell out your sister and her fiancé for."

"I don't understand. What's to prevent me from selling it now?"

"Not a thing. You might have trouble finding a buyer when they can read about it for fifty cents in *The New York Times*."

"What are you saying?"

"Joe's gone public with the file."

Peter stared at an architect's rendering on the wall. It showed the new shopping center he was building. "Looks like it's all over," he said quietly.

"Not quite. You're going to hear a lot about this little bundle of paper in the next few weeks. Some Indian reservations are going to be embarrassed. A few others may have to put their gaming plans on hold. There'll be a lot of power struggles going on in tribal councils across the country. Some politicians will get their fingers burned. A few renegades and a few Mafia types will go to jail, where they'll have lots of time to figure out what went wrong. Then the next scandal will come along, and everyone will forget about it."

"What about me?"

"Look on the bright side. The people you owe money will be too busy talking to their lawyers to collect on it. The bad news is that you're going to be busy, too, talking to federal prosecutors and singing in front of grand juries. I wouldn't make any long-term plans if I were you."

"I was thinking about Patty. And Joe."

"She doesn't want to talk to you right now. You can see Joe tomorrow on *Good Morning America*, but that's as close as you're going to get to him for a while. Nice knowing you, Peter."

I got up and went to the door.

Peter followed me. "Soc, I just want you to believe me. They said they weren't going to hurt them."

His face was as anguished as the Hopi death mask hanging on the wall.

"No," I said. "They were just going to kill them."

I opened the door and went out.

Thirty

NEAR MY BOATHOUSE is a break in the salt marsh grass that doubles as a combination landing ramp for my skiff, and a small but private bathing beach. I stood at the edge of the sparkling bay for a minute, digging my toes into the wet sand, then waded out to my waist and swam about fifty feet from shore.

The warm bay waters soothed my tired body like a salty balm, quieting the anger of the cuts and bruises, washing away the aura of perfidy, lies, and deception that clung to my skin like cheap perfume.

I dove deep into the dark emerald water, then swam up where I porpoised, breast-stroked, side-stroked, floated on my belly, and finally on my back. I squinted against the purple sunlight, watching a sharp-winged tern flit across the cloudless sky, and imagined I was in Lethe, the mythological river of forgetfulness. No boats passed. I was all alone, enjoying the sensory deprivation that comes when your eyes are closed, ears submerged, and you drift on the sea like a big jellyfish. It lasted only a few minutes—I had the feeling I wasn't alone.

I upended and scanned the bay. A few white sails were visible in the distance and the drone of a powerboat coasting along the outer beach came to me on the breeze. I swiveled the other way and looked back toward the boathouse.

A heavy-shouldered man in a blue suit stood on the deck staring at me. John Flagg. I waved. He lifted his hand in the desultory way Flagg moves in between fits of action, as if he saves his energy for a time when it really counts. I swam to shore and climbed the steps to the deck.

"Nice swimming pool," Flagg said, tossing me the beach towel from the back of a deck chair.

"I like it." I toweled myself dry. "Want some iced coffee?"

He nodded. When I came out with the cold glasses a few minutes later, he had taken off his jacket and tie and freed his feet from the confines of socks and shoes.

"You can roll up your pants. The neighbors won't mind."

"Thanks," he said, and did just that. He looked a lot more comfortable.

"How was England?"

"English. I was getting tired of bangers and mashed. High tea and low tea. Can't even get a good English muffin. Did you know that?"

"Like ordering French toast in Paris."

"Something like that." He leaned over and wiggled his toes, looking at them as if he were seeing them for the first time. "Good to be home. That Concorde is some kick-ass machine. Three and a half hours from Gatwick to JFK. Takes the same amount of time to catch the puddle jumper to Hyannis." He took a sip of his coffee, looked out at the bay. "Talked to Joe Quint. He says thanks."

"My pleasure. Last I knew, he was lining up press conferences."

"Yeah. Going cross-country after that. Going to save the world."

"You don't approve?"

"Joe does things *his* way. I do them mine." He touched the butt of a Glock 9mm semiautomatic that stuck out of a belt holster. "Looks like they're dropping the murder charges against Joe," he added.

"That's what I heard."

"Sorry I wasn't around to lend a hand. Duty called."

"No problem. Joe and I handled it okay."

"I knew you could. Looks like I owe you."

"Let's just call it even. No payback."

"Sounds good to me. Get me a bill for expenses."

"It's not necessary."

"Just do it. If you don't, I'll just send you money." He drained his glass. "Got to hit the saddle," he said wearily.

"I was hoping we could catch a bite. Mexican maybe. No bangers. No mashed. Tacos. Fajitas."

"Sounds good, Soc, but I'm supposed to be in D.C., debriefing. They probably think I've been kidnapped."

"Another time, then, Flagg."

He nodded and we walked out to his rental car where we shook hands.

"Oh, one more thing. Joe had a message for you."

"What was it?"

The makings of a smile played around the corners of Flagg's mouth. "Joe thinks it's pretty funny, you almost blowing up Plymouth Rock to save the *Mayflower*."

I could feel the color coming to my face. "It's not something I'll brag about the rest of my life, Flagg."

"Doesn't matter," Flagg said. "Joe says he's proud of you. It was the thought that counted." He got behind the wheel of his car and handed me a paper bag. "Says you're an honorary member of his tribe. This makes it official."

Before I could give him an answer, he started the engine and took off down the driveway leaving a brown cloud of dust.

Kojak, who had witnessed the transaction from his nest in the shade of an oak tree, came over, thinking I might have some cat food. As he rubbed against my leg, I went into the boathouse and opened the bag on the kitchen table.

Inside was a six-pack of Narragansett Beer.

After Flagg left, I made a long-distance call. Then I showered the salt off my body, changed into slacks and a shirt with a collar, and drove to Lowell.

The headquarters of Parthenon Pizza is in a converted mill building that you couldn't build for a million dollars today. Athena Kostas, who's been secretary-receptionist for the company since she got out of high school, said my folks were home, but George was in the bakery. George was in a playful mood. He grabbed a wad of dough from a vat, rolled it into a ball, then punched a dent in it with his fist and tossed it to me.

"See if you can toss a pizza, big brother."

I stuck my finger in the dent and spun the dough over my head, the way I'd seen the pros do it. It was like playing tennis; it looks a much easier than it is. The spinning dough disc got wider and thinner, wobbled out of control, spun off my finger like a Frisbee, and soared about ten feet before it crashed onto the floor. George picked it up and threw the mess into a waste container. He patted me on the shoulder.

"Still want to work in the bakery, Soc?"

"Give me a wad of dough to take home with me. I'll practice."

"Don't bother. That stuff's all done by machine, anyhow.

281

"How's Pop?"

"A lot better. I have to use a club to keep him out of the bakery. I was just telling Ma they ought to go on a vacation. Take some time off and get out of town."

"What did she say?"

"She looked at me like she didn't know what the word 'vacation' meant."

"She doesn't, George."

"Yeah, I know that. But it was worth a try anyhow."

"Just a suggestion. Stay off Pop's back on this. He won't listen, and you'll just end up feeling foolish. Let Ma take care of it. He minds her."

"Good idea. Look, Soc, I was just kidding with the pizza making a minute ago. I wasn't trying to make you look bad."

"I made myself look bad. Give me a chance to get back at you. Come out fishing with me, and I'll see if you can put bait on a hook without sticking your finger."

"It's a deal."

I went to the house where my mother stuffed me with a pasta dish called *pastitsio* that she'd cooked the day before. I smiled most of the way home. Part of it was seeing Pop make a comeback. The other part had to do with the Red Sox game on the radio. The Sox were playing the Yankees. And they won.

On the drive home from Lowell I detoured through Plymouth and stopped at Dr. Zane's excavation site. A dozen people I didn't know were gathered at the edge of the pond near the Day-Glo stake I had fastened the guideline to. They were sorting material into boxes, and there was a great deal of chatter and excitement in the air. Norma and Dil saw me walking toward them and came over to greet me with hugs and handshakes. I glanced around for a glimpse of Eileen's dark red hair.

"Where's Eileen?"

"She's in Providence looking for somebody to take her place on the project," Dil said.

"Is she leaving?"

"I guess you don't know about Doc Zane," he said. "He's in trouble with the law."

Norma put it more bluntly. "Our respected leader is accused of laundering stolen Indian artifacts."

"Unbelievable. Zane seemed like such a straight arrow."

Dil's hairy face fell. "He got a little bent in the making. From what we hear, he justified it on the grounds that it funded legitimate research."

Norma smiled. "The good news is that Eileen has taken over from Dr. Zane and will run the project while he's busy with his lawyers. Dil and I will be her assistants. That gaggle over there is mostly eggheads, but we need some grunts to dig and sift. Eileen is at Brown University rounding up youngsters with the usual qualifications: strong backs and weak minds."

I gestured at the activity. "Have you found anything interesting?"

"Absolutely incredible stuff coming up, Soc. We've got two new divers. Rick hasn't shown up for work in a couple of days. He left his gear at the house, so I guess he'll be back eventually to get it."

In ten to twenty years, I thought.

"Not that we really care." Dil smiled. "Rick was never our favorite person. He hated his work around here."

A diver was being helped out of the water. Then another. They handed their sample bags to the people waiting for them. There was a low murmur of conversation, then a yelp of triumph. Someone shouted at Dil to come over, pronto. He shook hands and rushed to see the latest find.

Norma said, "We're finding some pretty significant pieces, Soc. Want to see?"

"Thanks. I'll read about it in the scholarly journals."

She put her arms around me and gave me a warm peck on the cheek. "Dil and I will be writing the article on the cave's discovery. We plan to give you major credit. Screw Rick. Doc Zane, too."

"Thanks. Please tell Eileen I dropped by to say hello. Give her my congratulations."

"I'll be sure to do that. Don't go away just yet."

She reached into her shorts pocket and pulled out something flat and pale red. "Eileen wanted to give this to you as a souvenir."

It was a trangular-shaped pottery shard. Painted onto the faded surface of the pottery in thin black lines was a stick figure. The artist had drawn a quick short stroke between the figure's legs to show that it was a man. And he was running.

I drove into town, parked the pickup near the old church and climbed Pilgrim Path to the top of Burial Hill. Letting my eyes take in the tumble of old houses, narrow streets, and the blue sweep of harbor, I strolled along the crest of the hill through the quiet churchyard. Stopping here for a minute was my way of writing *finis* on the case of Joe Quint and company. It wasn't meant to be.

A woman was down on her hands and knees near the edge of the path. She was using a garden claw to weed a flower patch surrounding a cluster of ancient gravestones. She heard me walking toward her and looked up. We did a simultaneous double take. It was the steel-haired lady who had tried to keep me from warning the people on the *Mayflower II* that they were sitting on top of a time bomb.

She got up and stepped into the path, so I couldn't escape her and waited. Her hands and knees were dirty from her gardening. There were soil stains on her blouse and shorts and on the forehead that was shaded by a broad-brimmed straw hat with a flowered cloth band. When I was a few feet away, she said accusingly, "You're the young man who disrupted our dinner the other night."

I didn't need this. Not again. "There was a little problem," I said.

She drew her thin body up. "I'm well aware there was a bomb on the ship. Frankly, some of our members are so hard of hearing that they wouldn't have noticed an explosion unless it knocked over their martini glasses." The twinkle in the gray eyes hadn't been there on our first encounter. I relaxed. She asked my name and told me her name was Mrs. Collier.

"Socarides." She cocked her head. "That's Greek, isn't it?"

"My parents are both from the old country."

She gestured at the tombstones. "Just like my ancestors, immigrants all. My people just happened to come over an earlier wave. Which reminds me. I understand you almost blew up Plymouth Rock."

Word was getting around. "That's not exactly correct," I said.

Mrs. Collier picked up on my defensive vibes. "I'm not *scolding* you, for heaven's sakes!" she scolded. "Everybody appreciates your bravery. But you risked your life for what really is nothing more than a pile of floating wood, something that could be replaced. At great cost, admittedly, but still replaceable. Wasn't that rather foolish?"

"I've been known to be foolish."

"That's still no excuse, young man." Mrs. Collier fixed me

with a piercing gaze. "We're supposed to learn from our mistakes. That's the basis of building character." She took off her straw hat and wiped away the sweat, adding another streak of dirt to her forehead. The stiff gunmetal hair glinted in the sunlight. She replaced the hat carefully and pursed her lips. "That obnoxious Indian man who was going about town behaving so badly recently may have been more right than he knew."

"You mean Joe Quint?"

"I don't know the gentleman's name. Nor do I care to. People in this town would tar and feather me for this, but I'm just saying that some of what he said made perfect sense."

"He said Plymouth Rock should be broken up into a million pieces."

"It wouldn't be the first time. Years ago, our merchants chipped pieces off the rock to sell to tourists. The Indian fellow was right, but for the wrong reasons."

I would have paid a million dollars—if I had a million—to have Joe hear a *Mayflower* descendant agree with him.

"Quint said the rock was a symbol of the white man's oppression against the Indian."

"Compared to those who followed, the Pilgrims were practically progressive when it came to race relations."

"The Indians might disagree, Mrs. Collier."

"It is my firm view, Mr. Socarides, that those who claim credit for the good things their ancestors did should also acknowledge their venality as well. That goes for the Indians. Their ancestors were as Machiavellian, motivated by self-interest and eager for power as any one of the settlers. Miles Standish was a hard man, and his ruthlessness dismayed some in the colony, but they did what they had to do to survive. This Indian person, who sounds as pompous and self-important as some of the empty-heads I know, with his tirade against Plymouth Rock, the *Mayflower*, and Plimoth Plantation, missed the point entirely."

"Which is?"

"Let me ask you a question. What do you know about the Pilgrims?"

"Thanksgiving. 'The Courtship of Miles Standish.' Pilgrim Hall. The Pilgrims stepping ashore on the rock."

"Longfellow's poem is pure fabrication. Pilgrim Hall is full of rubbish. And if they tried to pull the shallop up to that rock in a December sea, they would have smashed it to pieces."

"What about Thanksgiving?"

"I make a turkey stuffing that is unequaled, Mr. Socarides." She swept her hand about. "The point is, those things don't paint a real picture of those whose bones lie beneath this hill. These were *real* people. They drank beer, lots of it, were quite lusty in matters of sex, and enjoyed a good joke. Not like the Puritans up near Boston. Stiff-necked and prudish, mean-spirited and holier-than-thou." She bristled. "The Puritans *hanged* witches, you know, Cotton Mather and his ilk. Our people *never* did anything like that. Do you know why?"

"No, ma'am." It seemed natural calling her ma'am.

"Because they were far too busy trying to stay alive. And eccentricity didn't bother them. What could have been more eccentric than sailing a small wooden boat across the ocean and settling in a wilderness?"

"I don't know, ma'am."

"My ancestor was a merchant adventurer who didn't give a tinker's dam about religion, and they understood that. The people who built a meetinghouse and fort behind the church over there didn't kill those who didn't conform. They told settlers like my ancestor they could believe what they liked, but if they lived here they'd have to abide by the rules and not cause trouble. Now do you understand when I say terrible things about the precious rock and all the theatrical attempts to portray the forefathers?"

"I think so."

She sighed like a stern schoolteacher trying to get the class dunce to say his own name.

"You made my point a minute ago. The Thanksgiving celebration has been perverted all out of proportion, but people still think of it as a time to give thanks for what they have. They don't need a *rock* to remind them of that. They require only an idea."

"And ideas last longer than rocks."

The gray eyes sparkled. "You may not be as unintelligent as you appear, young man."

"Thank you."

"You're welcome. Are you planning to be in Plymouth long?"

"I'm just passing through."

"Well, look closely at these *things* scattered about town. The First Comers would roar with laughter if they saw that rock in its portico, or the statue of Massasoit looking oh-so-noble on the hill. Or if they heard actors trying to imitate them. They didn't believe in monuments. They didn't look back. They were movers and shakers. Rebels. They cared about the problems of their day and the future for their children. They had an immense amount of courage. Above all, they were human. Remember that. Well, enough lecturing. I've got to get back to Obed and Prudence here. Their ghosts would never forgive me if I didn't pretty up their little flower patch."

I said good-bye. She called after me.

"Mr. Socarides, call me at the Pilgrim Society when you plan to be in Plymouth again. You must attend one of our dinners. Suitable attire and invited formally, of course."

"Of course."

She proved she had a nice smile that was rather human in itself, then got back on her hands and knees to tidy up Obed's and Prudence's resting place.

I was doing so well mending fences I gave Sally Carlin a call when I got home.

"How was your conference?" I asked.

"It was okay. Boring. How have you been doing?"

"I've met lots of Indians. When I wasn't going to see Indians, they were visiting me."

Silence. "Soc, have you been drinking again?"

"No. But that's not the problem."

"What *is* the problem?"

Pause. "I don't know, Sally."

"At least you're being honest."

I thought about Eileen. "Maybe."

Followed by a silence that was so sharp it hurt. "We're drifting apart, Soc. You don't inspire a lot of confidence in a girl."

"I'm sorry, Sal. I don't inspire a lot of confidence in myself."

"Which is ridiculous on the face of it. You do a lot. You help people. Try helping yourself for a change."

"Can we talk about it?"

Pause. "I'm not sure if it would do any good."

"I'm not either. We can always talk about Indians and whales."

"That wouldn't be solving anything."

"Well, think about it. Sorry I called you so late. Maybe we'll talk later."

"Maybe," she said.

I said good-bye and hung up.

A minute later, the phone rang. Sally. "I'm going to be really busy this week, Soc, but if you can wait . . ."

John Flagg called that night, told me to turn on the TV, and hung up. I flipped on the television set. Joe Quint was at a press conference answering questions about a report on corruption in casino gambling. Patty Hoagland was standing behind him. Joe was wearing the tall black Navajo hat. Correction. The *Hopi* hat.

Senator Alan Eaton's fishing rod bent like a bow. The monofilament line went taut.

"Wowee!" he said. "I've hooked onto Moby Dick." Even a U.S. senator becomes a kid again when he's got a big fish on the end of the line.

Sam leaned over his shoulder. "Reel him in real easy. Don't get impatient and lose him."

"For God's sakes, Sam, I know what I'm doing."

Sam shrugged and backed off to give the senator some room. The wheelchair was tied down so it wouldn't roll every time the angle of the deck changed. He reeled in fits and jerks. "Damn!" he said finally. "I've lost 'er." He gave me an exaggerated wink and whispered to get the gaff ready.

Sam, who had retreated to the wheelhouse, came out to offer an I-told-you-so. He'd barely opened his mouth when there was a flash of silver and black in the water. I leaned over the rail and with some effort, gaffed the striped bass aboard.

Sam got out a tape measure and measured the fish. The senator looked on anxiously.

"Too bad, Alan," he said sadly. "She isn't thirty-six inches."

The legal minimum for a striper was a yard from tail to snout. The senator looked crestfallen. "Sam, are you sure?"

Sam measured again with great ceremony. "Yup. It's thirty-*eight*."

"Yahoo!" the senator shouted. "It's a keeper. Blast your hide, Sam, making me think I had to throw that fish back in the ocean."

"*You're* the one who said you'd lost her."

"Count your blessings I didn't. I'm cooking this lunker for supper tonight. You know, I'll bet Maggie had something to do with me catching this fellow."

"Maggie would have seen that you caught a mermaid," I said.

He gave that some thought. "I think you're right, Soc. But, whatever. This calls for a beer."

"Did I hear somebody say beer?"

A large head more or less covered with ginger hair came out of the galley followed by the hulking body of FBI agent Rourke. He had three bottles of Harpoon Ale and a can of Coke in his hands. He gave Sam the Coke and spread the ale around. Sam was a good Methodist who wouldn't drink alcohol if you forced it on him. The senator glugged half a bottle and wiped his mouth with the back of his hand. It's amazing what a couple of hours fishing at sea with the boys will do to a person's decorum.

"Well, Rourke, what do you think of this baby?" the senator crowed.

"Maybe we ought to ask him if he's seen Jimmy Hoffa," Rourke said.

Eaton laughed so hard he almost fell out of his wheelchair. "I'm sure glad you and Soc got your little problem ironed out."

"Just a little misunderstanding, sir."

They clinked bottles and Eaton took another swig. "Are you really serious about wanting to get out of the Hyannis office, Rourke?"

"I've been there quite a while, Senator."

"Well, I've been thinking about it. I'll talk to a few people up in Justice when I get back on the Hill."

"I'd appreciate that very much, sir. If it's no trouble."

"Hell, it's no trouble," Eaton said. He drew in a deep breath. "Can't see why you want to leave God's country."

"Sometimes it's time to move on, sir."

"Yes, I know the feeling. But Lord, I envy you, all this peace and quiet. I guess compared to the rest of the world, it must get pretty dull around here sometimes."

I felt my scalp and lips gently. The bruises and cuts were healing nicely, but they still hurt to touch. "Dull isn't the word, for it, Senator."